DETECTING THE OMEGA DECEPTION

Notes From The Front

Metaterra Chronicles

Volume 1

Angela Brownemiller

Metaterra® Publications

NOTES FROM THE FRONT

DETECTING THE OMEGA DECEPTION

Notes From The Front

Metaterra Chronicles

Volume 1

Angela Brownemiller

Metaterra® Publications

NOTES FROM THE FRONT

Metaterra® Publications
METATERRA CHRONICLES
DETECTING THE OMEGA DECEPTION:
NOTES FROM THE FRONT
Metaterra Chronicles, Volume 1
Metaterra Chronicles Collection

Published in the United States by Metaterra® Publications.
Library of Congress Cataloging-in-Publication Data.
Brownemiller, Angela.
DETECTING THE OMEGA DECEPTION:
NOTES FROM THE FRONT
Angela Brownemiller/ 1st Edition.
1. Spiritual. 2. Metaphysical/Esoteric. 3. Consciousness.
4. Psychology. 5. Biology. 6. Ecology/Environment.
7. Future. 8. Inter-Dimensional.
9. End Times. 10. Apocalypse. 11. Inter-Denominational.
12. Science. 13. Science Fiction. 14. Survival.
15. Angela Brownemiller. 16. Angela Browne-Miller.
ISBN: 978-1-937951-56-6 (Paperback).
Also see Amazon for Ebook and Audiobook.
Published in the United States of America for U.S. and worldwide distribution.

EARTH IS CALLING

LISTEN

Nature Speaks
Earth Speaks
Species Speak
We Speak
Ancestors Speak
Those Beyond Speak

ALL CALLING US
THROUGH TIME
TO HEAR THIS NOW

NOTES FROM THE FRONT

dedicated to my beautiful daughter

and all the generations

NOTES FROM THE FRONT

Table of Contents

"We have a choice.
Collective action
or collective suicide.
It is in our hands."

United Nations Secretary General,
António Guterres
July 2022

NOTES FROM THE FRONT

We can step forward, lock arms, and march together into our rightful place in the cosmic order, as citizens of the cosmos. We can have a say in our own survival. We can assume control of this ship we call our own evolution, regardless of how it was earlier developed or controlled, naturally evolved or purposefully designed.

Dr. Angela Brownemiller
Excerpt from
Opening speech to UNDERGROUND RISING

NOTES FROM THE FRONT

Foreword:
The Politics of Earth Change

Some of you may recall the late 20th century movie, *Waterworld,* rolled out in the 1990s. *Waterworld* is set in a time where the polar ice caps have melted, the sea levels around the planet have risen to cover most of Earth's land, and where survivors are generally trying to survive while living on the water.

Roll the tape forward to the 21st century year, 2022, when many of the world's largest super yachts, many of these owned by Russian oligarchs, even perhaps by Russian leader Vladimir Putin himself, were confiscated by governments and agencies around the world. Some of these super yachts are virtually floating towns, some being 460 plus feet long, designed to house fifty plus guests (or residents). Their state-of-the-art high tech helicopters and helicopter pads, food and medical supply storage facilities, fuel holding capacities, solar energy generators, communication and navigation technologies, and water purifiers, are just some of the extensive and highly advanced functions carried by these floating towns.

These are perhaps the greatest Earth-based **survival vessels** of our times. (The jury is out on this however, as these vessels have not been tested against the most profound of Earth change events.)

Waterworld's lead character, played by actor and film producer, Kevin Costner, was restricted to traveling the flooded planet on a trimaran. Yet, the actual real life story we may see in coming times could be one where a ***small survival-centered fraction*** of the global elite may, in the face of severe Earth changes, move to their very comfortable even glorious super yacht floating towns.[1]

We must see that there is a *small yet powerful subgroup* of the generally highly humanitarian global elite who is, unlike others, simply looking out for itself, and only itself. Members of this subgroup are planning ahead, just in case survival is at stake, planning to corral their resources and information to be able to survive in even the most extraordinary circumstances. Members of this group are not restricted to any one nation or political system, rather to their common goal: survival of *themselves*. And indeed this group does have the absolute where-with-all to acquire – even to hoard -- survival-related assets and survival-related information.

At the same time, many others are, for the sake of all of us and of all life on Earth, protecting lands and resources that would otherwise be being harmed or destroyed. For example, Swiss billionaire steel magnate Hansjörg Wyss, who chose to live in Wyoming, USA, pledged one billion dollars to the effort to save a large majority of plant and animal species from extinction.[2]

---

[1] See: https://robbreport.com/motors/marine/largest-yachts-2837827/ and also: https://www.businessinsider.com/here-are-the-mega-yachts-belonging-to-russian-oligarchs-2022-3

[2] https://www.wyssfoundation.org/philanthropy

Another example of the good being done by many of the world's wealthiest is Bill Gates' Master Plan for Battling Climate Change.[3]

And yet, there is indeed also the other more opportunistic counter-survival trend taking place. And we are beginning to realize this is happening. We are sensing that some of those of the world's wealthiest who have the where-with-all to buy up survival resources and survival information, are indeed hoarding these, and even access to these, for themselves -- just in case these survival assets are needed at some point. This process is well underway and largely hidden from the public eye. Our detecting what I here on these pages define as this OMEGA CONSPIRACY is going to be key in the survival of WE THE PEOPLE OF THIS PLANET.

This is not a book about global politics per se, nor about military buildups and related tensions, although some of these will be discussed on the following pages. This is more a story about WE THE PEOPLE OF THIS PLANET realizing what is actually taking place on this planet as we face Earth changes of growing proportions. **The reaction of the *survival asset-hoarding segment* of the world's elite is already underway and must be monitored for what is actually taking place, and for what is actually driving this hoarding of information, access, and resources.** Here I take a moment to place the story told by this book, DETECTING THE OMEGA DECEPTION, into the context of recent modern events....

ΩΩΩ

---

[3]https://www.wsj.com/articles/bill-gates-interview-climate-change-book-11613173337

The global **omega conspiracy** I define herein is taking place as this underlying all powerful global drama slowly unveils itself for what it actually is. With historically increasing climate and Earth changes being the backdrop, the stage has long been set. And, among the primary actors has been one who strived to maintain a lead role, one who has led the autocratic regime controlling Russia. (Note that the Russian people themselves have as little access to the multimillion and billion dollar survival assets and super yachts as do any of WE THE PEOPLE OF THIS PLANET.)

Climate change is indeed already reshaping the world and its power structures. Certain powers are taking full advantage of the Earth change situation.

For example, as the polar caps and their ice shelves melt, we are seeing the militarization of the Arctic by Russia. While helping to foment climate change doubts and disbelief in the United States and elsewhere around the world, OR AT LEAST TO MINIMIZE THE SIGNIFICANCE OF THESE CHANGES, seeking to deny the reality and severity of what is taking place, Russia has nevertheless been laying extensive claim to the Arctic Circle territory. This has been taking place for years while Russian leader, Vladimir Putin, was consistently been publicly lukewarm on the matter, barely agreeing that Human activity has contributed to the vast Earth changes taking place, let alone to the idea that we face a global climate emergency.

WE THE PEOPLE OF THIS PLANET are being kept from access to key survival information and assets. As this is taking place, the emerging **global climate emergency** is reshaping global politics. For example, the Russian regime, steadily and with great stealth, while meeting comparatively little resistance

from the West, moved deeply into the Arctic to now lay claim to some seventy percent of the Central Arctic seabed, even reaching into what have been the exclusive economic zones of Canada and Greenland.[4]

Taking advantage of global warming while denying its significance, while several Arctic regions have become less ice-locked -- some even ice-free, Russia has engaged in unprecedented levels of military buildup in the Arctic Circle. And, a short distance east of Russia's Arctic border with Norway, nestled within the fiords there, Russia maintains the core of its vast nuclear arsenal.[5]

We as a planet, as a species, and as a people, are in a state of rapid and indeterminate flux. It was February, 24, 2022, when Russia began its escalation of the Russo-Ukrainian conflict which had been initiated at least as early as 2014. The revival of this 2014 conflict, more of a continuation and escalation of this conflict, took the form of the overt military invasion of Ukraine by Russia. This was, by and large, the most sizable attack in Europe since World War II – and the most profound attack yet on the Free World – even on the:

FREEDOM TO SURVIVE.

In response, economic sanctions on Russia and its oligarchs were implemented. The world waited to see whether these sanctions would have any real impact on what key Russian

---

[4] Refer to: https://www.cnn.com/2021/04/05/europe/russia-arctic-nato-military-intl-cmd/index.html

[5] See: https://www.arctictoday.com/as-tension-builds-over-ukraine-norway-grows-increasingly-worried-about-neighboring-russia/?wallit_nosession=1

leaders were unleashing on the world. Would they feel the pressure as their super yacht survival vessels and detectable accounts were being confiscated?

Or, are these visible vessels and accounts actually decoys for the still largely hidden extensive wealth and survival assets already established well under the radar?

How well are we recognizing the **omega conspiracy** that is so well underway?

Telescope-in to the Norwegian town of Kirkenes which lies north of the Arctic Circle, the town of Norway lying nearest the Russian border (only a few miles away). Note here that Kirkenes may be said to "owe" Russia, or at least the old Red Army, as it had liberated Norway, and Kirkenes itself, from the Nazi Germany back on October 25, 1944. However, rolling the tape forward to perilous now, we have witnessed (and even felt for ourselves) the great wariness Norway has been experiencing as it sits next to so called "Mother" Russia. And Kirkenes itself is on the line in so many ways.

The long term outcome and impact of the ongoing Russo-Ukraine conflict hangs in the balance.[6] **Questions are looming and racing to headline status within the collective consciousness**. In the long term, how will Ukraine and other "free" nations survive? How will freedom survive? **How will survival survive?** And how will Russia maintain its internal control over its own population as this conflict moves forward?

---

[6] See: https://apnews.com/article/arctic-europe-russia-business-technology-b67c5b28d917f03f9340d4a7b4642790

What levels of population control, **even of thought-policing,** will the Russian government implement?

How will the Free World, **even freedom itself**, survive in the face of such an assault, even violence upon, war upon, international agreements and conventions, even upon morality? **Is the king of the mountain entitlement model** (the **"it is one's right to do whatever it takes to be on top"** model**) sound justification for some of those at the top of the global economic pyramid now hoarding survival information, options, and assets?**

Are we aware of what is really going on here? Is this an eyes wide shut sort of assault upon the very structure and nature of our species itself?

Autocrats ruling China and Russia have argued that democracies will fail, that personal freedoms do not work, that autocracies are the model that will dominate as we move into these ever more intense times. Alliances between Russian and China represent a power alignment of *autocratic population control models standing against democratic control models*.

Yes, freedom is on the line. So is survival.

Yet, even freedom must be further understood for its many dimensions, so that true freedom can be protected.

Yet, even survival must be further understood for its many dimensions, so that true survival can truly be protected.

And while the leaders of some of the most powerful autocratic nations grow wealthier and wealthier to almost inconceivable extremes, we may wonder, how on Earth did they "legitimately" make their money? With Putin (for example) reportedly being one of the richest men on the planet, the populations supporting the build up of wealth in the hands of the global elite are under tighter and tighter control, **even purposeful information restriction and deception.**

And while the autocratic state control of the minds of the PEOPLE is being implemented, there is a **parallel disinformation process** being perpetrated upon all societies. (Dezinformatsiya = a tightly controlled false information system leaked to an opponent's social system or media to undermine, influence, and or control it).

In 2021, reports on Russia's major military buildup in the melting Arctic surfaced further into the lay press. Nevertheless, much of the Western World, much of the Free World, indeed even much of the entire world, remained generally unaware of, or at least largely unconcerned regarding, this development and its significance. It is as if blinders have already been placed upon us. We must ask: Do we blindly and obediently cooperate with those who are taking great advantage of major Earth changes?

However, at least some awareness is being acted upon. For example, in 2022, NATO nations (including the U.S.) were on a new alert. As of March 11, 2022, some 35,000 troops from some twenty-six countries began a Cold Response, a form of quick reaction military alert mission, in the High North region of Norway. Such a QRF in the military is a "quick reaction force" capable of responding to rapidly shifting situations.

Note that, generally the term "High North" refers to areas of Norway, Sweden, Finland, Iceland, Greenland (Denmark), Russia, Canada, the Yukon Territories, and also areas of the United States which are located above the Arctic Circle. China does not have direct access to the Arctic Circle, except through other nations, as the closest it gets to the Arctic is 900 miles. China has expressed great interest in the far northern Norwegian town of Kirkenes for its location and strategic possibilities. I will return to the matter of this pivotal point, Kirkenes, in later chapters of this book where I describe highly unusual meetings with key characters I actually attended there many years ago.

The notes in this Foreword point to just the tip of the iceberg, just hints of the **global omega conspiracy** and the politics surrounding it. On the following pages, we see how we can sensitize ourselves to signs of the great and growing EARTH CHANGE OPPORTUNISM being perpetrated upon us, upon WE THE PEOPLE OF THIS PLANET, and upon Earth herself. We must be highly alert to this great OMEGA DECEPTION already well underway. It is time for the case to become ever more clear.

Dr. Angela Brownemiller

NOTES FROM THE FRONT

A LOOMING QUESTION:
DOES THE GLOBAL ELITE
SURVIVE AN EXTINCTION-LEVEL EVENT?

"UN scientists ... delivered a stark warning about the impact of climate change on people and the planet, saying that ecosystem collapse, species extinction, deadly heatwaves and floods are among the 'unavoidable multiple climate hazards' the world will face over the next two decades due to global warming:

" ' This report is a dire warning about the consequences of inaction,' said Hoesung Lee, Chair of the Intergovernmental Panel on Climate Change (IPCC)). 'It shows that climate change is a grave and mounting threat to our wellbeing and a healthy planet. Our actions today will shape how people adapt and nature responds to increasing climate risks,' he said, adding: 'Half measures are no longer an option.'

"According to the report, **Human-induced climate change is causing dangerous and widespread disruption in nature and affecting billions of lives all over the world**, despite efforts to reduce the risks, with people and ecosystems least able to cope being hardest hit. ....

"UN Secretary-General Antonio Guterres called the first report, issued ... August [2021], a **'code red for Humanity'**, and said that 'If we combine forces now, we can avert climate catastrophe.'

"Clobbered by climate change ... His take on the latest [UN, February 2022] report is equally stark: he laments that the evidence detailed by IPCC is unlike anything he has ever seen, calling it an 'atlas of Human suffering and a damning indictment of failed climate leadership.' "[7]

---

[7] Refer to UN News, Global Perspectives Human Stories. PCC report: 'Code red' for Human driven global heating, warns UN chief. https://news.un.org/en/story/2021/08/1097362.
Also refer to Limiting the damage: UN helps policy-makers tackle climate change. Feb 27, 2022. https://news.un.org/en/story/2022/02/1111922

NOTES FROM THE FRONT

NOTE TO READERS: Those reading early editions of this book may find these footnotes incomplete at times. This is a result of the urgency of the release of this and its companion book, the novel, *REVEALING THE OMEGA KEY*. Thank you for your patience.

When the time comes for the

removal of ignorance,

the case shall become

more clear.

Nostradamus, 1555

NOTES FROM THE FRONT

Introduction To The Omega Deception

Right before our eyes, there are efforts to disguise and hide so much essential information from us. Some of those with the ultimate power, wealth, and thus capability to prepare for any possible eventuality we may face on this planet are doing just this: preparing for the possibility of a critical Earth Change phase, a life-endangering "End Time" or what I call herein, OMEGA TIME period.

Certainly, the time of the global Covid-19 pandemic alerted much of Humanity to the global and shared nature of our survival issues. And certainly, the increasing warnings, such as those from the United Nations, of Earth and climate changes becoming increasingly perilous, are calling our attention to the nature of this era, the riveting and perhaps even long predicted events we are witnessing around the planet.

Amidst the Russian invasion of the Ukraine which further advanced in early 2022, nations imposed new sanctions on Russian leader Putin and his inner circle of Russian oligarchs. With these, the world was reminded of the immense and largely hidden assets being collected by the world's most wealthy people. Of course, this is common knowledge. And of course, this huge collecting of wealth is taking place among global elite of many nations. And of course, this is a trend WE THE PEOPLE

OF THIS PLANET sense, both consciously do know about, and also subconsciously are sensing, tracking.

Let's again be clear about this. This is not an overall trend among all the world's most powerful, yet it is a trend among some more opportunistic members of this group.

Keep in mind that, the quite public sanctioning of Russia's most wealthy persons put the world on another level of alert. WE THE PEOPLE OF THIS PLANET sense, feel, ever more profoundly what this is telling us. These members of this *opportunistic fraction* of the global elite have already been moving assets, accounts, properties, access mechanisms, and even survival mechanisms such as sea worthy yachts the size of small towns, to locations around the world. Yes, some of the most visible and identifiable assets were seized. Others remain to be seized. OTHERS LIKELY REMAIN HIDDEN FROM THE PUBLIC EYE, PROTECTED, HELD UNDER THE RADAR OF HUMAN AWARENESS.

Yet, what is most apparent is that even analyses of cryptocurrency, dark money, dark web, shell ownerships, decoy labels, and other tracking mechanisms, reveal only the tip of the iceberg. Those with the greatest wealth have long prepared for eventualities where global access to their own and others' wealth and properties could be blocked or collapsed. Some of the global elite have been preparing for the possibility of an end time sort of global event, just in case one would occur, for quite some time. Deep pockets, private airlines, private armies, private security forces, secret and coded maps and directions, highly secreted holding mechanisms, private satellite communication set-ups, dark market fund storage and transmission accounts, secret currencies, private secret health care systems, and more have long been in place.

So, when in early 2022, Russian oligarchs were sanctioned and what could be located of their assets frozen or seized, WE THE PEOPLE OF THIS PLANET were made at least subconsciously more aware that something far greater than even what we have been told is happening is taking place:

The OMEGA DECEPTION
is well underway.

The collection and control of survival assets and survival territories by that *opportunistic fraction* of global elite coming from many different nations, likely including from the United States, has been and continues to be underway. WE THE PEOPLE OF THIS PLANET have been kept in the dark regarding the highest most invisible levels of survival planning the *opportunistic faction of the global elite* -- what I herein also term the OMEGA CABAL -- have been and are engaging in.

We have been the workers, keeping the Human endeavors running on this planet -- while being exploited by those who are simply using our existence where this benefits their long term survival goals.

We are now looking right in the eye at the GLOBAL SURVIVAL FEUDALISM we were not supposed to realize was so well underway. **It is time we consciously DETECT THE OMEGA DECEPTION.**

It is time we see the
OMEGA CONSPIRACY
already well underway.

DOUBLE
OMEGA
ALPHA

PART ONE

NOTES FROM THE FRONT

1

WE CAN SEE WHAT IS HAPPENING HERE

This book, DETECTING THE OMEGA DECEPTION, is not a memoir, although in some senses is a personal story. I leave my full memoir for other places, other times. What this book presents on the following pages is a brief look at the process of this case becoming more clear -- in this case, becoming more clear to me.

This growing awareness is coming to many people in various ways, through various avenues of realization. Yes, some of us are figuring this out, following our own paths to knowing as we are called to do so. Each in our own ways, we are coming to see increasingly more consciously what we have been knowing, sensing, and how very serious this is. What is happening here is becoming more clear day by day, moment by moment.

I must now step forward to share what I see: There exists a largely unseen cabal of global (and perhaps even inter-dimensional) proportions. I describe this as the OMEGA DECEPTION CABAL. Members of this cabal are developing, projecting, and sustaining a cover story, a blanket global deception, a story which we are all being told. This story is being

delivered in several forms, each form adapted to reach and deceive its particular audience.

The OMEGA DECEPTION CABAL holds us captive in its deceptive and even purposively confusing cover story of so many faces. We are presented the cover story the cabal seeks to plant within our hearts and minds via whatever reaches us, whether it be through political or religious views, or other philosophies, sometimes even through pre-packaged beliefs, sometimes even fads, and many other means of getting us to buy in to what the OMEGA CABAL wants us to succumb to: NOT KNOWING WHAT IS HAPPENING, and NOT HAVING ACCESS TO WHAT WE NEED TO KNOW.

We are held captive while members of the OMEGA DECEPTION CABAL are manipulating and profiting from: the increasing Earth change signs we are witnessing in these times; WE THE PEOPLE'S increasing instinct-driven responses to what we are experiencing; and, the increasing concern we feel registering within ourselves and others, both consciously and subconsciously.

This OMEGA CABAL is working to keep us unaware of its own existence and workings and purpose. This is what I describe as the *Omega Deception Cabal's People Control and Reality Denial Plan*. The denial of the severity, or for many even the actuality, of climate change, and of the immensity of the Earth changes taking place, promotes and fuels this OMEGA DECEPTION PLAN.

We are sitting ducks caught in the stupor being imposed upon the masses, while some of the elite form their own survival plans -- while this rogue elite group who have access to funds (and means to hoard and hide funds and properties and resources and information) continue to form their own secret survival plans.

While certainly there are many among the world's wealthiest who seek to do whatever can be done to help all humanity, it is important to see that this powerful fraction of the elite, this OMEGA CABAL, are not here for the safety and protection – let alone survival – of all of us.

Think about how this cabal can exploit the accumulation of both scarcity and wealth. Consider the reality that the world's wealth is indeed in the hands of a global elite. As of 2021, almost half of the world's wealth belonged to the top 1% of the world's population. The top 10% of the world's wealthiest owned 85% of the world's wealth. The top 30% owned 97% of the world's wealth. Meanwhile, over the past decade, the world's wealth itself has grown by phenomenal proportions. These calculations have been conducted by large financial agencies such as Credit Suisse.

While there is no reason to doubt estimates by these major agencies, there is reason to note that wealth is not always reported or stored in detectable ways. Hence even these agencies are reporting only some of what is taking place.

Nor is wealth itself all held in what are considered normal means of measuring and holding wealth. Underground and dark market monies, many of the most obscure designed to be virtually untraceable, are likely accumulating at almost immeasurable rates. Entire sub- and or supra-economies are well underway.

At the same time, the world's land is owned by fewer and fewer individuals. And where it is individuals (and or their privately owned entities) who own (or as the term is used for this, "capture") this land, they are in increasing control of use of, and even have increasing control of access to, these properties.

In 2021, the International Land Coalition noted that since the 1980s, the concentration of land ownership around the world has markedly increased. Currently, the wealthiest 10% own 60% of all agricultural land value in the world, while the poorest 50% of the population own (or capture) only 3%.

These astounding disparities are truly only the tip of the iceberg, are only what we can see, only what we are allowed to see. So much of the accumulation of monetary and land wealth is taking place beneath the surface. And while this is taking place, access to key territories is quietly being locked up.

So, extend this realization to the focus of this non-fiction book, and yes, also to the companion novel, REVEALING THE OMEGA KEY. Where 1% of the world's population is basically holding the overwhelming majority of the world's assets, and CONTROLLING the overwhelming majority of the world's access to these assets, including to the world's lands -- WE THE PEOPLE out here may already be being permanently locked out of these.

WE THE PEOPLE are quietly being blocked from opportunities to have what we need should there be a major global event we require protection during, and should we seek to survive this event.

We have long experienced significant, even wrenching, health disparities. Now the question regarding who shall live is

a still more pressing issue. Now we are truly on the brink of seeing how the *OMEGA CABAL fraction* of world's most wealthy have hoarded the financial and land resources that may be required for them to survive as the world faces profound Earth changes.

Clearly, access to great wealth and territory and options is a privilege, what I describe as a SURVIVAL PRIVILEGE. Who can be ready, really ready no matter what it takes, for any potential increases in survival pressures -- pressures in the form of climate, weather, fire, pollutant, epidemic, nuclear, political, and other pressure points?

Who has a right to be ready? Readers, we do!!! WE THE PEOPLE OF THIS PLANET do!!!

We are sensing the rising manipulation and disinformation processes designed for controlling us. We are experiencing the wall between us and what we have a right to know and access: the information and the resources required to survive major Earth changes and climate crises.

We are witnessing the downplaying, even the outright denial, of the pressing significance of, the truth about, the unbalanced concentrated accumulation of the world's wealth, land, top health care and medicines, access to safety, access to safe places, and other actual survival opportunities.

There are forces that understand that controlling us is easiest done by keeping us from knowing what is really going in. Keeping us unaware and locked out of survival opportunities in the face climate and Earth and other global changes is part of the OMEGA DECEPTION CABAL'S plan to dominate us in order for its own elite to survive.

Yet, we can and will rise above this suppression of WE THE PEOPLE OF THIS PLANET. We can and will confront, recognize, and survive the growing OMEGA DECEPTION being perpetrated by the OMEGA CABAL.

We have carried, deep within ourselves, within the consciousness of Humanity, the messages that are being activated now as we move into these times. We are carrying what we need to know, the informing and empowering survival messages that can carry us forward.

We all carry the knowledge, the truth about who we are, and what we can do to survive the coming grand cycle OMEGA TRANSITION the Earth and the cosmos will move through. Humanity, look DEEPLY within, as it is time to unveil the OMEGA KEY to survival of this coming grand cycle transition. We, Humanity, can and will override any extinction scenario[8] with which we are presented.

---

[8] See the accompanying novel, *REVEALING THE OMEGA KEY*. Also, refer to *Volumes 5 and 6* in the *KEYS TO CONSCIOUSNESS AND SURVIVAL SERIES*, titled *OVERRIDING THE EXTINCTION SCENARIO, BOOK ONE: DETECTING THE BAR ON THE EVOLUTION OF THE HUMAN SPECIES;* and *OVERRIDING THE EXTINCTION SCENARIO, BOOK TWO: RAISING THE BAR ON THE EVOLUTION OF THE HUMAN SPECIES.* See also other volumes in this series, as per reading list at the end of this present book.

REVEALING
THE OMEGA KEY

COSMIC LOVE STORY THROUGH ANCIENT END-TIME EARTH-CHANGE PROPHECY TO MODERN GLOBAL CONSPIRACY

ANGELA BROWNEMILLER
Metaterra® Publications

NOTES FROM THE FRONT

2
COMING TO SEE THE SUBTLE FORCES AND FACTORS SEEKING TO SUPPRESS THIS INFORMATION

We are seeing what appears to be an acceleration and intensification of Earth and climate changes. The gravity of this reality reaches us in waves. At the same time, it appears there are those who would prefer we not see the entire picture, not see what is taking place on this planet.

There are moments when we may cover our ears, when the rush of knowing is so very loud. We may grow overwhelmed or simply go blank in response to the pressure. We may try to hide from this stampede of messages coming in from us to ourselves, from Earth to us, and from beyond us.

What is going on here? Is there so much to know that it is too much to know?

There are those who have felt at times almost torn in half by conflicting pressures to either not share what they know, or to share what they know. And the pressures are real although largely difficult to detect. There are those who virtually for years retreat from their lives, from the world, from themselves, to protect themselves from others who seek to prevent them from sharing what they know -- even what may help Humanity survive in these coming times of geological, climatological, economic, political, and other upheavals. There are those who find themselves living in a virtual sort of hiding until they are ready to step forward to share important information, if they ever are.

In the years leading up to the formalization of my work in this space (on what became in some circles called my OMEGA WORK and eventually also my OMEGA DECEPTION DETECTION WORK), I found myself building a strong foundation as a professional and expert in several very mainstream social and psychological fields. I built this foundation as it gave me valuable information and tools to help people dealing with psychological and social issues. As the years went by, I saw another reason I had developed this strong foundation: this gave me the means of establishing myself as someone who had truly arrived at what I am saying through very solid intellectual pathways.

As time went by, my work in the mainstream fields seemed to converge with my more esoteric work, the latter which for years I indeed kept somewhat in the background to protect my professional reputation. Although I felt and continue to feel my areas of work are all related, I understand how some boundaries are insisted upon by some leaders of some fields.

I cannot capture in words the various pressures I felt pressing me to both withhold my more esoteric work, and to not only suppress it but to simply shut it down. As a lecturer at a university, a psychotherapist, a corporate consultant, and so on, I was frequently faced with both implicit and explicit pressures to simply close off one side of myself and my work. Nevertheless, all along the way, I could feel that I was being called to express what I know no matter who told me not to. My DETECTING THE OMEGA DECEPTION was underway long before I formally knew this is what I was doing.

When I first began pulling together and really hearing, connecting the dots among and across, the messages that have been coming in to us through science, literature, religion, modern and ancient teachings, I incorporated these into a story, a novel, as these messages felt best presented as fiction. I therefore wrote the novel, REVEALING THE OMEGA KEY. Even the early draft and test versions of this fictionalized story were confronted by both visible and invisible, explicit and implicit, forces and factors (such as attacks and warnings from some members of media, religious groups, academia, scientific research communities, government (such as persons saying they were representing the NSA), and others I will not name, to suppress the release of these truths.

Apparently presenting this as fiction, in story form, did not stop those forces and factors seeking to suppress these messages. On the contrary, these forces and factors appeared to become activated once I started speaking up about the meaning of and experience of writing the work of fiction, REVEALING THE OMEGA KEY.

NOTES FROM THE FRONT

3

DESIGNATED MESSAGE PROTECTORS

Undisclosed Location, 2001. It was a heavily attended ticketed speaking engagement. I had been honored to be invited to be the keynote speaker that night. I arrived early as is my practice before speaking at events.

There apparently had been some casual screening of attendees at the entrance, as the person who had set up this event had been concerned. He had explained to me, "This topic you are working on, your speech tonight about the converging of scientific and ancient messages speaking to us now about the coming Earth changes and the political forces that will work these, well this seems to have activated people. We have a great turnout. We have also had some threatening calls and messages, which is why the security screening at the entrances is taking place. Right before I introduce you, I will let the audience know that we have taken some basic security measures and simply say that this is customary these days."

I was only somewhat unnerved. It is not that I had developed nerves of steel. But this producer of this event had ensured me that my safety was "entirely guaranteed." And, as I had been dealing with milder versions of such threats during my various speeches on this early version of my OMEGA WORK, I had grown somewhat used to this.

NOTES FROM THE FRONT

As I collected my notes and prepared to come out from behind the curtain, I was stopped by an old colleague--actually three old colleagues. I say colleagues here as these were scientists I had known for years in other circles, such as academic circles. A few years earlier, they had asked me to work with them on an independent remote viewing project, one they had developed based on related U.S. Department of Defense work. When first approached about remote viewing, I had told these men that I was not inclined to do such work. One of them had replied, "We are quite aware that you do related work on your own. We sense you out there, you do know this. We are asking you to join our team as you have skills we very much need." I will say more about the work of that team in later chapters of this book. Here, let me go back to what they said to me as I was about to go on stage that night.

"We are here to protect you. You need this protection. There is no time to explain right now. We will simply walk out with you and sit near the stage, one of us on each side of the stage, and one of us in front the stage. We will be watching the audience, yes, but more than this, watching the energies and presences coming at you, and warding off those who wish to stop you from sharing the information you are bringing in."

I had little time to reply as I was being ushered out and up onto the stage. But these men were scientists I had known for quite some time, and I very much respected their professional work in their very mainstream fields. So I simply said, "Sure, and thank you, and you can tell me more later. Can you do this quietly and somewhat discreetly while I speak?"

They told me they would try to be unseen, if possible, however this was not going to be entirely possible. Then they

went on and conducted their protection work. As unusual as this was, as out of the norm as this was, I felt I simply could not say no.

I was still getting used to some of the powerful reactions to this OMEGA KEY, OMEGA TRANSITION, EARTH CHANGE material I was working on. Speaking on this early draft of the novel, REVEALING THE OMEGA KEY, was a big step away from my more traditional work and presentations. I found these new audiences were reacting to what I was saying quite intensely, to put it mildly. Therefore, I was not surprised that night when I could practically physically feel the various energies of the audience members coming to me in waves. I say energy here, for want of a better word. Whether this was imaginary or actual can be debated according to your, my Readers', preferences. However invisible this was, it was virtually tangible. I could feel these waves of energy washing over and through me. I tried to tell myself this was basically the adrenaline surge performers feel when before large audiences. I also tried to tell myself that this was "simply" a neuropsychological experience I was having. The waves of energy washing through me, including through my throat and voice box area, increased when I read to the audience pieces of dialog I had written based on dreams I had had where I was hearing from my book's characters such as Einstein, Hermes, Nostradamus, even EARTH herself, what they wanted me to include in this book.

As my talk proceeded, especially when I got into talking about my experiences writing the voices of certain characters who virtually came into my dreams and showed me their ideas, I could feel the audience responding. Waves and rays and maybe even balls of energy seemed to come to me. Some of the rays seemed to be individual rays of light, some more like streams of light, and others felt somewhat like energetic weapons. That night, I was quietly glad that my physicist friends were there surrounding the stage with what they described as their "energetic screening and force field work."

I could see that members of this very large audience were aware of these three men and the motions and gestures they were at times making as their hands moved through the air. No one asked me or these men what they were doing during or following my speech. It was as if there was a recognition of the importance this highly unusual yet very subtle activity.

For quite a few years, these men and others they worked with would appear when I was presenting my work and quietly conduct their energetic protection. I was grateful. It was in those same years that for reasons of this OMEGA WORK as well as for other reasons, there had been various threats made against me. I will address just some of these later in this book.

What became clear to me, no matter how much I at first resisted thinking this, is that various forces and factors prefer I not share my OMEGA WORK. Clearly there is something here for us to know, something we have a right to know. Readers, on the following pages I tell the story of how I pieced together my DETECTING of the OMEGA DECEPTION, a story of opportunists taking advantage of the increasingly precarious condition our biosphere, even our Earth herself, is in.

4

WE CAN ACCESS THE TRUTH

We know, we just know, we already sense this: If the time comes when our survival depends upon our access to the greatest degree of information regarding what is actually going on, then those with this access may indeed have the greatest chance of survival. If this access is being tightly controlled, we cannot gain this access. Or at least that is what those controlling access want us to think. But we CAN gain increased access by watching very closely what is taking place, and by looking very closely at the effects of this process upon our own minds and spirits.

We carry the access we need deep within our own minds, our own consciousness-es. Readers, we do not need to give up! Our own ancestors stored the knowledge we need at this ***grand cycle turn of time*** deep within the consciousness of Humanity. I have come to call this the OMEGA KEY. It is time for us to access and activate this knowledge. This knowledge we carry deep within was not restricted to some modern day global elites who may be suppressing this knowledge.

Some of the access we require we are aware of, and much of the access we require is largely out of our awareness BY DESIGN. This is about access not only to opportunities and resources, but also about access to knowledge about what is really going on, and even about access to safe places where survival of climate and other Earth changes may be most likely. The *opportunistic faction* of the global elite, the OMEGA CABAL, who control this access will decide who survives -- **unless we understand what is taking place and move ourselves into ever more heightened awareness, and so do now.**

That we have arrived here is not surprising once we delve into the messaging we have been told to be giving ourselves (and others have been giving us) through time. Both modern science and ancient teachings, both awareness and instinct, have been telling us this OMEGA TRANSITION time of mounting shifts in our environment is coming, that *we approach the end of a grand cosmic cycle* (or at least the close of a long term astrophysical, climatological, or other process).

At the same time, elite of many eons (rulers, leaders, controllers of various governments, institutions, economies, religions, and other groups, and even at times cult-like functions) have chosen too frequently to restrict access to knowledge, access to teachings, in order to control people. So many times in history, we have seen that the design was to restrict access to key information, technologies, mysteries, secrets, to allow only so-called "chosen ones" to know what was needed to know, even to have what was needed to survive.

Those of you who have followed my work over the years have watched this story evolve. Many of you have been pressing me to step forward now, in these times. Others of you are new to this message and to this OMEGA WORK. However you have arrived here, welcome to seeing BEYOND what we have been allowed to know by those forces and factors who prefer we not know – yes, who prefer we not know about the OMEGA

DECEPTION being perpetrated upon we, the masses of Humanity, upon WE THE PEOPLE, here on Earth and BEYOND.

Readers are encouraged to see the companion book, the novel, REVEALING THE OMEGA KEY, where ancient teachings and modern messages are told in the form of an interdimensional love story, where a leading global environmentalist meets a key perpetrator of the OMEGA DECEPTION. Together they eventually come to terms with what is really taking place as the Earth undergoes predicted changes on so many levels.

Please know that this is NOT an extinction story, this is a SURVIVAL STORY, as I have detailed in numerous books written for these times, as found in the KEYS TO CONSCIOUSNESS AND SURVIVAL SERIES.[9]

---

[9] Among the numerous *KEYS TO CONSCIOUSNESS AND SURVIVAL SERIES* books are: *Volume 3 - UNVEILING THE HIDDEN INSTINCT; Volume 4 - HOW TO DIE AND SURVIVE; Volumes 5 and 6 - OVERRIDING THE EXTINCTION SCENARIO, PARTS ONE AND TWO; Volume 8 - NAVIGATING LIFE'S STUFF; Volume 10 - SEEING BEYOND OUR LINE OF SIGHT; Volume 11 - HOW TO DIE AND SURVIVE, BOOK TWO.* See reading list at the end of this present book.

5

TIME TO FLIP THE HOURGLASS

The hourglass sits so still on the desk, the sands of time moving oh so slowly -- so slowly we almost do not see them move. After long hours and days and weeks and months and years and decades, centuries, millennia of watching, do we start to notice the creep, the creep of time passing, the creep of time moving -- the sands moving down to the bottom of the hourglass more and more rapidly, more and more rapidly, rapidly, rapidly, rapidly, until we are almost at the end of time?

What happens when the last sand drops? Do we simply just flip the hourglass and start again? Or have we reached the final end of time, the end of the last cycle? End time? What in the heck is end time? Do we know? Do we really know?

NOTES FROM THE FRONT

6

THE LAST THING

The last thing I want to do is be a conspiracy theorist. I think there is too much grassy knoll thinking, too much "they're out to get us," too much jumping to conclusions about what's really going on to jump to conclusions.

In my work, I have resisted -isms and movements and memberships that meant just believing without examining the belief for oneself. In other words, I find that the necessary *moment of uncertainty* (or many moments of uncertainty) before believing something is too often eliminated. Too many conclusions are jumped to without examining the information or what may appear to be information available.

I say this here because I am talking about what I am calling the OMEGA CABAL. I use this term in both this present non-fiction book and in the companion novel, REVEALING THE OMEGA KEY. The latter, a novel, brings together a storyline and characters with ancient teachings and mythologies and scientific findings and current events, looking at what we can pull out of what we are seeing and hearing and feeling. What can we actually know? And what may we actually need to know to manage our existence? And yes, to manage, even NAVIGATE, our survival in these times.

NOTES FROM THE FRONT

7

WE MUST LOOK CLOSELY

As I noted on previous pages, this book is not intended to be a grassy knoll, conspiracy theory, sort of presentation. Not at all. Yet, we must be aware to protect ourselves. We must try to take in what information we can access, and then decide for ourselves what we think is going on.

The companion book, the REVEALING THE OMEGA KEY novel, portrays a lead character who is a multinational real estate developer. He is either trying to exploit (and make money on) people's fears of global disaster or even apocalypse, or is himself preparing to be safe no matter what, ***and to be safe at the expense of everyday people who unwittingly do what he causes them to do:***

surrender their assets and power

for the sake of survival.

Are the most wealthy making plans in case the apocalypse or some sort of dangerous event takes place, affecting life on Earth, and access to resources and safety? Do those elite at the highest levels of wealth and power have plans even media and researchers cannot find out about, cannot fully DETECT?

NOTES FROM THE FRONT

Those of us who are not members of the global financial and power elite must look closely at what is taking place around us, even for signs of what we may not be being allowed to know. Of course, so much of what is going on is taking place out of sight, not reported on, done quite undercover. While this book is not a research document, here in this brief chapter I do want to share just a few examples of how the media tries and of course barely discovers what is really going on. However, even these brief quotes from various sources serve as the tip of the iceberg, of hints of what I call THE OMEGA DECEPTION.

Just before and during the Covid-19 Pandemic years, beginning early in 2020 (or according to some, before this, in 2019), various news pieces surfaced about the major preparations being made by the very wealthy to survive major disasters and other great pressures. While this sort of thinking is nothing new, and while the world's elite have long been making elaborate and costly "back up plans" in case needed, as the times predicted in so many prophetic visions and doctrines have approached, the monies going in to this sort of thing have exponentially mounted.

We can only see the bits of information regarding so-called "terror scenario" island havens, apocalypse retreats, and survival bunkers that have made it to the surface, such as via media, for example in those rocky years from 2017-2021:

Quotes from article: "Wealthy Persons Buying 'Apocalypse Retreats'." Mark O'Connell. 2-15-2018. The Guardian:[10]

> Everyone is always saying these days that it's easier to imagine the end of the world than the end of capitalism. Everyone is always saying it, in my view, because it's obviously true. The perception, paranoid or otherwise, that billionaires are preparing for a coming civilizational collapse seems a literal manifestation of this axiom. Those who are saved, in the end, will be those who can afford the premium of salvation. And New Zealand, the furthest place from anywhere, is in this narrative a kind of new Ararat: a place of shelter from the coming flood.
>
> Because this is the role that New Zealand now plays in our unfurling cultural fever dream: an island haven amid a rising tide of apocalyptic unease. According to the country's Department of Internal Affairs, in the two days following the 2016 election the number of Americans who visited its website to enquire about the process of gaining New Zealand citizenship increased by a factor of 14 compared to the same days in the previous month. In particular, New Zealand has come to be seen as a bolthole of choice for Silicon Valley's tech elite.

----

[10] See this: https://www.theguardian.com/news/2018/feb/15/why-silicon-valley-billionaires-are-prepping-for-the-apocalypse-in-new-zealand

Quotes from the article: "Doomesday Prep for the Super-Rich." Evan Osnos. 1-22-2017. THE NEW YORKER:[11]

> In private Facebook groups, wealthy survivalists swap tips on gas masks, bunkers, and locations safe from the effects of climate change. One member, the head of an investment firm, told me, 'I keep a helicopter gassed up all the time, and I have an underground bunker with an air-filtration system.' He said that his preparations probably put him at the 'extreme' end among his peers. But he added, 'A lot of my friends do the guns and the motorcycles and the gold coins. That's not too rare anymore.'
>
> Tim Chang, a forty-four-year-old managing director at Mayfield Fund, a venture-capital firm, told me, 'There's a bunch of us in the Valley. We meet up and have these financial-hacking dinners and talk about backup plans people are doing. It runs the gamut from a lot of people stocking up on Bitcoin and cryptocurrency, to figuring out how to get second passports if they need it, to having vacation homes in other countries that could be escape havens.' He said, 'I'll be candid: I'm stockpiling now on real estate to generate passive income but also to have havens to go to.' He and his wife, who is in technology, keep a set of bags packed for themselves and their four-year-old daughter. He told me, 'I kind of have this terror scenario: Oh, my God, if there is a civil war or a giant Earthquake that cleaves off part of California, we want to be ready.'

----

[11] See https://www.newyorker.com/magazine/2017/01/30/doomsday-prep-for-the-super-rich

Quotes from the article: "The Wealthy Are Moving to These 5 Mountain Towns." Emma Reynolds. 1-14-2021, FORBES:[12]

> While there's no conclusive evidence that people are permanently moving out of cities, it's no secret that secondary markets across the country, namely mountain towns, are seeing an influx of rentals and sales.
>
> Both rentals and purchases, including vacation homes, were up in 2020 in Aspen, Colorado; Jackson Hole, Wyoming; Park City, Utah; Big Sky, Montana; and Lake Tahoe, California. Similar to the mad dash for the Hamptons in the wake of Covid-19, these towns are seeing an influx of people coming in and scooping up the most sought-after real estate.

Quotes from the article: " 'Billionaire Bunkers' That Could Shelter The Superrich During An Apocalypse." Aria Bendix. 6-10-2019. BUSINESS INSIDER: SCIENCE SECTION:[13]

> The Vivos Group, a company based in Del Mar, California, is building a 'global underground shelter network' for high-end clients. ... Their fanciest compound, known as Europa One, is located beneath a 400-foot-tall mountain in the village of Rothenstein, Germany. ... The property is designed to withstand a close-range nuclear blast, airline crash, Earthquake, flood, or military attack. ... When doomsday

---

[12] See https://www.forbes.com/sites/emmareynolds/2021/01/14/the-wealthy-are-moving-to-these-5-us-mountains-towns/?sh=508b461810a6

[13] See https://www.businessinsider.com/billionaire-bunkers-shelter-wealthy-during-apocalypse-2019-6

arrives, the company envisions residents arriving in Germany by car or plane. From there, Vivos will transport them via helicopter to their sheltered homes. ... There are only 34 private living quarters, so space is limited ... But the price will likely preclude most people from buying. Private apartments start at $2.5 million and fully furnished, semi-private suites start at around $40,000 a person. ... If billionaires can't find space at Europa One, there's also xPoint, a compound in South Dakota that's almost the size of Manhattan. ... xPoint comes with its own electrical and water systems, so residents can survive for at least a year without having to go outside. ... The company has yet another shelter in Indiana, which can house just 80 people.

8

REACHING THROUGH TO TELL ME

1990s, Northern California. One day I received a call from a woman, her voice somewhat distraught. She said, "May I make an appointment to come and see you?" And I said, "Sure, so are you calling regarding consulting or perhaps therapy?"

And so we discussed what she might be looking for. She said she really wanted some mental health assistance. The reason she had contacted me, she explained, was that she had found one of my books on death and dying in a recycle bin where she worked (at a major newspaper). She said she had taken this book out of the recycle bin, then had taken it home and read it all in one night, and now felt she very much needed to talk to me.

She came in to see me. We did some very deep work on anxiety and sleeplessness, and then on issues of grief, and then also on fear of death. This woman described her fear of death as "maybe general" rather than regarding the death of anyone in particular.

Toward the end of this discussion, she started to cry. She said, "Why? Why now? Why all this now? Why is there all this pain? Why is there all this fear?" Then she went on, "And, the bigger issue is, the bigger question is, why is everybody getting so worried about what's going to happen to the Earth now? All this planet stuff."

There was so much I wanted to say at that moment. I simply began with, "You know, that's a great question I think many of us are asking. I'm hearing from many people, clients included, that there is stress, and for some even pain in this question, pain and sometimes also fear."

The woman sitting in my office across from me was tearful as she asked, "Why would all this be affecting people more and more these days? Why would all this be affecting my own state of mind so much?"

At that moment, for some reason not then clear to me, I wanted to get up and go to the closest in the hallway just outside my office, and grab a rolled up ecology poster that I knew I had in there. I said, "Will you excuse me a minute? I want to find something, I have something I want to show you."

So I went out to that hallway closet. I opened the sliding door of that closet and reached down to the back of the closet for that poster. That was when a box fell from an upper shelf. This was an open file box, the kind of vertical file box that is designed to stand open so you can stack papers into it. On its way down, this vertical file box actually nicked me in the head. Luckily, it was just cardboard. And a few papers fell out of this file.

I picked up the first fallen paper, the paper that was on top. I was going to quickly put these fallen papers away so I could quickly return to my client sitting in my office. But, as I started to do this, I looked at this first fallen paper. I saw it was a single typewritten page that had been typed by my father. In that moment, I remembered that this vertical file of notes to me was

one my father, who had died some months earlier, had a year earlier put together and given me, telling me to "wait and read it all someday in the future."

I looked at this top paper that my father had typed up on his old typewriter. There he had written me a cryptic message, one telling me that as a great universal cycle comes to a close, we may not be realizing this is happening. Yet, again and again through the ages, the wise elders have tried to tell people what was taking place. They tried so hard and few listened to them. So they knew they would have to go through yet another cycle, and be back at this point all over again.

At that moment, I knew that this paper falling out of that file box had somehow (coincidentally or otherwise) fallen to give me and my client a message. This message had knocked me in the head to get my attention, opened itself to me. I somehow just knew that I was intentionally being given this message at this moment. Whether this was I myself, or my father reaching from beyond, or some other source, there was something meant to be about this message. I told myself that this surely was at least a strange coincidence, so strange this was not coincidence.

I went back into my office. I brought the ecology poster and also this note I had once received from my father. I explained to my client what had just happened.

I explained that a file box had fallen and knocked me in the head, that this falling cardboard box hadn't really hurt me, but that it had dropped this paper right in front of me. I said that, in looking at this paper I realized, right in that moment, how very aware my father (who had been an engineer and an intellectual) had been of ancient esoteric teachings and how he had hinted at these things to me, many times during my childhood and young adulthood, although he had never directly imposed his beliefs upon me. I noted that this was a page my father had once typed up and told me he would eventually give me, telling me to read it sometime much later.

As I explained, I noticed that my client's mood elevating. She now appeared quite relaxed. She said, "Well, you know, if you're getting these messages yourself, if you're having this stuff come to you, and you're sort of all OK with it, then I can be too." At the time, I felt that this client's reasoning was a wonderful and fascinating process, one this client had sort of automatically undergone.

What a subtle yet profound chain of events. A newspaper had put one of my books in its recycle bin. A newspaper staff member had found this book, taken it home, read it, and then made an appointment to see me. When that woman had come to see me, asking about why now, why were people so stressed about life and death, and ecology issues, I had been put on some kind of inner alert. I could feel I was being called by something. Then somehow when I went to get this client an ecology poster from my closet, my recently deceased father's notes to me fell right onto me, hitting me in the head to get my attention. Then there I was, reading this message -- something about how the great Masters try so hard to tell us what is happening at the approaching end of a great cosmic cycle, but we generally do not listen and are destined to repeat it all over again. (It is after all, a cycle.)

So, I had to hear this message: What is going to be happening on Earth now in these times is part of a far larger cycle, one we are going to move through one way or another. I would begin to see that part of my work in this lifetime (in at least this lifetime) was to be helping us understand that we can have a say in how we move through, NAVIGATE, the close of this grand cycle, this TURN OF TIME, into the next epoch, what I have come to call the coming ALPHA EPOCH.

That moment there in my office, all this raced through my subconscious. I blinked, as for a moment I could hear someone in my ear telling me that yes, we are moving into the next turn of time, the next OMEGA TRANSITION. I also heard myself or someone else deep inside my inner mind telling me the choice was ours, that we now have the opportunity to transform this experience, this moving of ourselves through this cyclic cosmic event, not as pawns but as CITIZENS OF THE COSMOS. We have the option to do this consciously, to make this a NEW FORM OF OMEGA TRANSITION -- whatever we can make this be. I would come to know the meaning of this message more and more as the days and years went by.

Sure, this could all be coincidence. And on the other hand, this was so oddly, even startlingly, random that this was not random. I was being given this message, and made to hear it now.

NOTES FROM THE FRONT

9

IS THIS THE END OF THE WORLD OR JUST A STORY?

Here, I say more about the companion book to this one. Writing that work of fiction titled, REVEALING THE OMEGA KEY, was a profound, eye opening experience. Being the author of that novel continues, on an almost daily basis, to be a remarkable experience. This is putting it mildly.

Writing the novel, REVEALING THE OMEGA KEY, was a profound and unexpected experience that changed my life. Although an established expert in numerous "mainstream" fields, having authored several other books, I was nevertheless unprepared for the extremely unusual experiences of writing that novel.

Unusual is putting it mildly. The wall the brain has between the conscious and the subconscious, even between so-called present and past realities, between real and so-called imagined messagings, can become porous. When carefully managed to avoid both personal disorientation and social ostracism, powerful, essential, critical information can be brought to our attention. This can allow the brain's perception functions to break through the brain's programming to not see, not know, not hear what is calling us to listen: voices calling through time, seeking to reach us now, at this critical juncture in Earth's, in our biosphere's, in our evolution.

NOTES FROM THE FRONT

One does not feel compelled to write a book like this novel, and then remain untouched by what emerges from between the lines. When I tell people that the novel, REVEALING THE OMEGA KEY, is about *the meaning of the meaning* of images of global cataclysm, I am being perhaps understated. REVEALING THE OMEGA KEY is about far more than this.

For cosmic eons, there have been grand cosmic cycles of which our own journeys are small parts. Again and again, there are great endings and beginnings. Again and again, as a great cycle closes, a new great cycle arises. ***Again and again, there is a crashing of the time wave, and a releasing of energies locked in old systems, triggering movement into the next beginning, the new*** **ALPHA EPOCH.**

We can learn to see what is happening and to ***override all this being manifested in the physical plane*** where so many life forms, ecosystems, biospheres are at stake. We can survive this great transition through this time wave, this OMEGA TRANSITION-- when we understand what this is and means.

Once we understand ourselves as ***the interdimensional beings who we truly are,*** we can NAVIGATE this next OMEGA TRANSITION into our survival without vast and complete destruction along the way -- we can move ourselves into the overriding of physical plane DISASTER into what is clearly the arising opportunity for manifesting the new <u>META LEVEL</u> OMEGA TRANSITION.

Images of apocalypse themselves are messages from us to ourselves. On some very deep inner level, we know this, our instinctual awareness-es are already being triggered.

DETECTING THE OMEGA DECEPTION

I frequently say that REVEALING THE OMEGA KEY is a novel, is certainly fiction, and I continue to want to know this to be true. And, as we are still here to read that book, we know that what we read there likely has not already happened (or happened all over again). After all, within the pages of REVEALING THE OMEGA KEY, the apocalypse may seem to have already taken place for the characters, but not for the Readers. "Is this the end of the world?" our heroine asks our hero already early on in that book.

And I have to ask myself exactly this, if for no other reason than that I had to live through the apocalypse on some very profound imaginative level in order to write this. I have had to convince myself in order to be convincing. And so, a part of me has already walked through -- on walkways of words, passageways deep into the mind and soul, and journeys so far beyond I have no words to describe -- in great detail exactly the predictions that are explored herein to write this book.

And now, another part of me, being convinced of the validity of the messaging in this book, REVEALING THE OMEGA KEY, is somehow telling myself the events discussed there are somehow remaining in the past (or in parallel present is it?): in the time before the coming of the apocalypse predicted by many great religions and ancient teachings of the world as they tell their members to prepare for the coming, and to see the signs.

I debate with myself whether the coming is metaphorical or actual. If I really believe all this, what should I say to my friends and my family? If I only believe some of this, which parts? Do I follow what seem, on some days, to be my rising instincts, disrupt a settled life, and guide myself and those who will join

me to *safe lands, survivor territories,* as this book's heroine describes these?

Or is the metaphor of all this the message? Is this about the possibility that we can survive the next OMEGA TRANSITION? We can, this time, move through this cyclic galactic, even cosmic, transition, awake and aware of our options to survive, to transcend, to evolve more rapidly than the events unfolding before our eyes already now. Can we move this whole process to another level, into a META LEVEL OMEGA TRANSITION? Is there the time and the will to understand what this means, and to shift the physical plane experience into a whole other space and dimension where increasing physical plane harm and devastation may not be done as we move through this next grand transition?

I have shared in other books details of my definition of interdimensional awareness and migration.[14] Here, let me simply again say, our instincts are already being triggered. ***If we listen we know, we know how and when and where to go.*** We can sense what it means to gravitate geographically to what seem to be *safe lands,* geographical locations most likely to endure a global catastrophe of profound proportions. We can sense on some level the same for seeking spiritual safety, safe lands, domains, where the mind and spirit can survive.

Can we sense how we can prepare ourselves and our loved ones to make the conceptual, dimensional, and spiritual leaps that may be required to survive the 3-D tumult that may be

[14] For example, see *Volume 3* of the *KEYS TO CONSCIOUSNESS AND SURVIVAL SERIES,* titled, *UNVEILING THE HIDDEN INSTINCT.* (See also the reading list at the end of this present book).

coming to the Earth in the form of geological, climatological, societal, and other forms of upheaval?

Is this a life and death matter, OR NOT?

Quite some time ago, when attending a first book talk regarding an early draft of this novel, I found myself insisting to a very large audience that this was fiction, a novel, perhaps science fiction or even historical fiction -- if time travel was part of history. While I was honored to see such a large attendance, I was rather overwhelmed.

People there had arrived from several areas and even countries, some in tears, some praying, others arguing with each other regarding their ecological views, and many watching others and wanting to know what this anxiety was all about. I insisted several times that this novel was just a story bringing together some ancient teachings, drawing from several mythological and religious stories, and including some history and some science, then knitting all this together via a love and corruption story. I do continue to hope that I was right about this, that this is just a love story wrapped in a mystery, wrapped in a conspiracy, wrapped in esoteric, ancient and modern, mysteries.

Yet, as time continues to continue, the stakes here on Planet Earth are growing higher. The survival of our Human species, and of other species here on physical plane Earth, is moving to front and center of all issues on the plate of our planetary drama.

DrrStrrttt Xula NdnNdnDah
Welcome to The Portal
Dr. Angela Brownemiller

NOTES FROM THE FRONT

DOUBLE

OMEGA

ALPHA

PART TWO

NOTES FROM THE FRONT

10

WAKE UP CALL: FALLING THROUGH TIME

Central America, 1970s. There I was, very young and adventurous, perhaps too young and adventurous. I was hiking over rugged terrain on a roughly carved dirt trail, tripping over bumps, stones, and branches, following a new friend who I some years later discovered was a CIA consultant (actually agent). This charming gentleman had suddenly appeared and befriended me as I had been quickly avoiding an area further south where there was a malaria outbreak.

A bit of background. I had been wandering Central America alone in my 20s. Wise or unwise, there I had been when my passport had been taken from me for three weeks, with no explanation as to why. When I finally was given an explanation, the officials told me that there were European terrorists hiding in Central America, and that I had been mistaken for one. While this seemed highly unlikely to me, I was in no position to argue and was grateful to have my passport back. So I said nothing.

Not long after that, I joined this gentleman who had suddenly appeared in my life right after my passport was returned to me. He agreed that avoiding the malaria outbreak was a good idea. Upon hearing my plans, he said he would join me on my visit to some ancient ruins I had been planning on

secretly hiking into, which were at that time not yet accessible to the public.

In the back of my mind, I found it strange that I had met someone who wanted to get into the same as yet undeveloped ancient ruins as I did. What a coincidence, I said to myself, and only wondered about this coincidence many years later.

I was uncertain regarding how this man was able to openly access this area. However, he had explained that he had connections in many countries because he had traveled so much.

As we hiked in to explore these ruins, I, in my naïve and independent way, had fallen far behind this man I was with. I wanted to move very slowly, to carefully take it all in. So I was out there hiking along, pretty much alone. But, there seemed to be nothing to be concerned about. Of course, while nothing about this experience appeared to be anything unusual, there was also nothing usual about this experience.

What happened next changed my life, or perhaps was my life. It all happened so quickly. I fell (or was pushed by unseen hands) into a hole and blacked out.

It was in that fall that so much took place. In those moments of falling were stuffed lifetimes of impressions and eons of knowledge. I know this all happened very quickly, but time practically stopped along the way down.

Downward, hitting my back and shoulder and head several times on the way, each blow seemed harder and hit in quicker succession than the one previous. Each jolt filled my head with color and pictures – pictures of some kind of ceremony, some kind of very intense last moments of my life -- or of someone's life.

My entire life seemed to rush before my eyes in that instant. However, it was not entirely my life I was seeing, rather the life of a young woman living in ancient times. She knew she was about to die in a ritual process and was in close contact with the spirit realm that had already opened for her before she was killed. Killed? I am not being killed, my consciousness screamed at itself. This is not me. No. No. No.

As I fell, an extreme slow motion sensation kicked in. Everything almost stilled, moving ever more slowly, until time finally did seem to entirely stop, the immense gears of the universe seeming to come to a grinding but gentle halt. I thought I saw a very old woman reaching out to catch me in her arms. The last blow to my head as I toppled deeper into that hole was so terrifically hard, I passed out. The world went blank.

For quite some time, I was aware of nothing. Was I dead, I heard myself wonder. Once I heard myself wonder this, I realized I was aware of myself. I was about to ask myself how I could be aware of myself if I was dead, when suddenly I was distracted: There came a blinding flicker of brilliant light in which I saw seven women with their arms extended what seemed to be upward toward me. And then again the old woman appeared, again reaching for me and then catching me in her arms. Wake up, I thought I heard her say, wake up.

I flickered in and out of consciousness, feeling unclear as to what was happening and whether I was alive or dead.

****

I temporarily came to in this dry *cenote*, which I later was told was a site where young women had been ritually sacrificed in ancient times. Still caught in the unusual near death experience I had just had, I had expected to open my eyes – wake up dead – in the next world, and see the spirits, ancient spirits, all around me. Instead, I felt the gush of warm blood roll down my forehead into my eye, and down from the area under my right eye all over my cheek. Now I knew I was alive, alive in this lifetime I had been living and was still living.

Still, there was a concurrent moment of internal chaos, a moment of what I later came to call ***inter-dimensional shock*** and fierce confusion.[15] It seemed I had been with, or even had been, that ancient girl being sacrificed by that leader or medicine man, right there at that sacrificial site, at that cenote where I now laid injured and stuck at the bottom.[16]

I tried to summon the strength to call out for help. But it would be a while before my voice came back to me. I tried not to fear the jungle snakes, or whatever it was I could hear moving in the ground around me. But I had no place to go and no way to move out of the hole in the ground.

I lay there in pain and bleeding, wondering how injured I

---

15 I define diagnostic conditions such as these in the *KEYS TO CONSCIOUSNESS AND SURVIVAL SERIES* books.

16 Refer to books in the *KEYS TO CONSCIOUSNESS AND SURVIVAL SERIES* and in the *METATERRA CHRONICLES COLLECTION* where I further discuss various easily assimilated, and some perhaps more challenging, states of mind, and guidance for these states of mind that can develop during experiences beyond what appear to be the boundaries of the physical plane. See reading list at the end of this present book.

was, and whether someone would find me there and save me soon. As I did, a strange yet insistent sense came to me, an awareness that I had willingly given my life back then ***in order to return to this time where I was now***. I could hear someone telling me that this time now was the *dawning of the time of the Great Return*. Where was this voice coming from, I wondered.

I was somehow made to understand that this is the time, this is what I and many others are here for now. This is the time we have returned for.

Although at that time, none of this made much sense to me, as I was still mostly blacked out at the bottom of a hole in the ground, I have never forgotten this message, and never forgotten under what strange circumstances I heard this message:

> ***We are coming back, returning, as we have known we would do at this perilous moment in Earth and Human history.***
>
> ***We have to come back to safely guide Humanity through this coming turn of time. We have to be here now for Earth, for Maka, and for all her people, for the Human species and all living things on Earth and in the Cosmos.***

I looked up out of the hole, right into the old woman's immaterial face still appearing there. "You're just a ghost," I silently told her, "you can't help me out of here. You can't save my life, can you?"

She pointed to my heart and I gulped. I suddenly remembered I had seen her before. I had once dreamed I stored

a crystal drop she had given me. Yet, it was not really a dream. I had been alone, a teenage girl, laying in despair, there on the bed of a survival commune leader (who had called himself Leader, as is discussed in another, later, chapter of this book). It then flashed through my memory that this crystal drop had been handed me and other women at other sacrificial events longer ago, in ancient times.

Now the light of truth gleamed before me. Again I was unsure whether I was alive or dead. As if it had been a catalyst, the light of this truth illuminated a passageway. I found I could see through time as I lay bleeding at the bottom of that hole, that old once water-filled hole where ancient priestesses were once sacrificed, where their hearts were once cut out right before their bodies were thrown down, down, down into time. I could see priestesses of so many ancient cultures, women from all over and all eons – now gathered around the hole I was in, close to this old woman who had caught me in her arms.

Of course, they were telling me – communicating to me right through this hole in time. They were saying that for us to give our lives back then was the way to carry the power of ancient women directly to this time where we are now. ***This is how we are coming back now, back for the Great Return, for the next OMEGA TRANSITION. The Earth needs us, Mother Earth needs us, and Humanity needs us, as we must tip the balance back to save all Humanity and all life.***

* * * * * * *

When finally I actually came to, I realized something immense, something that I would not have been able to accept before this fall: The young woman I had heard screaming in the jungle – I was this woman, and so were many others. That had been *my* and others' voices calling at *me* and all of us through time. I and others had been that young woman being sacrificed right there. I and other women had given my and their lives back then in order to return to this time where I was now. Where we all are now.

The time is coming for the removal of ignorance.

NOTES FROM THE FRONT

11

STORY OF A LIFE COMES INTO FOCUS

We all may have moments when we try to understand what our lives are about. The story of a life is like a developing picture, every moment coming into focus, more into focus. What you think you see clearly right now (if you do) may not be what you see clearly about all of this a little while later. Whether we look again in a moment or a week or a month or a year or a decade or a century or a millennium, whenever it might be, we as individuals and as a species are seeing just what we think we see at the moment we see it.

We are describing what we think we have experienced or observed or studied for a time period, what we have studied with the tools we think we are using to study it. Yet, there is so much more going on here, so much more that we never really see the whole picture. Still, we may find that things are becoming increasingly clear to us. Realities are coming more into focus, surfacing into our understanding.

In this sense, the time is always coming for the further removal of more of our ignorance, of more of our not knowing, of more of our inability to see the whole picture. We are only

Human and we only have biological brains and biological eyes, right? Or is this right? I suggest we may be seeing or perceiving more than we realize we are. I suggest it is time for us to listen to our deeply buried instincts. The time is coming for us to see more. We must see more in order to survive.

I think of that graphic artist, M. C. Escher, and his detailed Escher prints portraying relationships between shapes and space, generating illusion to detail more about reality. Those of you who have gazed at an Escher print understand this concept of looking at a picture -- and then looking at it long enough that the picture beneath the picture, or the actual picture, begins to surface -- and suddenly you see things that your eyes weren't telling you were there when you first looked. So, what we see at first glance or first look isn't all there is to see.

We think of the Escher prints as working with optics and optical functions, calling on our ability to see through optical illusions. Whatever we see (or perceive) via our physical biological senses (seeing, touching, tasting, smelling, hearing) -- is basically an illusion. There is so much more going on around and within us. We've reduced what we can take in down to what we can biologically process. Or so we think.[17]

Those of you who know my work (or will know my work) will see that I frequently discuss the matter of the Human brain and its brain functions, which I cherish. I refer to this brain of ours in all kinds of my work, ranging from scientific research to

[17] Refer to books in the *KEYS TO CONSCIOUSNESS AND SURVIVAL SERIES*, such as *Volumes 5 and 6*, the *OVERRIDING THE EXTINCTION SCENARIO* books.

psychological and clinical work, to the more esoteric aspects of my work and writing.

Many of you have heard me so often ask:

Is the brain controlling us
or are we controlling the brain?

My question here is linked to the larger questions I also return to again and again:

Who is in charge here?

And, how did we get to this place where we actually have just a limited perception of the reality in which we live, of the place where we exist?

How did we arrive at this place in our evolution where we have such great implanted restrictions on our perceptions?

Is this random evolution,
or is this something more questionable such as
a design and control we cannot detect?[18]

So, anything we think we see, or say we see, or are told by our brains and senses we see, is but a small piece of reality, if that, a fragment of what is really going on. All we sense and think we see is just a still shot of a moving picture. Anything that we sense is always in process. Everything is always moving

[18] Refer to *Volumes 5 and 6* in the *KEYS TO CONSCIOUSNESS AND SURVIVAL SERIES,* titled *OVERRIDING THE EXTINCTION SCENARIO, PART ONE* and *OVERRIDING THE EXTINCTION SCENARIO, PART TWO.*

even when it appears still. I use the word "moving" knowing that this is just a word, that I am using a word to address something so immense no words can capture its reality.

And of course, we all know that nothing is simply moving in a straight line. Moving is not just moving forward, the way people drive along a street in a straight line. (Well, many people drive in a straight line on a straight street. Some people don't. But that's grounds for another discussion.) What I am saying here is that we are moving, yes, we are moving in a linear way.

We are also moving backward and forward and round and round. We are also moving in directions that we don't necessarily consciously perceive with our biological brains. In other words, we are moving through many dimensions at the same time. Of course, for some reason, our five biological senses are not designed to sense the full reality of this. As I have explained in other books, we have been evolved or designed not to know.[19]

So the journeys we take are not direct and straight. We are not moving directly in a straight line. Nothing is entirely linear about our reality, about our pathway in time. Of course, linearness is a good shorthand, as it lets us work with complex ideas, for example here in sentences. Note that many of my sentences, although not all of them, are seemingly linear; they have beginnings and endings. So, we can shorthand and reduce our

---

[19] When I use the word "moving" here, that is shorthand for a vast interdimensional expansion I define in other books. I describe expansion and the concept of expansion and what it means to perceive expansion in books in the *KEYS TO CONSCIOUSNESS AND SURVIVAL SERIES,* such as *Volume* 3, titled *UNVEILING THE HIDDEN INSTINCT.*

realities in order to work with them. Yet, we have to remember we are really moving on multiple tracks at all times, in multiple dimensions. We live in, within, and without and around, all through, an interdimensional matrix or spectrum.

Nothing is linear. In fact, nothing is 3-D, nothing is only physical plane third dimensional. Nor is our reality only 3-D. Nor is our consciousness. Nor are our identities as individuals and as a species. So of course our survival is not only a 3-D matter.

So things are pretty vast. And we know this. And of course the vastness of the cosmos is both joyous and probably impressive, while also rather daunting. Those of you who have jumped off a boat into a big ocean to swim for a moment may have had that experience of feeling so, so tiny, so infinitesimal in this gigantic immeasurable space of the cosmos. How minor we are, we little blips here. And this is a lot to know. We are minor dots in this vast reality. And yet, each of us has this tremendously profound experience of existing while we are here in these biological bodies in this 3-D physical plane on Earth. And I believe we are also elsewhere at the same time, right now as well as later, beyond this thing we think of as now.[20]

So, when we talk about what some people are calling END TIMES, we are sensing something that is so vast, so beyond what our biological brains can fully comprehend. To work with such an idea, we must reach beyond traditional modes of knowing.

Yes, we do need all the scientific and psychological and spiritual information we can take in. Yet, there is so much more

---

[20] Refer to *Volume 10* in the *KEYS TO CONSCIOUSNESS AND SURVIVAL SERIES,* titled *SEEING BEYOND OUR LINE OF SIGHT.*

to know, to sense, to be aware of as we approach this coming end of a grand cosmic cycle and movement into the next one. Although there may be forces and factors seeking to keep us not knowing what we need to know about what is going on, we have the right to know and indeed can know.

The more conscious we can become of what is taking place, of how this is taking place on so many levels, the greater our possibility of shifting these END TIME developments -- events of this next OMEGA TRANSITION -- to a higher level transition, a META LEVEL OMEGA TRANSITION.

We do not need to follow this end time wave through on this physical plane. We know how to move our experience of this transition out of the physical dimension. We carry the key to navigating this transition through to survival. We carry the OMEGA KEY.

With each passing decade, year, and day of my present life, it has become more clear to me that I have come in to this time on this planet to help identify, understand, protect, and REVEAL to WE THE PEOPLE OF THIS PLANET, the OMEGA KEY to surviving this OMEGA TRANSITION time.

It has also become clear that there are those who would prefer that this KEY to survival here and beyond is restricted to their control.

12

BARBED BORDERS

Kirkenes, Norway: 1979. I was young, in my mid to late twenties, and was quite interested in adventurous jobs. I had become a research writer and editor for several persons working in global business and information intelligence fields, including for the gentleman I had earlier met in Central America (who, as noted earlier, I had much later discovered worked for the CIA). Over the years, I traveled with several of these persons to take notes, conduct research, edit, and write for them. While I at that time maintained moderate conversational levels of various languages (as my parents had spoken several romance languages and I had studied Mandarin, Chinese, Russian, and Spanish as a child and teen), I wrote and edited for these persons in my first and primary language, English, which is what they wanted. Many of them appreciated assistance with their own translations of their own notes into English.

My work for these people involved a significant amount of travel, which suited me well, as I was young and curious and wanted see and know this world from as many perspectives as possible. To this day, I continue to ponder the way I had somehow been found and offered this work.

One of the major projects involved doing writing, editing, and research for the gentleman I had met in Central America.

One year, this work took me on a trip up the coast of Norway on a large fishing trawler, where I was working with this gentleman and a few of his colleagues who told me they were documenting their findings on what they were observing. I was told I was helping to research North Sea and northern nations' transportation and commerce issues such as fishing and shipping. For several days, I traveled through relatively rough seas with these persons I was writing for, while living on a rather claustrophobic fishing trawler. I was told they were there taking photographs and notes, and also interviewing the fisherman and the captains of the ship. I was to take copious notes, and to help them to write up their reports and articles.

That project then took me by other boats, then by train and plane, to far northern Norway, to the town of Kirkenes on the border of Norway and Russia. It was becoming somewhat clear to me that the projects I was writing reports for were somehow involved in intelligence collection of some sort. However, the purpose and goals were unclear to me at that time. I did notice that a great deal of the notes I edited included detailed observations regarding what were apparently highly sensitive locations, latitudes and longitudes, and areas where there were certain fiords, ports, shipping lanes, submarine routes, ocean traffic activities, ocean mining activities, and movements of military forces' supplies, among other things.

I rarely asked for an explanation and in fact it was almost unspoken that I would not ask for an explanation. I was always to turn in all notes, even scratch copies I had made, at the end of each day.

Already back then, I did glean from conversations among these people I was working for that there were quiet tensions between those northern nations and what was back then the Soviet Union (and of course now is Russia).

Many years later, around the year 2020, I would hear Kirkenes was caught in what was then being called a building "spy war" as tensions between Russia and NATO were themselves building. By then, I had become more aware of the East West tensions that had been at play already back when I was working on these early so-called "Kirkenes Projects."

Back then, I somewhat naively arrived in Kirkenes to continue my work as note taker, editor, writer, researcher, and perhaps at times also errand girl, for these various persons I had been working with. I was provided a room in a hotel-like building, although tourism was not anywhere evident there in those years. The environment was rather grim.

I had earlier that day been taken by auto just a few kilometers away, to the well armed, and well layered with many many rows of barbed wire, border where Russian guards stared out at Norway. Intensely and forbiddingly ominous was the phrase I quietly gave myself to describe this setting.

I was glad to return to the hotel, or perhaps somewhat elegant barracks is a better description. There I was invited to dinner with the gentleman (who I later found out worked with the CIA) along with someone else he apparently knew, a man named Yan who said he sold Polish farm equipment to Russia. When I politely asked Yan what business brought him there, to this far northern location very close to the North Pole, where there was little farming and little farm equipment at least as far as I could see, he chuckled a little.

He made some kind of wry joke about: how one never sees

what is really going on; how nowhere in the world can we see what is actually taking place; how we cannot even know where to go and when to be there; how so much is so very hidden from everyone except the global elite. His joke made little sense to me at that time. I laughed a little anyway. A moment later, and then more so years later, I would realize none of this was very funny.

After I laughed a little, he added to his commentary rather sternly, "Excuse me for making light of a life and death situation. I am wrong to explain it that way. Let me put it this way: As you will see in the years to come, there are those at the top echelons of global control who quietly beneath the radar are already securing what they need to survive in the future when it will be needed. The rest of us on this planet will not have access when we truly need it unless we take action before then."

Yan was staring so hard at me that I had to blink several times to ease the tension.

Yan leaned forward, looked me still more intensely in the eye and with stone cold determination continued, "You will always remember what I say here today, you will always know this in the years and decades to come. You are now part of this understanding which we are calling the Kirkenes Project, in honor of this location on this blessed planet, Kirkenes, and in honor of so very very much more."

I had no response. I was trying to absorb what this man had just said, to register this on deep levels. I could not make sense of it all. But I could feel the profound significance.

Silence.

Then Yan shifted gears, lightened in mood, and asked how

good my Russian was. In those years, my Russian was good enough to carry on some pieces of conversation, especially when sprinkled with English, which he was quite fluent in. He told me he was impressed by the accent in which I spoke Russian. I explained that the team of two Russian teachers I had studied Russian with in high school had fled from the Soviet Union and landed their high school teaching jobs in Cupertino, California where I grew up. For some reason, both men at the table nodded as if they already knew this. I ignored my own surprise at this.

As we continued talking, I realized that I had seen this man's face before, in an airport in another country. The coincidence hit me, and, at the same time I told myself it was best not to say I remembered his watching me somewhere else. Why, why had he been watching me, and who was he? What was he doing there in Norway? If he was watching me, how did he know I would be in Norway, let alone in this out of the way place, Kirkenes? I did want to know, but did not ask.

The conversation with these gentleman moved on to other matters as we continued with our dinner. They continued to discuss matters of location, including various latitudes and longitudes. This was supposed to be a social dinner, so I was not there taking notes. And, it was clear as usual that location information such as latitude and longitude was nothing I should try to remember or know.

What also caught my attention during that dinner conversation were references to the matter of safety and security of what these men were describing as "protected territories." It became clear to me these territories being referred to were not particular states or nations. Rather, as one of them said to the other, these were viewed as UNLABELLED CRISIS SPACES.

Then something still more strange was suggested, although for many years I placed on the back burner of my mind the powerful inference made by Yan that night: These crisis spaces, which I would later come to call SURVIVOR TERRITORIES, exist both here on Earth in the physical plane, *and beyond -- not in what scientists call outer space, but in the Human consciousness itself.*[21] And even back then, that night, I had recognized the concept as one I had carried with me since I was a child.[22] So that night, I had known exactly what Yan was talking about or at least inferring--as if he and I had already discussed this matter sometime earlier. However, we had never before that night met.

It would be over time, as I grew into my career as a researcher, clinician, and author, that I would see how again and again in my life, I was for some reason being presented with the notion of locations AND ACCESS TO LOCATIONS that might be protected from discovery. It was not that we did not have world maps. It was that where we could be safe in the event of profound global events was being kept secret, as was the long term storing of plans, access mechanisms, and resources in these places.

In what later became called my OMEGA work, the SAFE

---

[21] I have further developed this SURVIVOR TERRITORIES AND PROCESSES BEYOND concept in various chapters of the books in the *KEYS TO CONSCIOUSNESS AND SURVIVAL SERIES,* such as chapters in *Volume 3* of that series, titled *UNVEILING THE HIDDEN INSTINCT,* and in *Volumes 5 and 6,* the *OVERRIDING THE EXTINCTION SCENARIO* books.

[22] As a child, I had already known I would decades later write books titled, *HOW TO DIE AND SURVIVE,* which are *Volumes 4, 11, and 13* in the *KEYS TO CONSCIOUSNESS AND SURVIVAL SERIES.*

LANDS and SURVIVOR TERRITORIES concepts were certainly influenced by my connection to the Kirkenes Project. Over the years, certain people kept showing up in my life and presenting me with the notion that the designations of certain areas, and accesses to these areas, were being unlabeled to keep them secret from the general population, from WE THE PEOPLE OF THIS PLANET. This I would eventually say and more deeply explain in the esoteric-scientific global crisis story portrayed in the REVEALING THE OMEGA KEY novel, and also on the pages of this present book, DETECTING THE OMEGA DECEPTION.

That night in Kirkenes, I said something, something I worked through in my mind before saying, making sure I dumbed myself down just a bit so as not to alert anyone that I was thinking about this very much. Still, I remember the quizzical looks on their faces when I naively asked these men my question. "Is it that specific information, plans, places, and spaces are unlabeled to keep them from being identified by the enemy? And if so, who is the enemy in this case -- IS IT THE PEOPLE OF THIS PLANET, WE EVERYDAY PEOPLE OUT HERE? Are WE THE PEOPLE out here those a rogue faction of the global elite identify as being: people they do not want to allow access to, or even knowledge of, plans for and locations of safety and survival?" I immediately felt I had said too much. I was actually shocked that this question had come out of my mouth, that this question was in my mind.

Silence.

One of the gentleman at the table finally said, "It is that there may be a time when such spaces are the most precious on the planet, and beyond. This will become more clear to you, and thus to all of us, in the decades to come, certainly in your present lifetime. You will eventually be working daily on this matter, as this will become your raison d'etre, you will see."

I nodded. It would be years later when I would write about how my OMEGA WORK was already most certainly addressing this matter.

When I wanted to continue with this conversation, the other gentleman at the table changed the subject of the conversation to dessert, which by the way was surprisingly delicious.

It would be approximately a year later, when I was back living in my cottage near U.C. Berkeley where I was completing one of my PhDs, that Yan would show up at my door and demand I come to Moscow with him. This was surprising as I had never given him my address.

I said no and never went to Moscow. He left for Moscow, then continued for several years to write me from Moscow, insisting I join him at his expense in Moscow. Finally, the gentleman, perhaps I should say CIA agent, I had met in Central America, one of the people I had been working for when in Norway, told me he would make sure that Yan never approached me again. But Yan did later contact me again, although it was much later. And others did as well.

13

MEET THE NEW OMEGA PICTURE

When I began publicly speaking about my early draft of the novel, REVEALING THE OMEGA KEY, I saw that these book talks and events were quite different from those I had been doing regarding my other books. I saw that some persons were taking this work of fiction quite seriously. Many of these people were focusing on the concepts of *apocalypse* and *end time.* Some were even calling my work the new *Book of Revelations.* I continued to insist this was just a book of fiction. I was taken aback, actually stunned, by all this. *What is going on here,* I kept asking myself.

I wanted to know the people who really believed, whether for scientific or for religious or for other reasons, in the apocalypse, and also those who were either actively preparing for it or actively working to prevent it.

As if by magic, although I knew it was not magic, I was found by many different strongly persuaded people, with many different perspectives on the situation -- again ranging from scientific to philosophic to religious to political to other forms of world views and beliefs.

Some who approached me even told me they were "armed

and ready to go." When I said, "Go what, where?" they insisted to me that my work would be something those in power would want to stop, that they would protect me. I responded, "Please, please know this: what I have written is a novel, just a novel." When that was not convincing enough, I would add, "Look, what I am talking about is not about fighting with arms and weapons. This is about responding to the suppression of information and access we may all need in order to survive coming Earth changes -- responding by becoming as informed and aware as possible. Information is the weapon, not guns, please."

In the decades since I first began speaking on my OMEGA WORK, I found the pressure so great that for a time I took my work on this material silent or at least somewhat underground. Yet now, some decades later, many people from different walks of life are still calling me to step forward and resume my OMEGA WORK.

Beginning when I first began writing the OMEGA novel, even its early drafts, and continuing to this day, I could and still can feel some kind of calling pressing me to write this novel and its related material, and to share it with the world. At first, I tried to avoid this sensation, to reason it away. Yet, over time, it was clear that there are some experiences that are simply not entirely explained in conventional ways.

Parallel to this OMEGA WORK, I was called, literally by a demanding voice washing into my head, to write a book about death and its true nature. I understood that Humanity needed to understand that ecological and planetary disaster could mean large scale risk to the lives of the Humans and other animals on this planet. I saw that we need to understand the risks we may perhaps someday face and how to respond to these. And while doing this, I saw that we need to change our understanding of death itself. And indeed, over these years, driven by an insistent calling, my books on death and dying have come to me and insisted I write them, in the form of titles such as *How To Die And Survive* and *Seeing Beyond Our Line Of Sight*.[23]

At the same time, I have experienced various social and other pressures, some even quite threatening, not to make available this information I have written to help people. The pressure not to share this information with WE THE PEOPLE OF THIS PLANET has been both subtle and the opposite of subtle, and has been ongoing. Among these pressures are those visible and invisible pressures, pressing me to keep silent any knowledge of this OMEGA DECEPTION PLAN that I write about on the pages of this present non-fiction book, and also in the companion novel, REVEALING THE OMEGA KEY. I have pretty much been told not to inform WE THE PEOPLE OF THIS PLANET. Basically, I have been told to shut up.

Over the years, it has occurred to me that those persons (such as myself and others) who may be consciously sensing what is taking place are being tagged, noted, perhaps watched, for what they do with this information, and for how much of this information they are actually consciously processing.

---

[23] See *Volumes 4, 10, and 11* in the *KEYS TO CONSCIOUSNESS AND SURVIVAL SERIES.*

NOTES FROM THE FRONT

14

HOW I GOT HERE

Many times I've been asked how I got here, how I reached this point in my life where DETECTING THE OMEGA DECEPTION and its partner book, the novel, REVALING THE OMEGA KEY, have been pressing me to step forward.

Generally speaking, being asked how I got here is a nice question. Of course I often reply, "Do you mean how was I born?" This is perhaps the best approach, as I remember being born. I didn't like it, those fluorescent lights blasting into my eyes,. Even though my mother had me by natural childbirth, I was born in a hospital and the fluorescent lights were the first sight. This was a yellow kind of light I found very unpleasant. This shocking light was the first thing my biological eyes perceived of this world outside the womb.

However the birth was conducted, I, as most of you, got here by what seem to be rather normal means: biological birth. Yet, like many of you, I have also had experiences that tell me we have all arrived here by many means, not just biologically.

I remember clearly much of my childhood, even my early childhood, such as being four years old. That was when my grandfather brought us a piano and I quickly learned to play Chopin, the music of the dog chasing his tail. For some reason,

playing the piano felt like something I had done before. I still remember sitting at the piano and kind of knowing it. I let my father give me some basic piano lessons, but I also kind of knew the piano. I was young and didn't know the phrase déjà vu. Yet there were so many such déjà vu's I remember having in those early years and also later on as I grew up, and even now as an adult. (Indeed, this OMEGA WORK itself feels so much like a grand déjà vu.)

Bless my parents. They were sort of artistic intellectual esoterics, themselves struggling with being 3-D biological Humans, although I didn't know this until much later in life, when they were already gone. They also were pretty strict, no white sugar and no TV. I was the oldest kid, so the strictness was imposed upon me longer and faded as the years went by. By ten years of age, I got to see television about an hour a week and that was the Sunday night Walt Disney TV show.

We didn't get much white sugar. So when the Sunlight Bread truck would drive through our neighborhood selling other people fresh greasy donuts full of sugar, I didn't get them but I craved them. And once in a while, I would sneak out with a few nickels and dimes, get a donut and hide it and have it bit by bit, very carefully. So while I didn't get much sugar, when I did, it sure seemed like a treat.

My parents were also funny about school. While they were glad to send me to school, and were proud parents of children in public schools, my father would say to me many times a week, "Just go to school because you have to, it's the law, and when you come home, I will teach you something." My father had a fascinating attitude. By the time I was nine years old, he was giving me books to read about every major religion in the world.

He also gave me the book titled, *Project Blue Book,* which definitely held my attention.

As a child, I was having dreams that I was out of my body at night. I remember one night being in the air, looking down and seeing my father working in the garden. I was floating above him. I can still see this all these years later. At that time, I just took this experience for granted, and as normal. My father had a serious nine-to-five job working at Jet Propulsion Laboratory, dealing with science and engineering issues and all kinds of related things, like space rocket fuel propellant. But, he would like to do relaxing things at night after work. I would sometimes go to sleep and fly around in the sky, look down, and see him working in the garden.

I did other things when I was out of my body at night. Sometimes when I would fly out of my body in my dreams, I would tell my dad about it the next day. I wasn't really sure how to describe what was happening, but I tried. The best I could do was grab onto something that I knew about.

I would say, "Daddy, last night Walt Disney took me through the air in the Sunlight Bread truck." To this day, I remember that my father never scoffed or laughed at me, and he never looked surprised at what I was telling him. I can still see his face. He would say, "Oh, OK." And this would happen a lot. I'd say, "I had that dream again. And, there were people there but they didn't look like people, but I talked to those people."

Then things moved into further communication with these beings or dream beings. I told my father, "Last night they told me they are my real parents." And I remember my father looked at me very kindly and said, "Oh, OK. Well, they may be your real parents, but while you're here, your mother and I are taking care of you, and you are going to be *our* child. And you're going to stay here and do this."

There were times when I wondered if my father meant that I should not fly off into the sky for good, go away with those beings who said they were my real parents. I did not ask this question, but decided if the opportunity to fly away arose, I would stay here at least for many many years. Yet, I continued to wonder, these beings who said they were my real parents, who are they? Where are they from? Many years later, I would ask them this question.

I remember my father basically telling me to stay here. First of all, this was wonderful, this gave me some security. But I also remember my father telling me, and he didn't say this, but the implication was, "You can do this. You can dream this. You can be aware of these unusual things and beings; however, you're going to live this physical plane life the way it is here, and do this with this mommy and daddy, find out what it's like to live here on this Earth."

So that became an awareness I had even before I was aware I had the awareness. I do remember knowing pretty clearly, at the ages of four, five, and six, that I would someday write books about traveling beyond, and one or more books about dying and surviving. I began seeing pictures of book covers with these words on them. I saw myself writing the pages of these books. And sure enough, many decades later, I wrote these and other books that you see now in the KEYS TO CONSCIOUSNESS AND SURVIVAL SERIES. The HOW TO DIE AND SURVIVE books are presently a three book set (Volumes 4, 11, and 14) within that series. In fact, I wrote an early pilot version of HOW

TO DIE AND SURVIVE at the end of the 1990s -- responding in part to my early work on the early draft version of my OMEGA story – and responding in other part to a series of most unusual experiences during which I felt quite clearly called to write this material that itself wanted to be titled, HOW TO DIE AND SURVIVE, of all things.

As the years have gone by, I have come to understand that these books are also about the notion that ***there are territories we have a right to access, both here on Earth in the physical plane, and BEYOND.***[24]

I have also come to understand that there have been those throughout Human history who have sought to suppress knowledge regarding access to what I call ***after-life domains***. This realization has surfaced within my mind, heart, and soul as I have worked to make the OMEGA WORK and the *KEYS TO CONSCIOUSNESS AND SURVIVAL SERIES* available to people living in these times when we are approaching the turn of time. This realization is profound and requires deep commitment on my part, as this is why I am here on this planet at this time. I have somehow known this since I was a child.

It is in doing this work that I have encountered those who wish to keep us from knowing what we have a right to know about survival here on Earth and BEYOND. Standing up to this OMEGA DECEPTION is a challenge, and I thank all those who are also engaged in parallel work. And to those who would suppress this knowledge and awareness, well, we are developing other routes of knowing, many ancient messages

---

[24] Refer to *Volume 10* in the *KEYS TO CONSCIOUSNESS AND SURVIVAL SERIES,* titled *SEEING BEYOND OUR LINE OF SIGHT.*

coming to us through time, and much data surfacing from deep within our consciousness-es where we placed it for safekeeping. (See the *KEYS TO CONSCIOUSNESS AND SURVIVAL SERIES* books for more on this.)

15

CALLED IN FROM THE COLD

Silicon Valley, California, 1990. Among my various work activities, I had developed a consulting business addressing workplace mental health and related matters such as employee substance addiction. This work frequently took me into what was then and still is called Silicon Valley, where at that time many employers were addressing serious addiction issues, such as the poly drug addiction issues of cocaine and alcohol. This in itself was both fascinating and demanding work. Several employers had hired me to come into their workplaces and assess the extent of the substance use issues there, and to then conduct workplace seminars on addiction.

One evening after one of these long consulting days, I was on my way back up to my home in Northern California. A windy storm had hit and driving was becoming difficult. As I decided to pull over for a while, I realized I had not eaten all day. So I made my way to a cafe located right off the highway. It was a clean and quiet place, where a few other customers had gotten off the freeway to eat something and wait out the storm. I was glad for the rest and dinner, and pulled out my notes to review them.

Deep in my work, I did not notice someone approach my table until he was already sitting down there. As he placed his coffee cup on my table, I looked up and said, "Excuse me, please sit at one of the other tables, I am working. Thank you."

He sat down anyway, saying in a low tone so as not to be heard by others there, "Excuse me, I think I know you."

I really did not appreciate this pick up line and let him know with a frown. "No you do not."

He leaned forward in his chair and said very quietly, "Kirkeness."

I immediately was on alert and telling myself he should not know I was on alert. I looked at him as blandly as I could and responded also very quietly, "What? I do not know what this is."

He simply nodded and quietly replied, "You do, however it is good you say you do not."

We were quiet for a while. The hostess came by and filled the two coffee cups on the table. "Anything else?" she said.

The two of us at this table said at the same time, "No thank you."

When the hostess was out of earshot, the man said, "You knew we would want to meet with you for updates at some point."

I realized I was not going to be able to pretend I did not know what he was talking about much longer. I knew, however not very much, about what he was referring to. This was something about that strange work I had been doing, and that related dinner meeting I had attended, in Kirkenes, Norway, some years earlier.

All I then said was, "What do you want with me?"

"Time to check in, you know this," he said.

"No, I do not know this. I have never agreed to any further work related to Kirkeness, or to any other project with those people, for that matter."

"Certainly you recall making this agreement."

"Again, I say no I do not. And whatever this is about, my answer is no."

"Sorry, but *it* does not work like that. You are committed for life once you are identified and brought in."

I tried not to raise my voice, as I did not want to attract attention. I practically whispered my quite irritated response, "IT? What is this IT you are talking about?" But just as I said this, I recalled something about being in a situation where I was told I had been brought in to "the work" and would always belong to "the project" from that point on. So I did know a little about what this man was talking about, but only a little so far as I knew.

Silence for a few minutes.

"Look, I am not sure what this is about. Who are you and how did you find me? Are you following me? Stalking me?"

"Who I am does not matter. How I found you? Well, you are not hard to find, you have for years been getting quite a bit of coverage for your work, your articles and books on various psychological and social issues. Plus, you do know we've been tracking you for a long time."

"Seriously? Ever since Kirkenes?" I asked still irritated, but I sort of knew he was right.

"Actually tracking you much longer than this. You know this. Since your childhood in Cupertino."

I was floored, yet somehow I knew that he was right. I had been tagged and tracked for years. So I simply said as quietly as I could, "What in the hell do you want with me?"

He looked me in the eye somehow both coldly and kindly and practically whispered his reply, "Just a reminder there is work to be done."

"Whatever this work is, I quit. I am not available. I have a very busy life and I do not want to do whatever this is you want."

"We want you to do nothing but what you do, at least for now."

"What in the hell does this mean?"

"Simply that we will continue to track you, to be in touch from time to time, that there is nothing for you to do but continue to do as you feel you are called to do."

I simply stared at him and raised my eyebrows.

"You are plugged in, and you serve by following your instincts."

"And what if I choose not to serve who and whatever the f-- this is?"

"There is no choice to be made. Simply by existing you are in service."

"I cannot accept this dictum," I said. However, as I spoke I felt the imperative. It was the Project Kirkenes thing.

"Times will move forward. Things will change in the coming years, powerfully intensify. You will understand your calling as you mature further into the knowledge you carry."

"Oh come on, give me a break. This is ridiculous and I need you to leave now."

The man grinned just a little, seemed to be trying not to chuckle. "You are like the spy who does not come in from the cold, ever, yes?"

I could not help but laugh. All I said was, "Please let me get back to my work now. I myself would leave, however I am going to wait to drive until this storm backs off."

"Understood, and good evening," was all he said. He then stood up, put a few dollars on the table to cover his coffee, closed his coat, and walked out the door. I watched out the window as he got into his car, and drove off in the storm.

NOTES FROM THE FRONT

16

SO THERE I WAS

1990s, California. For years following that strange meeting off the highway during that storm, I decided to work even harder at what I was doing in my then present life, to be less and less available for whatever it might be that that man had been talking about. Of course, I did know what this man was talking about, as this was Project Kirkenes. This would become still more clear to me later in my life.

Some years after that meeting, I was still more engaged on several career tracks at the same time. I was co-operating a clinic, maintaining a private practice, had worked with a large number of people experiencing mental health and chemical dependence crises, was still doing a great deal of consulting inside corporations regarding workplace mental health and substance use issues, and among other things, was teaching as a lecturer in the Hass School of Business at U.C. Berkeley where I taught the topics of mental health in the workplace, and employee well-being. I was also parenting one of the most amazing children to come into this place, physical plane Earth, in these times. (I will leave this amazing part of the story for another book.) Concurrently, my work as an author was streaming ahead with my several new books on social and psychological issues. And, at the same time, my earlier and very first book, which had been on child day care, and child care for working families, which had taken me onto the Oprah Winfrey Show, was now resurfacing. So I was quite busy, to put it mildly.

I found I had what felt to be limitless energy. Of course, this was not the case, yet I was so intensely motivated that I found I could do more than expected much of the time. So, I was in the middle of several big careers when at the same time, most nights between midnight and six in the morning, I also wrote the first draft of my OMEGA WORK, in the form of this end-time mythology novel. I felt driven to get this written, and did not find the writing in the middle of the night tiring. At the same time, also during the night, I was drafting the first of many books I would write on death and dying. For me, my death and dying work was closely tied to the OMEGA WORK in that looking at threats to survival, possibilities of extinction, resonated with death issues. However, for me, both the OMEGA WORK and death and dying work I was doing were related as ***I was writing about survival, not death***. Later, I indeed did write my *How To Die And Survive* books, which even by the title were clearly looking at surviving, surviving whether it be death of the body or extinction itself.

Somehow this all fit into my life. My OMEGA novel was incorporating ancient teachings from religions and mythologies and other sorts of worldviews, as well as scientific findings, and also incorporating my experiences with numerous experts on various global warming issues. The novel opened describing a major oil spill, much like one where I had years earlier actually been present, helping with the cleanup of oil-covered birds on a beach on the North Sea (off the coast of France).

Suddenly, various people started contacting me, asking me to write disaster books, some romantic and some more terror-oriented. I said no each time. My OMEGA WORK was of a far different ilk and had a far different purpose, and would stay that way. I had to protect and further develop the essential messages coming in.

I had not expected much attention would be given my first draft of my OMEGA story. So much other coverage had been given, and was being given, to my nonfiction mainstream work and writing. I was glad of this as my non-fiction was my primary work. Yet suddenly, I was asked to do a book signing for this new novel, right there in the San Francisco Bay Area. Ironically, or should I say oddly, this pre-scheduled book signing ended up taking place when the air in that area, the entire sky, was suddenly filled with heavy smoke as the result of a major eighty-thousand-acre fire raging out on the coast. Perhaps this fire would have been irrelevant to my book talk that night, were it not for the fact that this novel ended in atmospheric fire following what this novel described as a range of global climate and geophysical Earth changes and catastrophes.

Although I had quite a bit of experience doing book talks and appearances, I was truly unprepared for this particular book talk on this particular book. Even getting to this event proved difficult. Leaving my home was difficult because at the last minute there was a person in my home who did not want me to go, who suddenly invited dinner guests and wanted me to cook for them. And, when I said no to this, that I had someplace I had to be, my feet were stomped on in the pantry. It was quite difficult to get out to be at my book talk. I arrived at the book talk a little disheveled, with bruised arms covered over by long sleeves, and with bruised feet luckily covered by my boots, although I was limping. I was met there by people who had been

expecting me, not just by the host and hostess of the book talk at this major setting, but by others who had heard I would be there.

The moment I arrived, somebody said, "Let us buy you some tea so you can relax before you talk." Since, thank goodness, I was a little early as I always try to be before I give a talk, I was able to say yes.

I had tea with these kind people who turned out to be an American businessman with another gentleman he wanted me to meet, someone he had hosted to fly up to California from Peru. This man was from the southern Peruvian Amazon area, at what he called the beginning and the end of Peru, the spot of a special intersection of ley lines where various sacred waters of the Amazon flow together.

That night, this businessman had brought this Peruvian tribal leader there to hear me speak. It turned out that they wanted to hear me speak, and then to ask me to let them pay me to come to Peru to learn what they had to say about the Earth, and the ancient prophecies, and what was happening on the planet now. I thanked them and said that this invitation was all very interesting, quite an honor and so wonderful, yet I had a very busy schedule. So I would think about it and get back to them.

Then I went in to give my book talk. As I looked around the room, I saw that it was wall-to-wall people, so crowded that many were sitting on the floor as the chairs were all full. But then I saw that many of the people were also in tears. Some were actually lightly whipping themselves and engaging in other apparently ritual behaviors.

My first response was that I had better make it clear to everybody that "*This is fiction*. This is a novel." So I did that. Yet many people nodded no. And I said, "Look, this story came to me, pretty much demanded I write it. This has been and still is a powerful creative experience, to be so engrossed in a project that it almost drives one to get it done, even fills one's dreams with characters, voices and visions, messages and directives, very real experiences in other locations and eras. But this does not itself make all this nonfiction, not at all. Yet, this drive to write this book made it easy for me to write this story between midnight and six in the morning every day, or night should I say, for a very long time. I felt I had to tell the story. But I do want to call this fiction."

There were a lot of questions and there was a lot of interest. This was the beginning of my still more deeply realizing that what I was working on was being taken so very seriously, as if the Human spirit was speaking through the hearts and minds of my audiences. My voice, the voices of my book's characters, my audiences' voices, were all speaking to each other. I could feel the voices in the novel speaking to the readers and to me, through me, through the words on the pages and out to this world This meta-level dialog was at first both exciting and unnerving.

The calling, the mandate, to identify, protect, and help REVEAL THE OMEGA KEY began and has continued to call me throughout my life. Even when at times I stepped back from this work, I was again called to return to it.

Sometime after a speech about all this I had given to a very large audience (approximately 2,000 people), I received a call from someone who wanted to fly me to another state, I won't name the place or the location. He said, "We'd like to meet with you. We want to sponsor you and your great work on what's happening on Earth." I replied, "Well I'm a clinician, have a private practice. And I write in many fields, and I'm lecturing at U.C. Berkeley, and this isn't my major venue." And they said, "Nevertheless, this is very important and it's all you'll ever need to do your work. We guarantee you that our offer is solid and lasting."

I asked, "Can you tell me more about who you are?" And the gentleman answered, "At this time I won't give you our name. We will of course be providing you our name. But the reason we want to do this is because we have been part of a major long term global crime syndicate, and we feel that part of why the Earth is suffering so much is because of all the," and now the man used the word sin, "sin that our organization has been involved in for a very long time. God is reacting to what we have been doing on Earth and is punishing the world for our sins."

I said, "This is all so very profound, and thank you for contacting me. Yet, I don't get on private jets with strangers out of the blue. So, it's an incredible offer and I understand you want to do some good for the planet, and maybe there's another way we can come at this." ... I did receive many more calls from these people, and I did continue to turn their offers down. But as time proceeded, I became ever more aware that this material was being taken very seriously by many different groups with many different world views.

Around the same time, a publisher contacted me and wanted me to write a book, but not really this book. This publisher wanted me to remove the science and history, along with many ancient teachings, and to have me write a lot more sex and romance into my OMEGA story. I didn't want more sex in the book, and I did not want to remove the information, the key messaging, from the book. They wanted the book to be racier and more Hollywoodish. They basically wanted a whole different book. They told me that they would pay me to "TAKE YOUR OMEGA WORK OFF THE MARKET RIGHT AWAY."

I was stunned. Here again was that great AND GROWING pressure not to put this information out. I could feel this pressure coming at me from so many directions. I had to say, "Look, if you want the essential messaging in this OMEGA STORY, my OMEGA WORK itself, removed from the world, I have to say no. How can I say yes when I have been called through time to step forward in this lifetime I am living here, to bring this KEY information in to this world? Clearly there is some distinct pressure to suppress this essential messaging coming to us through time, TO STOP ME FROM REVEALING THIS OMEGA KEY." I would feel the economic consequences of this pressure, and of my not selling out, for many years.

Meanwhile, the calls about this book increased, running parallel to calls I was also getting about my mainstream work. There were times when I was told to drop my OMEGA STORY, and my related OMEGA WORK, as this was taking away from my mainstream career. There were times I was told the opposite as well.

Again and again, there were forces and factors pressuring me to take my OMEGA material away from the world, and to suppress release of the messages coming to me.

There I was, being invited to speak on my OMEGA WORK, with invitations coming in from all over the country and even the world. I could not keep up, as I had a mainstream career to maintain and protect. I also had myself to protect, as some of those who wanted to shut me down were indeed quite threatening, demanding I be quiet. I was constantly surprised at the intensity of this effort to keep me from sharing my OMEGA WORK -- and also at some of those who were pressuring me to be quiet, as some of those persons projected themselves to the public to be of the opposite inclination.

The duplicity and double messaging of those threatening me continued. I could feel there was something about the messaging in my OMEGA WORK, about the OMEGA KEY itself, that various forces and factors wanted to stop from being disseminated into the awareness of Humanity living in this physical plane on Earth. I kept telling myself this was not happening, and yet it continued.

I agreed to be a keynote speaker at a major conference being held on a reservation in South Dakota. I was surprised at this invitation, but felt I wanted to be there and needed to be there. So I got there, traveling to Santa Fe, New Mexico, where I had clients, then to Denver, Colorado, where I had clients, then to the Lakota Sioux reservation in South Dakota.

When I arrived, the conference chairman, Standing Elk, who later became a good friend, was quite gracious with me and introduced me as a keynote speaker. Before I went on stage, I asked Standing Elk, "I'm assuming this is a fifteen-minute talk, yes?" He said, "Oh, half an hour or as long as you want."

Well, I went up to the stage, saw the unexpectedly large crowd I would be facing, took a deep breath, silently said a prayer asking for guidance and strength as I did this presentation, then started speaking, opening with a statement similar to my hourglass words at the opening of this book. I did however add this sentence:

We watch every day another species dying out. What makes us think we are not in line? What can we do to wake ourselves up? What can we do to survive both here and beyond?

Over an hour later, I paused my speech and looked at Standing Elk who was still sitting in the front row in this very crowded amphitheater. I whispered, "Haven't I gone on far too long?" He said, "No, we're all very fascinated, just keep going."

I apparently spoke for a couple hours, and spoke about how time may be running out. We should watch the clock. The planet is calling us. We must pay attention. And that was the beginning of my truly knowing on very deep, even cellular, even neural, level that this piece of fiction, and my OMEGA WORK itself, was far far far more than fiction.

This is no game, this is reality. No es un juego, es realidad.

So here I am to tell my story. Not because my own story is in itself an important story, but because I have been told that I must tell my story so people understand who it is that is sharing this information and writing these books, and all of the books in all of these series that I have been writing and publishing and making available to people everywhere to help us make this great LEAP in our evolution -- and therefore in our survival.

DOUBLE
OMEGA
ALPHA

PART THREE

NOTES FROM THE FRONT

17

SEEING BEYOND

Earth or Beyond, undisclosed location, 2010. "Nightly, the next few weeks, 0300 to approx. 60 min before dawn, PST." I had come to know quite well what these messages were talking about, and of course I would join in. I would be available nightly from 3AM on, for a few hours. This worked for me, as somehow I did not feel exhausted the days following these telephone meetings, and this work did not interfere with the rest of my life. If anything, this work enhanced my growing perception of what was really going on, of the **interdimensional drama being played out everywhere, with Earth and her biosphere one of the key the theaters, one of the key battlegrounds.**

There was really no one I could tell about this work -- certainly not my colleagues in various workplace settings. Certainly not my friends and family. The scientists who had organized this project had asked me to agree to never communicate with them about this by telephone or email or any electronic means. Paper mail to private mailboxes was the only option. That and yes, burner phones.

Other than this, there would be times when one or two of these scientists would sort of bump in to me somewhere, have a quick cup of tea with me, and quickly discuss anything that needed be said in hushed tones. And, as noted earlier, there would also be times when one or two of these scientists would show up where I was presenting or speaking on my OMEGA WORK and protect me as they had been doing for years.

I had long accepted that there was some meaning in this adapted or enhanced remote viewing work, that this break off group and its modification of the previous remote viewing activities was for good reason, essential reason. Whether I was engaged because I was fascinated, intensely intrigued, or even felt the work being done was profoundly important to life on Earth, remained unanswered -- at least in my conscious mind. However, on a deeper level, I knew this was somehow part of the work I had committed to years earlier, part of the original undercover Kirkenes Project.

There are forces and factors, here on physical plane Earth AND BEYOND collaborating to further their own survival agendas. As I began to ever more focus on what this meant, deeper recognition of the vast reaches of what I had come to see is the OMEGA CABAL became increasingly clear to me.

18

WE HAVE A CHOICE

Petersberg Climate Dialogue, Berlin, Germany, July, 2022. United Nations Secretary General, António Guterres made himself heard around the world (and likely even BEYOND) when in mid 2022, he told the nations of this planet, "Half of humanity is in the danger zone, from floods, droughts, extreme storms and wildfires. No nation is immune. Yet we continue to feed our fossil fuel addiction." Guterres then added those words that will forever resonate in Human history,

"We have a choice. Collective action or collective suicide. It is in our hands."

The dimensions of this dictum are immense, well beyond words, well beyond our everyday, physical plane lives. And, between the lines of this dictum, beyond even these profound words of Secretary General Guterres, there is something more we must see now.

It is quite possible Guterres recognizes this vast reality, senses the role of the global elite, who are already working both on and off planet, in the fate of Humanity. It is quite possible Guterres senses the interdimensional elements of all this. It is quite possible he, as many of us do, feel the pressure not to openly talk about all that is in our awareness.

There was a time when those who said the Earth was not flat were ridiculed, even persecuted. Now today, when I am saying Human evolution must most rapidly reach into other domains, even into non-physical domains of Humanity's consciousness, FOR THE SAKE OF OUR SURVIVAL, the risk of ridicule and persecution, retaliation for speaking this truth to this power, is present.

What is also present is the risk that there are indeed those with a stake in keeping WE THE PEOPLE OF THIS PLANET unaware and uninformed of the extent to which they:

**a self-selected segment of the global elite,
members of the OMEGA CABAL,
have already reached beyond the norm of our given realities
to hoard both here and beyond,
opportunity and resources, and access to these, for themselves.**

How far can those who see what is actually taking place go? How much can they safely say, even when they do recognize what is happening here -- even when they do see the role of some of the most globally powerful top of the food chain actors, members of the most powerful wealthiest elite of the global elite, who are driving Humanity to the eve of destruction? What truth can safely be told?

19

THE CHARACTER AS BOTH SYMBOL AND VOICE

When I first created and then later expanded upon REVEALING THE OMEGA KEY's lead female character, Sheeyah, I somehow knew that Mother Earth was actually the main character. Yet Sheeyah was, in so many ways, the star antagonist, or was it protagonist, a question answered differently depending on who was describing her. I chose to portray Sheeyah as the founder of an organization I named Earthcult, and thus the leader of a global environmental movement standing up to corporations and exploiters, mega exploiters of the environment and deniers of what was happening. The opposing character, also either a protagonist or an antagonist or both, who she fell in love with, had a completely different position (or so it seemed) regarding the Earth and increasing Earth changes.

As founder of the major global underground movement, Earthcult, the character, Sheeyah, was stepping up to the Earth change challenges of our times, becoming a voice for WE THE PEOPLE OF THIS PLANET, for all life on Earth, and even for Earth herself. Sure enough, on the last pages of the very first draft, pilot, version of this OMEGA novel, a newsletter advertisement was included. It was called *"Underground Rising*

-- *The Global Underground Newsletter*." The newsletter advertisement read, "Free our species from bondage. Don't let true Humanity die. Be connected to the growing network of persons who seek liberation from the historical, political, philosophical, spiritual, geophysical, medical, and economic illusions that have been so long forced upon us by those planetary and off-planet entities who have controlled Human evolution. You have a right to know true freedom. You have a right to your position as a potent citizen of the cosmos. You have a right to the truth. *Underground Rising* serves as a checkpoint, a source, a form for the ideas upon which your true freedom depends. Give Humanity liberation or it faces obliteration. The proceeds of all subscriptions to this newsletter go to the production and distribution of this newsletter and to the cause it represents."

The results were astounding. Clearly, I had touched a nerve. I began hearing from people around the world that I was tuning in to the strong need of WE THE PEOPLE OF THIS PLANET EARTH to connect and know what is really taking place as we move into these times. It was becoming more and more apparent to me that, on a deep intuitive and even gut level, Humanity is sensing this profound transitional time period we have entered. What I had been describing in fictional terms was front and center now: We are looking at the approach of the GREAT RETURN, the CLOSE OF THIS GRAND COSMIC CYCLE, the coming of this NEW OMEGA TRANSITION.

Responding to that first *Global Underground Newsletter* announcement, I received letters from all over the world with promise of payment for subscription to this newsletter. I was astounded and immediately began outlining several issues of this newsletter. Then quite suddenly, and I was not in any way expecting this, I received contact from what I was told was the NSA, the U.S. National Security Administration, telling me I must take this newsletter down, and do so immediately.

I was floored. First of all, I had no idea that anyone that official was watching. Second of all, I certainly didn't know how to verify for sure this NSA was the contact it said it was.[25] And third of all, I did not really want to make myself more visible if a newsletter like this, the concept of Underground Rising, was catching the attention of those who wanted to stop me.

After doing some deep soul searching, I decided to cancel the newsletter. So far, in terms of publication, that newsletter did not occur and has not occurred. However, were this newsletter to occur now, it would be presented in another way. Readers are encouraged to watch to see whether this newsletter exists and what form it takes at this time.

Readers are also encouraged to search other underground sources for related information being posted by scientists and researchers, many who continue to wish to remain anonymous. Of course, some of you have attended private meetings of UNDERGROUND RISING where we have met directly, where we have discussed how high the stakes are now. Continue to protect this knowledge and yourselves and Humanity as we work to REVEAL THE OMEGA KEY.

---

[25] "The NSA is responsible for global monitoring, collection, and processing of information and data for foreign and domestic intelligence and counterintelligence." See https://www.nsa.gov/about/mission/

20

THE GREAT DEBRIEF

During many years of my adulthood, the CIA (and another intelligence organization that never actually fully identified itself) were both attempting to recruit me. As I noted earlier in this book, in the earlier chapter, *Called In From The Cold,* there were even a few occasions when I was being told I had already been recruited and had apparently accepted.

However, to my knowledge my acceptance never took place. Again and again over a period of at least ten years, I was invited to events and told along with the invitation that while I was there I would meet with members of the CIA who would like to talk to me about possible positions, jobs I might be interested in. For example, I was invited to attend a space shuttle launch and told that following it I would meet with various officials regarding my placement within the CIA. These numerous invitations continued to surprise me, as I had never actually applied for a job with the CIA or with any other intelligence organization.

Could I have somehow been identified and tagged as a potential agent? Over time, I even wondered whether I should be asking myself whether I had actually been identified and tagged as an *actual* agent. But agent of what, and how could it be that I would not know if I was an agent? I would continue to dismiss all this as simply government recruiting efforts, something many people out there were likely experiencing.

Still, I did wonder what about me, if anything, was being looked at, let alone tracked. Could I have been identified early on, as a Cupertino sixth grader in a class of children who had been extensively screened by group and individual tests that none of us had asked to take?

One day, one of the teachers of the unusual class I was placed in told me that I and a few others there had been further identified based on testing and interviews. Soon after that, a few of us were being sent in for more interviews. I say "we" here; however, those of us involved were told part of this new test was to see how little we would say to others about these interviews. So we could not talk to each other about these interviews. What a test to give children.

Additionally, these additional interviews were rather strange ones. The questions we were asked made little sense to a young person, unless these were treated as games. And indeed, some of these questions were treated as games. For example, we were asked questions such as: here is a situation, think of three possible chains of events that will follow and stem from this situation. Then draw or diagram or talk this out for us, however you think will be the best way to explain what you see. They told us to, "Think of how you can be the fastest one answering these questions." I still remember all these years later the atmosphere created for each of us who were being interviewed alone, without other children, and without our parents or regular teachers. Nothing about it felt like a game; there was more a rat in a maze sensation.

I said nothing about these interviews, except to one day sort of talk to my teacher about them, while making it clear I was not really talking about those interviews but wanted to know "if we could be done with all that now." The teacher looked at me, showing what appeared to be sympathy, then said nothing except, "Yes, done for now." I did not realize that these sort of interviews would later appear at various times in my life, and frequently feel like debriefings.

Soon after that, the teacher I had asked whether those interviews were finished gave me a copy of a novel by John Hersey, *The Child Buyer,* which had first been published back in 1960. This is the story of a government committee investigating a corporation's buying of a precocious genius-like child (among the many other children it had bought for use in defense industry-related work). This novel looks at the uses of intelligence as well as at how far we will go to defend democracy. What captured me as I read this book during my sixth grade year was the idea that children's minds could be used, and used as weapons. (There is much more to this fascinating novel, and readers are encouraged to check it out. It would be many years, later, in the 1980s, when a stranger would walk up to me after I had been giving a speech, place a book in my hands, telling me, "This is next after *Child Buyer,*" and walk away without giving me his name. I was stunned when I later checked the book out and saw that this was the story of an Earth-wide military force recruiting children to play virtual war games, which were actually wars taking place out in space.)

It was six years after I completed the sixth grade when a number of us who had been in these classes at various stages of our 6th to 8th grade educations were asked to speak and answer questions at a meeting of government directors of these programs. I was the youngest speaker, age seventeen at that time. Instead of praising the program, I said to the large group of adults in the room that I had been placed in that program without my permission, and that that program had put me so far ahead in school I could never fit in again. I had been socially and educationally and emotionally isolated. When I had finished that special accelerated sixth grade year, I was pretty much done with high school, but still had to go through junior (or middle) and then senior high school. And at the same time, the years since that program were a complete let down I told them, as nothing was as challenging and interesting as that class had been. I saw them all furiously scribbling notes as I spoke. Afterword, several came up to me and gave me their cards, asking me to meet with them. I never called them. And, so far as I know I never met with them unless they had found ways to present themselves in later years as representing other causes.

If so, were there others in this class who were now as adults having this same experience of being contacted by the CIA and other intelligence agencies for interview or even recruitment? I knew I could not ask anyone, as I was at risk of being retaliated against for disclosing. But for disclosing what, what, for God's sake? (Note that over the years, certain others I had known during my school years found ways to infer to me that they had had the same sort of experience.)

Eventually, I became more alert to the subtle forms of contact and questioning that I was experiencing from time to time. I began to ask myself whether there could have been other experiences where I had not only been contacted, but even been interviewed or even been debriefed. Indeed, there have been a few debriefings I later was told I had experienced. Each time, these were questionings that seemed somewhat coincidental, informal, accidental. As I note in a few different chapters of this book, I have at times been questioned and then later informed the questioner was indeed a CIA debriefer. Could it have been these instances where I was tagged? When if ever did this tagging begin?

Could it have been my family history? My grandfather had worked for the State Department, apparently for some of his years there for the State Department Intelligence Agency. He certainly had been at some key places in modern history. For example, he'd been on the last plane out of Shanghai in 1949, when the city fell to the Chinese Communist Party.

Could it have been the work of others close to me, some working in top secret research and engineering areas? I really can't pinpoint any one incidence of my being tagged, nothing for sure. But again and again, when I was presented with questions by those who were appearing to question me in various unusual circumstances, these were questions about what was going on with regard to current thinking about the planet, about the Earth, but more than this -- about survival, about what people were thinking about their own survival should times get very difficult. Again and again and again in my life, I saw these questions surfacing.

However all this was playing out, I liked to tell myself it was taking place in the background of my life. At same time, I was developing a solid career in the social and psychological services, sciences, clinical and policy fields. Still, concurrently I was continuously aware of the more undefined areas of Human work and investigation I was engaged in, areas relating to the survival of our and other species, for example.

21

SACRED WATERS OF TRUTH

1996, Peru. There I was at one of the key intersections of the sacred waters of the Amazon in far southern Peru. I was with people I'd never met before -- except for the leader, the Curandero and Runa Simi priest, who was leading this specially planned sacred ayahuasca ceremony event. This priest had sometime earlier been brought to me back in North America, at a talk I had been giving on my OMEGA WORK and its relationship to the work I had been doing on death and dying – or as I explained it, on death and **surviving.** (Indeed, as explained elsewhere, I did eventually write several books titled, *How To Die And Survive.*)

When I arrived, I met with this priest who had invited me to attend and as he described it, "Be trained in this tradition to see the real thing, to be trained the way I was, already as a boy."

I agreed to this training, replying in Spanish (the language we both could speak), "Thank you, I am honored. You know I want to learn of the real rituals. I want to learn to conduct these sacred processes the way that you do, and in the place that you do."

This priest responded, "All right. And, we want you to help us with these visitors." There were two other Americans there,

several people from Germany and Japan, and others from a few other nations. Few spoke Spanish but most did speak English, hence I was asked to translate for this priest so he could work with them through the rituals he was going to be conducting. He would translate his Runa Simi into Spanish, then I would translate for him his Spanish into English. I was also asked to be ready to help in any instances where participants might have difficult moments during their ayahuasca journeys. I agreed, as I had had extensive experience doing this sort of thing in other settings.

(A note here: Traditional use of ayahuasca among indigenous cultures along and surrounding the Amazon is said to trace back at least a thousand years. As a psychoactive and hallucinogenic medicinal plant, ayahuasca has long been used as ceremonial spiritual medicine, as well as socially, and apparently sometimes also in war. As an entheogen, this medicinal psychoactive is imbibed in ceremonial and sacred settings, frequently by those seeking insight, even visions, even healing. While in more recent times, ayahuasca is also being applied in some treatment settings with the goal of bringing on clinically measurable changes in emotion and behavior, or extensions of perception and consciousness, the effects of the ayahuasca experience are said to be most profound in traditional ceremonial and ritual settings.)

My agreement with my host was that, at a certain point, I would also participate at the level and dosage their own tribal leaders participated, not the lower dosage guests were given. I would be trained as their own curanderos were trained. It was important to this priest and his fellow curanderos that I understood that far too many others conducting such rituals both in Peru, and in North America and Europe, were not fully understanding what this was actually about. (In the years since, many have been trained in the sacred rituals by those living in the Amazon, guiding those they have been training to adhere to the authentic ceremonies and processes.)

At some point, I was asked if I was ready for the real experience, the one they themselves participated in. I said yes, at which point I was handed a deep huge cup of what I can only describe as sludge-like material. They explained that this was made from the ayahuasca plant, or as they called it, the "cord of death" or "vine of death." Many of these gentlemen said they had grown up there, living in the dirt next to these plants, had been in communication with these plants, with this soil, with this water, with this Earth, all their lives. Many of them said they were well over a hundred, even over a hundred and thirty years old. Some said that some of them had been there for centuries, and had come and gone from Earth, and were here again. Indeed, some of these people certainly did look older than any people I'd ever seen anywhere before.

So I took part in this journey. As I did, already early on, there were a number of people, guests, that appeared to be having a very hard time. Fortunately, many of these people did speak English. I could share the guidance of this curandero, this Runa Simi tribal leader who was leading these ceremonies in his Runa Simi language and in Spanish, as I could translate his Spanish into English.

At one point, when there was clearly some difficulty being experienced by some of these guests, the leader said to me in Spanish, "Please state this prayer for these people." And he began in Spanish reciting the Lord's Prayer, which of course I

knew, I had known since I was a child. I was quite interested in the bringing in of what at that time I assumed was mainstream Christianity to this ritual experience. I did go ahead and recite this prayer for the guests in English, both translating it from the Spanish it was being spoken in, and of course reciting it from my own memory. I saw that this prayer allowed the people having a difficult time handling their experiences to give these a spiritual framework, one they were familiar with. I could see that phrases such as, "Thy will be done, ***on Earth as it is in Heaven***" were helping guests to give context to their experiences. What became clear to me was that the messaging in this prayer was itself universal. I was later told that these men there leading this ceremony believed that Cristos, the first Christ, had actually walked their land some 30,000 years ago, back when Pangaea was their continent.

I asked the Runa Simi priest leading this ritual, "Is this prayer part of your belief system?" He smiled and responded, "You ask about our belief system, yet this is bigger than any one belief system. You know this. Your OMEGA WORK shows that you can understand the Earth speaks through prayer, calls us. Your death work shows you know there is more than this life here, and that we can live on. We brought you here from North America so you can help build a bridge between our worlds." I said, "Thank you, I am very grateful and honored, but why me?" He said, "Because of the work you are doing. Trying to bring Earth's teachings to the world at this time where the whole world desperately needs these. People need to know they can live."

So we continued in this work for many days. While I was there, I explored the journeys of these people coming to this

place for their own various reasons. I also explored the call to this place experienced by these Runa Simi Priests -- and I say men because it was all men performing this ritual. At least they appeared to be Human men. Their ongoing shape shifting, both during and outside of ceremony, seemed to reveal their other faces and forms. Some of these men said that sometimes they even shape shifted to become the ayahuasca vine itself.

[A note here: Shape shifting is generally thought of (in various ancient and modern beliefs, rituals, traditions, and practices) as being the shifting of the self into another form – perhaps for visionary, or exploratory, or empathetic, or healing, or other purposes. The concept of shape-shifting has been both positively and negatively applied by various belief systems. Some shape shifting is said to be self-willed; other shape shifting is said to be brought about by particular animals, or by out-of-body spirits, or even deities. Some out of body beings have been said to be seeking to come in and use the body of a person – such as in walk-in events. Some shape shifting is said to be a reward or advancement in awareness and capacity, in the ability to come and go from human form. Other shape shifting, at least in some traditions, is said to be a punishment where a god or other being forces a Human to become an animal. Many cultures and belief systems have had terms for the shape shifting their various gods (such as Zeus) can do, and that various mythological animals and beings (such as werewolves) can do. Other terms are regarding what individual people apparently may be able to do. Many terms for shape-shifting have appeared throughout history, ranging from one who changes shape, to skin-walker, to changeling.]

There I was with some of the most powerful teachers I'd ever imagined meeting. They generously shared their wisdom, insights, and visions. As I explored the Runa Simi traditions, I also had occasion to explore my own experience, which became quite intense as I had taken the heavy, heavy dose that they regularly give themselves.

I can still recall many moments of this experience which did change my life. Much of my work since has reflected this. Although I have participated in numerous other related experiences, this particular experience was one of, if not the most, profound and life-changing of all of them. What a wondrous journey, travel to way beyond, beyond any imaginable territories, to places and planets and visions of light so pristine and distinct and present – and to voices, astounding presences meeting me and speaking to me about my work on Earth, showing me Earth from far out there. I was so suspended out there, so engrossed in the luminous realities and so connected to the powerful presences, I was unaware that I had left my body back on Earth for so long.

I finally caught a glimpse of myself back down on Earth. Even all these years later, I can still see myself looking down on my body. I can still see my body way down below me, which was, as best as I could tell, vacated, just empty down there below me on a bench in the jungle. While I had been having out of body experiences since I was a child, that particular out of body experience, which as I was later told lasted for over twelve hours, changed my life. I found myself communicating with myself about those books I knew already as a child I would eventually write, the *How To Die And Survive* books. Presences, beings made of light, wise elders speaking through time, then told me I had to commit to my work and go back to my Earth life to do the work my Earth life was about.

I made this profound commitment while out there, way out there. And sure enough, just as I had found myself navigating the way out of my body, traveling so far out I visited other planets and universes for that matter, now I would have to navigate the way back in to my physical body, in to my physical plane life. I agreed to do this. But I waited and waited, in what I have come to call a **suspension in the exhilaration of the beyond.**

At one point, while still way out there, now looking down upon my physical body, I heard a voice calling me, calling me, saying, "Angela, Dr. Angela, come back. You have family, a beautiful daughter in North America, you must come back. You have work to do for Earth. We on Earth still need you." I realized that this Runa Simi priest who had invited me down to the sacred waters to join him was speaking to me. I heard his voice, and it was most definitely the word "daughter" that pulled me back. This would not be the only time this precious child would save my life.

So I found my way back. This in itself was quite a journey. I found a long seemingly infinite cord extending from me, the me who was way out there, to my physical body lying back down there on Earth. I realized that I had followed this cord of death out, and now would follow this cord of death – which was now this **cord of life**, back in.

Navigating my way back was a fascinating process, one I will never forget. First, I had to choose to make that return journey. Second, I had to feel what it was like to return to physicality once expanded so far beyond it.

That day, the trip back into my Earth life became part of the gateways and agreements and deals I was making in order to do my work. If I was going to travel that far out and see what I had seen that far out there, I had to take the responsibility to share this knowledge, a responsibility to bring this knowledge in and to do this very carefully.

I would also have to learn to protect myself as I did my life's work. Indeed, while I was suspended way out there, out of my physical body, as I decided to return to Earth, I found myself **negotiating with life itself** to return. I would come back, yes, and commit to doing this OMEGA WORK and the related death and dying work, which was actually death *and surviving* work. I could see the books I had as a child known I would someday write. These books were there in my mind writing themselves in my mind as they had been all my life, the HOW TO DIE AND SURVIVE books.

Ayahuasca, also known as the cord or vine of death, had been a means of accessing and clarifying what this lifetime I am living here on Earth is about.

All these years later, I understand more what it means to commit oneself to one's purpose. At times, I have walked away from the responsibility or at least taken a break when I felt threatened for conducting my work in these fields, even for conducting my thinking in these fields. But my work has continued to call me. I eventually came to understand that I would not and could not walk away from my OMEGA WORK, and the related HOW TO DIE AND SURVIVE work, as this is why I am here.

Over the years, there have been times when I was under attack for my work. Such attacks were actually rather frequent during my adulthood, including during some family, and some family-related business, legal issues. It was in those legal processes that I actually sat on the stand in a courtroom and was forced by the opposing side in a legal case to defend (for some reason) -- and even to read excerpts of – my writings and books, such as the early version of my OMEGA STORY, and my early writings on consciousness, and on death and dying.

Somehow, the opposing side's attorneys sought to discredit me based on my work, as a way of allowing them to try to argue that I was not mentally sound and therefore my claims were not valid. This was a cruel yet ridiculous argument, attacking even my first amendment rights. This was an argument which of course they did not win.

However, such an intrusion into my thinking, such an attack on my life's work and purpose, was something I had never imagined could happen to me. I also understood that my work is what had called attention to the possibility that I was not only an unusual thinker, but a thinker that could be portrayed as something other than I was, as a way of the opposing side trying to win a legal case.

Some of the attorneys who battered me while I was on the stand, who attacked the early version of my OMEGA STORY novel, and who also attacked my death and dying work, later found themselves facing life threatening illnesses. I was told by some of their own family members that they were actually taking comfort in my books.

While being attacked on the stand for my death and dying work, I explained that I had used metaphor quite frequently, and that all my writing was done to help people through difficulties. I was demeaned on the witness stand. At one point, while I was sitting on the witness stand being slammed for my OMEGA WORK and book, I said again and again, "This OMEGA STORY, and I emphasize the word STORY, is just a first draft, and is a work in progress, but it is fiction, a novel. And, why is this relevant to my seeking justice after being defrauded? This has nothing to do with this legal case." I was then loudly ordered by the judge not to speak out of turn.

So somehow, not only I, but my ideas and my work on issues of extinction, and on death and dying or surviving, and even my OMEGA STORY itself, were all on trial. What this meant was going to become ever more clear over time:

There are forces and factors seeking to stop empowering survival information from coming in to people living on Earth at this time. Key in standing up to these forces and factors is seeing them and saying:

YOU WILL NOT STOP ME,
YOU WILL NOT STOP US.

WE CAN SURVIVE.
WE HAVE A RIGHT TO SURVIVE.

22

THE OMEGA DECEPTION IS WELL UNDERWAY

Meeting With Undisclosed Researchers, 2021. I answered a call from some scientists I had met with some years earlier at a meeting I had been hosting, a sort of get-together status-report regarding my and others' work. At the time when I was first approached by these persons, they had shared with me some of their, what was at that time something we decided to call, "climatological economy research." They and I then agreed that what we were together working on were the "psychological, economical, biological, political, and yes perhaps even spiritual, impacts of geophysical and climatological change."

Now, years later, they returned, asking me to someday be ready, when the time came, to help move forward information regarding the efforts of some of the world's wealthiest and most powerful to protect themselves in advance of possible life-endangering climate change and other geophysical events. They explained that even now, all these years into growing awareness of climate and other events indicating conditions on this planet may be becoming more extreme, they would face reprisals for presenting themselves in this light, in their professional circles such as at the universities where they worked and taught.

This pressure not to talk about their and their colleagues' concerns regarding what is taking place right before our eyes, while this is not being acknowledged, is out there. I myself have experienced some of this, even at times having my so-called mainstream professional writing being called quote "apocalyptic," when there was nothing in that material anywhere approaching anything apocalyptic, let alone relating to my *fictional* OMEGA STORY. Note that I emphasize the word *fictional* here as apparently writing a book of fiction can allow detractors to attack one's nonfiction work based upon the stories one tells in a separate novel.

What has become clear to me is that any communication regarding what for some people are highly disturbing concepts regarding potential Earth changes, is unsettling on a deep level, unsettling to the point of some wanting to quiet about, or even deny, what may be taking place, even if only being examined in our imaginations via fiction.

This plays into the larger OMEGA DECEPTION I am discussing right here on the pages of this present book: WE THE PEOPLE OF THIS PLANET are being denied our rightful access to possible survival options, survival territories, survival resources, and even to potentially essential survival information. Messages coming to us from many directions and levels, even from deep within our own consciousness, are being suppressed, blocked, denied, in effort to control our access to the survival knowledge which is our birthright.

It appears that those speaking up about what may actually be happening, attempting to alert the Human species about all this, or about even just some of this, experience various forms of negative feedback. This appears to be denial, plus a sort of stop the messenger response.

Even on the stand in a courtroom where I had brought an entirely unrelated case, attempts were made to discredit my testimony based upon my entirely unrelated work of fiction, the early version of the fictional OMEGA STORY, as well as to attack me regarding proposed diagnostic categories I suggest in several of my psychological books, such as what I have termed, *Earth change anxiety*, and the *apocalypse syndrome*. I explained that more and more I was (and still am) seeing people coming in describing their anxieties and other emotional responses to what they are sensing may be increasing climate and Earth change events and effects.

It is time we allow for the reality that the Human species is experiencing survival pressures, even where largely subconscious and seemingly, supposedly, irrational. (Nothing about discussing or proposing a psychological issue or a diagnostic category should be grounds for attacking a witness on the stand, as this is a common part of professional work.)

When I was again contacted by these scientists I mention at the opening of this chapter, I definitely understood their concerns regarding reprisals for speaking up about what they see happening in our world as we move into these times of what I have called the OMEGA TRANSITION. Here I simply share their surface comments, as they have asked I wait on releasing their more detailed findings. Apparently, they feel the time is coming when it may either be safe for them to release their findings, or be too late to be useful to release their findings. In the mean time, we can glean from media those tips of the iceberg available for us to know about. This (below) is some of the

general surface information that is already available to WE THE PEOPLE, if we dig for this.

WE THE PEOPLE can allow ourselves to become aware that:

Certainly, some of the wealthiest 1% of the world's population are likely to have access to generally undisclosed information about what is expected in the coming years. Clearly, they have the options and the resources to ensure themselves and their families the greatest chance of survival should times become more challenging. We cannot and do not know what conversations and planning meetings they have had and continue to have with each other. However, it makes sense that those with the greatest access to resources will want to have the greatest access to survival options and information.

Nothing about what I say here is an attack on members of the elite who are buying up huge tracts of land and resources, generally with the result of protecting these places. However, WE THE PEOPLE OF THIS PLANET must realize on some deep level that most of us will never have the opportunity to own such large tracts of land, let alone to access these should times get very difficult. Already now, access to most of these places and resources is almost impossible as these are all under heavy guard.

It is well known that numerous members of the global elite have secured part or even entire islands for themselves and their inner circles, such as Larry Elison who owned 98% of Lanai Island, which he purchased in 2012 for $300 million. Much earlier island purchasers include: the Barclay brothers of Brittan who acquired the Channel Island of Brecqhou in 1993; and

Ekaterina Rybolovelevna, daughter of Russian oligarch Dmitry Rybolovlev, who acquired Skorpios Island off the coast of Greece (acquired from Aristotle Onasis), after others such as Bill Gates, Madonna, and Giorgia Armanni, tried to buy this island but did not succeed.[26]

Islands are perhaps the more visible of many of the large acquisitions taking place. A range of purchases, exchanges, communications, even SURVIVAL STRATEGIES, are underway and taking place beneath the radar, far out of the awareness of the general population of this planet.

Do the world's wealthiest 1%, or even the world's wealthiest 10%, communicate about their Earth change knowledge and plans among each other? Do they know what each other is thinking and planning and doing? For example, are "share deals" being made such as, I will have this available for you and your family if you have that available for me and my family?

What resources are being sequestered without WE THE PEOPLE OF THIS PLANET asking why? Again, this is not to criticize anyone of any financial means for acquiring property. However, as many people have no access to funds that would allow them to do such, all they can do is try to know a bit about who is doing what and why.

For example, to begin trying to detect what is going on out of earshot and eyeshot, we may want to ask questions like this: Did the Bush family communicate with others when it chose to purchase 300,000 acres of land in the remote Chaco area of

---

[26] See https://www.loveproperty.com/gallerylist/62241/pristine-private-island-hideaways-owned-by-billionaires

Paraguay, sparsely populated heavily deforested land which no one seemed to want? Few talk about or know about what is so very valuable under this land: an ocean of fresh grade A water, part of one of the largest freshwater aquifers on the planet, Acuifero Guarani, which stretches across parts of Paraguay, Uraguay, Brazil, and Argentina. There are a few under land, underground, oceans of fresh water around the planet. Fresh water will become increasingly rare and increasingly valuable.

Already now, when the Earth's water is 98% salt water, fresh water is a precious resource. Regarding the remaining 2% of the world's water, almost 90% of this is trapped in glaciers, which as they melt disperse their little amounts of fresh water into the sea, which is salt water. Less than 1%, actually no more than 0.25%, of the world's fresh water is found outside glaciers, such as in lakes and rivers, and underground seas such as this one underneath the Bush family land.[27]

There are many members of the global elite communicating so much to each other with no requirement that they report to a public place, or to what I suggest we might call the MANDATORY INTERNATIONAL EARTH CHANGE INFORMATION AND ACTION REGISTRY. We are not being told what all the global elite are doing and thinking regarding surviving potential life-endangering climate and other biospheric, even geophysical, Earth changes.

And, while we find surface details if we dig through the news, we are left in the dark regarding the actual secret research findings, the hidden purchases of land and resources, the untold

---

[27] See https://5minforecast.com/2015/04/24/why-did-george-bush-buy-nearly-300000-acres-in-paraguay/

actions and plans, of the most powerful OMEGA CABAL – whose members are dedicated to their own survival.

Do we have a right to know what is taking place when we are perhaps talking about survival of our species, even perhaps of life on Earth?

We do hear bits and pieces of lesser efforts to pay to survive climate change issues. For example, we hear that Kim Kardashian and Kanye West had hired private firefighters to protect their $60 million dollar home from a California wildfire.[28] We generally say this is good as it protected more than just their home. We also say this is good that wealthy spend their resources protecting their neighborhoods and communities. I do agree. However, note that those elsewhere who could not afford private firefighting teams may have lost their homes, some their lives. Clearly, access to resources can help respond to survival matters.

Again, this is not to say it is wrong of those who can pay for some increased protection to do so. However, it must be made clear that wealth may help address the coming climate and Earth changes most of us are not rich enough to pay to deal with.

Let's think of some other well known wealthy personalities. For example, we see that former U.S. President Donald Trump has had and continues to have business dealings all around the world. His net wealth remains difficult to entirely detect, however reports say that Trump's net worth "slipped to about

---

[28] See https://www.firerescue1.com/wildfire/articles/kim-kardashian-and-kanye-west-hire-private-firefighters-to-save-homes-lqlx9LKcNSEOmQcX/

$2.3 billion during his presidency compared to about $3 billion before he took office, according to Bloomberg." And in 2021, *Forbes* estimated that his current wealth was $2.1 billion.[29] While he was U.S. President, Donald Trump placed his assets in a blind trust managed by his two sons, under the auspice of insulating him from conflicts of interest while president. However, this distancing from his assets and their use and value was only a heartbeat away so to speak, as his sons were family and were able to get their father funds or other help if ever needed or wanted at any point.

This in itself would not necessarily be pertinent to the discussion of the arising OMEGA TRANSITION the Earth may be facing. However, persons at even Trump's level of wealth, and those at higher levels, must be watched for indications of how some of the very wealthy are planning to protect themselves if climate and Earth Changes become more severe. For example, where so many of the Trump business dealings around the world have been internationally known, such as the locating of Trump Hotels and other Trump properties in many nations, so much more has been taking place out of sight.[30]

Many will recall the one-of-a-kind private (with no other officials present) meeting in 2018, between the then newly elected U.S. President Donald Trump and the Russian President Vladimir Putin. Of course, there were many international matters to be discussed (apparently also including discussion of the then recent presidential election in the United States).

---

[29] See https://www.investopedia.com/updates/donald-trump-companies/

[30] See https://www.trump.com

However, we cannot know what these two may have said to each other regarding their plans for survival if needed during the mounting climate and Earth change crises.

Recall that this is the climate change which Trump was generally denying and which Putin had largely downplayed, even as late of 2019 when he did finally say that some climate change was perhaps caused by Humans. It would make sense that persons with this level of access to resources, money, and land, will have given great thought to their own survival plans.

Yet, their consistent denying of the gravity of this climate crisis is loud and clear. We must realize that while the gravity of our situation on Earth is known to the global elite, and while some even publicly deny this gravity or its full extent, they are already protecting themselves and planning ahead in every way possible. WE ARE BEING DISTRACTED BY THEM WHILE THEY ARE DOING THIS, AS THIS IS THE OMEGA DECEPTION.

If we read between their lines, they, much like the lead protagonist in the novel, REVEALING THE OMEGA KEY, are seeking to deny what is taking place while they, in their own private realities, are securing as much property, wealth, and access as they possibly can so as to be ready if needed to take care of themselves -- while WE THE PEOPLE out here have been told by them that climate change is nothing much to be concerned about, or at least that climate and Earth changes are nothing to make much noise about. We are being purposefully distracted.

What is happening in Russia is but one sad example, yet so to the point. Let's take a moment to look at this situation: As of early 2022, Vladimir Putin, President of Russia, was seen as the single most powerful determinant of Russia's future. However, it is climate change itself that will be this. The Center for Strategic & International Studies reported in 2021 that:

> Russia is warming 2.5 times faster than the rest of the world. In 2020, regions across Russia have experienced the hottest temperatures on record, contributing to forest fires that burned through acreage the size of Greece and emitted one-third more carbon dioxide into the atmosphere than in 2019 (Russian forests account for one-fifth of the world's total). Flash floods in Siberia destroyed entire villages and displaced thousands of residents. Snow coverage was at a record low in 2020, and Arctic sea ice coverage shrank to its second-lowest extent in over 40 years.
>
> Permafrost, which covers nearly two-thirds of Russian territory, is rapidly thawing. More dramatic freeze-thaw cycles in the subsoil are eroding urban infrastructure in Russia's Arctic cities, home to over 2 million people, and pose a mounting risk to Russia's 200,000 kilometers of oil and gas pipelines, not to mention thousands of miles of roads and rail lines bridging some of Russia's widest rivers. Permafrost thaw recently toppled a diesel storage tank near the Arctic city of Norilsk, spilling 21,000 tons of diesel into the Ambarnaya river and surrounding subsoil. It has been linked to outbreaks of anthrax and the discovery of vast methane craters. At its current rate of thaw—about 1 degree Celsius per decade—Russia's permafrost layer will stop freezing completely in three decades. This could result in a potentially catastrophic, one-off release of carbon into the

atmosphere which will no longer be Russia's problem alone. According to one study, a 30 to 99 percent reduction in near-surface permafrost would release an additional 10 to 240 billion tons of carbon and methane into the atmosphere and potentially put the globe "over the brink" by 2100. Russia is already the fourth-largest emitter of greenhouse gases, accounting for 4.6 percent of all global emissions. Its per capita emissions are among the highest in the world—53 percent higher than China, and 79 percent higher than the European Union.

Dramatic shifts in global weather patterns, accelerated by warming Arctic waters and a diminishing ice cap, are expected to increase droughts in Russia's rich southern agricultural 'bread basket' regions encompassing Stavropol and Rostov. This could pose food security risks and threaten a primary Russian export: wheat. Though climate change will expand arable land in Russia in its northern latitudes, the northern topsoil tends to be thinner and more acidic than in Russia's most productive southern regions and would not make up for its losses. In fact, arable land shrank by more than half to just 120,000 acres in 2017. In June of this year, regional officials in Stravopol, one of Russia's major wheat regions, projected a remarkable 40 percent decline in wheat crop in 2020 as a result of droughts. This too has global implications: Russia is a core part of global food chains, accounting for 20 percent of global wheat exports, so climate disruption to Russian agricultural output will have strong effects well beyond Russia's borders and budget coffers. As agriculture shifts north, scientists are concerned that the cultivation of carbon-rich soils will create a separate carbon feedback loop and expedite global warming. ...

The threat to the Russian economy from climate change is twofold. An increase in droughts, floods, wildfires, permafrost damage, and disease could lower GDP by 3 percent annually in the next decade, according to Russia's Audit Chamber. Climate damage to buildings and infrastructure alone could cost Russia up to 9 trillion rubles ($99 billion) by 2050, according to Deputy Minister for the Development of the Russian Far East and Arctic Alexander Krutikov.

Meanwhile, Russia's overreliance on hydrocarbon production is a conspicuous vulnerability as the world shifts toward low-carbon sources of energy and carbon neutrality. Natural gas and Arctic liquified natural gas may serve as bridge for Russia into a lower-carbon future, but global demand for gas is expected to be in sharp decline by mid-century. Russia's top-down federal policy strongly favors state-led and managed industrial oil and gas giants. Though Russia has immense potential as a source of renewable energy, the share of renewables in Russia's energy mix is negligible—under 0.1 percent for wind, solar, and geothermal—and there are no clear plans to invest significantly in their growth. Nor do current strategy documents foresee a major growth in nuclear and hydropower, which currently account for 36 percent of Russia's electricity mix but under current plans will only climb to 43 percent by 2050. (To limit global warming to 1.5

degrees Celsius, renewables must account for 70-85 percent of global electricity by 2050.)[31]

Imagine what crosses the minds and desks of such moguls who are doing whatever they can to amass key wealth and key properties which will be available to the chosen few, if these are ever needed as places of safety during climate and Earth change crises.

When those scientists I refer to at the start of this chapter approached me again in 2021, they mentioned that the reprisals they may face for disclosing information they feel the public should have would be so serious it could shut them up for life.

The complex suppression of survival-related information is already well underway. The OMEGA DECEPTION itself is already well underway.

---

[31] See https://www.csis.org/analysis/climate-change-will-reshape-russia

NOTES FROM THE FRONT

23

PROCESS OF DISCOVERING

Keys to Now Radio Show, Internet Radio, Global, 2022. I found myself sharing these thoughts on several of the shows I was hosting:

> *Awareness of the condition of Earth and her inhabitants has grown significantly as we have moved into this phase of this grand cycle, into this phase of what I have described as this OMEGA TRANSITION. This awareness is coming ever more into focus within us as it clarifies itself within the conscious realms of our consciousness-es. What we know, what we have carried through time to know now, to be able to access at this time when we greatly need it, is here for us, calling us, like a developing photograph becoming more clear. If you have ever lost your car keys and searched your home for them, finally to discover that they were in your pocket the whole time -- you may have a sense of what it is like to be REVEALING to yourself THE OMEGA KEY you carry so deeply within.*

Listeners wrote in from around the world to tell me they understood, and that they were feeling these pressures from within themselves, pressures to recognize deeply buried messaging coming in through time to be here now. Profoundly grateful to hear from these people, and deeply inspired by what this was telling us, I began to delve more deeply into the matter of what I have found to be a ***profound species level instinct, a deeply resonating, increasingly emerging, instinct.*** (I delve deeply into this instinct in the volumes of the KEYS TO CONSCIOUSNESS AND SURVIVAL SERIES, such as Volume 3, titled UNVEILING THE HIDDEN INSTINCT: UNDERSTANDING OUR INTERDIMENSIONAL SURVIVAL AWARENESS.) Actually, I had been tracking this rising awareness within our species for quite some time, for what felt to be many lifetimes. For example ....

North of Estes Park, Colorado, 1996. Sometime into the process of my becoming aware that there was a demand for this creative fiction/non-fiction I was writing to share my OMEGA WORK, I began seeing more about this process. I was moving into a genre that really can't be defined, writing and speaking about what's happening to and on this planet, and perhaps even speaking (fictionally) for the planet itself (HERself). I was invited to speak, as I had been many times already, at a major event. This one was a conference in the Rocky Mountains. I only realized after I had arrived there, that the location of the event was very close to the place where my OMEGA novel had ended, where the heroine survives to lead the people and the Earth herself into a new form of survival. So I was, at first without realizing this, geographically arriving at a place I had included in my fictional depiction of a profound prophecy revelation and prediction process.

There, I was asked to speak about my death and body-exit meditations and exercises. As I made clear to all of them, as I make clear in all my books, as I make clear to everybody, I do not teach suicide, I do not teach euthanasia, this is not at all what I am talking about. However, throughout history there have been teachings and practices telling us that we can become increasingly able to move our focus in and out of what we perceive as being our physical experience or our physical bodies.

I explained this to the group, and I led some of the exercises that can now be found in my HOW TO DIE AND SURVIVE books. The audience was quite receptive. It was a large audience again, who had all signed up to be in this half-day event. Actually, this was a two-part workshop; they could be there for the whole day or the half day, and most of them were with me all day.

That day, one of my previous clients surprised me and showed up there with his mother who lived in a nursing home about a hundred miles away. As he brought her in, I saw that his mother was in a wheelchair. He nodded at me and said, "I brought my mother so she could listen to you. She's not really here very much these days, but I believe she hears." He told me he wanted me to conduct my death and body exit exercises with her. I responded, "Well, I really don't do this without an individual consciously requesting this, so the individual conducts the exercises for her or himself." He understood and agreed, saying that they would stay and listen to my presentation anyway.

I then moved on into my presentation of my metaphorical body-exit and body re-entry exercises and methods. As I worked this through with the audience, this woman who was in her wheelchair there with her son, sitting there near the front of the stage, literally woke up. She had re-entered herself doing these exercises, her son later told me. It was as if the collective group, working on moving their own personal focuses in and out of their own physical bodies, had brought this woman into her body to wake and up be present there.

Her son was overjoyed and astounded and in tears. He later told me he had thought he would never be able to talk with his mother again. As she woke up, she calmly asked, "Oh, where am I?" And I said, "You're here with your son and with me, Dr. Angela, and with these other people." Then I explained where this was, showed her the place, let her look at her son and then my face. Then I went on, "and we're talking about how to be more aware of our bodies, how to feel what's going on with our **selves**."

And she was awake and alert for hours. When later in the day, she and her son were leaving, I said good-bye to both of them and thanked them for coming. They both thanked me. Apparently some weeks after that, this woman who had bravely woken up that day did die peacefully back in her nursing home.

That day was a fascinating experience for all who were present. During the break, a couple of the participants came up to me and said, almost tearfully, "This is so important. We understand what this is really about. We know what you are really thinking about." And I said, "You do, oh my. Well, thank you, I think. Maybe you can share with me what you're seeing and feeling about this." And they said, "We will, but we'd like to tell everybody after you start up again this evening in your after-workshop closure time." So I said, "Sure." Only later would I wonder about this.

That evening, I invited them to come up to the stage and speak about their perceptions. They said, "We're here to share what we are feeling, which is that we're all learning this because someday we will all need to know this, because the suffering in this biosphere is going to increase. We don't know how bad it'll get, but we might all need to leave our physical bodies someday, to move somewhere for safety, and do this peacefully."

I was startled and silently gulped. How apocalyptic was this going to get? How were people arriving at this based on my work, including the novel, my OMEGA STORY. That novel was fiction! What was I to do now? So, I thought it best to just say here, "Well, let's see. This is an interesting perception. Let's hit the pause button for now, and those of you who wish to continue this line of thought, come and talk to me later tonight after this meeting is over if you like. Thank you for sharing." I had to say more here, so I went on, "I want to again remind everybody that <u>none</u> of my work or books are teaching suicide. And, this is <u>not</u> teaching euthanasia. If you're saying people can learn to shift their awareness-es and their focus-es in and out of their own physical bodies, to shift their own degrees of physicality, yes, likely so."

Later that evening, a group of about ten persons came to me to further discuss their perceptions. They told me that they believed enough of the teachings in my OMEGA book, and enough of what climate and other scientists were already saying, to know that environmental disaster may be inevitable. They said they knew I knew this, and they knew that the material I was offering was training just in case we did have to know how to move in and out of our bodies. I told them I somewhat agreed, and that it was far too early to present things this way. They asked if they could start working with me to be trained to do these trainings. I told them I would take their names and contact information for future reference.

I asked them to wait a couple of decades. They agreed. All these years later, many of them are calling upon me to step forward again, and many are now studying the books in the KEYS TO CONSCIOUSNESS AND SURVIVAL SERIES, as well as the newest advanced and expanded OMEGA book, REVEALING THE OMEGA KEY. I continue to advise that this information must be carefully understood and presented safely, with safety central at all times.

Let's me say again here: In the REVEALING THE OMEGA KEY novel's fictional depiction of the climate and Earth change drama, there are some key characters who have already left or are now choosing to leave this dimension, as in that novel physical plane life on Earth is growing more difficult to breathe in, live in, survive in. I want to insist there is still time to turn things around.

There is also still time to learn new methods of physicalizing and de-physicalizing to rewire (or what some say is heal) problem energy arrangements.

As I explain in the KEYS TO CONSCIOUSNESS AND SURVIVAL SERIES, there is growing awareness of our need to know more about the great capacity of the Human consciousness to shift and change its energy arrangements, to SURVIVE. We all carry important messages, frequently in the form of stories, in the subconsciousness, and in the sub and collective consciousness of individuals and of our species.

Surviving this next OMEGA TRANSITION is surely on our minds. That we may face extinction or at least profound survival pressure is something our species senses. A critical mass of the population is on some level already feeling this. I have become increasingly aware of this. In fact, every day I'm increasingly more aware of this. (Refer to my discussion of MIGRATION INSTINCTS in *Volume 3* in the KEYS TO CONSCIOUSNESS AND SURVIVAL SERIES, which is titled, UNVEILING THE HIDDEN INSTINCT.)

NOTES FROM THE FRONT

24

PROJECT KIRKENES CALLING

Denver International Airport (DIA, which later became DEN), Denver, Colorado, 1996. I left that conference in Estes Park and went to Denver to head to California. Dealing with a delayed flight, I found a quiet spot in the airport to hide and think about the intense experience of this recent conference. I was actually about to doze off when I heard someone sit down near me. Of course, I made sure I kept my eyes open and my hands on my bag.

I turned to see who was sitting too close to me before I shooed him off. I almost fell out of my seat when I realized this was a much older now white haired Yan, who I had not seen in person for many years.

He saw me realize who he was, and stopped my startle reflex with a couple silly comments spoken in Russian: "Давно не виделись. (*Davno nye videlis* -- Long time no see.) "Что но́венького?" (*Shtoh novyenkogo* -- What's new?)

I glared at him, then thought I would back off on the hostility and see what he wanted, and how he had found me. I at first responded, "I do not know" in Russian: "я не знаю" (pronounced: yah nye znayoo).

Yan switched to English. "You haven't responded to our efforts to contact you."

"Why should I?"

"I think it's time we stopped this attitude. You do know what we are doing. You know you do, and I know you do."

Actually, I knew more than ever what Yan was talking about. I even felt I understood the issues better than he did. But I wasn't sure I wanted to be formally involved in this so-called Project I had somehow signed onto years ago. "I just cannot fit this into my life."

"From what we can see, you *are* already fitting this into your life. So how about you just cut to the chase and give me a short synopsis."

I nodded yes and surprised myself with my quick overview: "Here's the short version, Yan. ... Everything I've done so far in my life brings me to this same understanding, and I see this is a long term, lifelong, probably many lives long, project. ... I've been digging deeper into this concept that there are extensive subliminal, for want of a better word, although subconscious may be better said here, invasion, directing, and suppressing of streams of essential information that should be retrieved by Humans everywhere, should be surfacing into Human consciousness now. ... Yet, there are extensive, powerful, yet mostly covert, efforts being made to block this advancement in awareness, even in evolution of the general Human population. ... All this is taking place while survival -- even extinction -- will become the ultimate issue. Who shall live when times get tough? Who shall survive major changes coming to Earth? ... Should only some elite somewhere have access to what is needed to survive? By what is needed here, I am referring to information, assets, resources, territories, medical care, security, and also to quite subtle forms of consciousness, *access to quite immaterial knowledge*. ... The competition for control of our minds, of our awareness, ***even of our evolution into survival domains*** is clear to me. ... And, what I have come to see is most important here is that these survival domains are both here in this 3-D physical plane on Earth and also far far beyond, deep into the reaches of the Human consciousness. ... Humanity's access to its own rightful survival domains both here and beyond is already being affected. ... This is the point, as I see it. We must stop this effort to control Humanity's reaching into its own survival territories here and beyond. We must stop efforts to block the next step in Humanity's evolution, and Humanity's expansion into domains of its own consciousness for the sake of its own survival."

I looked Yan deep in the eye. I could see he had been listening very closely. I saw now that he had tears in his eyes. "You are so right on. You are taking this project to the next and most essential levels where it must go in coming years. We were right to bring you in early in your life."

"Yan, I see you understand what I am saying here: this is far more interdimensional than any of us ever discussed."

"Yes, it is. This is an understanding that we each have to arrive at on our own before being certain that this is so profoundly relevant."

"Agreed," I said quite matter of factly. "I see myself moving into arenas where the forces are working hard to prevent their own detection and disclosure, to prevent realization of what is really taking place. But I must do this carefully, as there are many around me that are seeking to stop me, even some who are quite close in."

"I know, you have already been threatened both explicitly and implicitly several times. And even now, in your personal life, you are experiencing some very complex emotional, physical, financial, even also professional, *chantage (shan-tazh),* blackmail, extortion. Just know you are protected, although there may be, and even already have been, hard hits along the way. I feel for you and wish those hitting you so hard would come to their senses, or if not, then meet their justice. Yet, they have big enough assets that they can even influence the justice system, as you will see. Just know that you will be still standing."

Suddenly, I was fighting back tears. I did not want to tell Yan how difficult my personal life was, how hard I had been hit. It seemed somehow he did know though.

Yan reached out and touched my hand. Then, he shifted gears a moment, which surprised me, "You know I have always loved you. Just let me know if you ever decide we can be together."

"Please, let's not go there, Yan. Please. You live on the other side of the world, or somewhere, it is never clear where you are. And I have a life, and people I love. Whether or not I feel for you, I cannot be with you. I do have a well established life I want to continue." As I spoke, I felt my profound loneliness, but chose not to speak to this.

Yan gazed deep into me. I could feel he knew my pain. "I know you do, and I will stay on the periphery of your world, if this is where you want me. Just know I am out here if you need me or want me. I do love you, but this is not our work, is it."

"Thank you, I do know how you feel, I do." I was so grateful for the lifelong care and protection of this person, Yan, and of his colleague, the CIA agent I had met decades earlier in Central America.

Later, just when I was truly going to reach out for protection and help from these men, I found out that Yan had been killed and that the CIA agent friend had had a stroke which later killed him.

By then the stakes were ever higher, and I realized I was going to have to find a way to protect myself while I did this work that had once been called the Project Kirkenes Mission.

25

STUMBLING INTO DEBRIEF

Across the U.S., 1971. There we were, having hopped freights and hitchhiked across the United States, my eighteen year old teenage self and these two eighteen-year-old boys I had been traveling this rough road alongside. Suddenly, we were in a beautiful home with one of the boy's parents. We were in Pennsylvania near Temple University. His parents were so kind. They gave me a lovely room to stay in. I had a wonderful shower to use which I did use many times over that three or so day period, and they fed us so well. We had been traveling a long time, with little food and no shelter to speak of.

After a few days, we were nevertheless preparing to leave. That last night we were there, at dinner with these wonderful people, overjoyed to be eating some delicious food, and to be clean, really clean after hopping freights and hitch hiking across the country.

Our host and hostess were so gracious despite the fact they quietly disapproved of what we were doing. They were quietly trying to get their own son to stay home and get ready for college, however he was not agreeing to this.

We found out quite late in our stay that the father there had contacted the parents of the two of us from California, and discovered my father was working on top security space, defense, and other engineering management and documentation matters, and that the other boy's father was head of a pioneering state wide desalinization project. When this contacting of our fathers became clear to us, the father of the boy from Pennsylvania whose house we were guests in made some kind of friendly comment, something to the effect of, "Well, you certainly are in good company. All three of you, myself included here, have fathers doing very important work for the world. And all three of you have been accepted to and received scholarships to colleges. Don't you all think it is time to move on and return to your paths in life?" We all said no.

After dinner, the kind host then pulled me aside and said he had not only called my father, but had spoken to him in depth. I was surprised, not only as I had not given this man my father's number, but also as I had not asked that he talk to my father. He said my father was ready to buy an airline ticket for me to come home, and that I would be taken to the airport the next day.

I cried and thanked this man, saying, "I just cannot go home right now."

He then told me that my father had told him that my mother had recently died and that the year before I had also lost my grandfather who I was very close to, and that I simply was unable to be in the family house. My father had asked him to tell me that he could find other places for me to stay near home if I would just come back and get ready for college. I cried and thanked this man, yet wondered how he felt he could reach into my life so deeply.

In any case, later that night, back at the dinner table for desert, we three young people began talking about our experiences crossing this country, and then about the times we had while living in a so-called survival commune. That commune was full of well-intentioned people, we explained, people who wanted to help themselves and others survive the so-called "predicted" changes that were coming to the planet. But things had gotten difficult there, we said rather calmly, not wanting to alarm my friend's parents about what that environment had really been like. Yet, we then went ahead and talked about how we were not able to get out of that commune, that we had not been able to leave when we wanted to, and that a visiting school teacher had secretly gotten us out late one night when it became clear I needed hospitalization and wasn't being taken to get any medical care of any sort.

As we were speaking, the boy's father, a very wonderful, very kind, very intelligent man, began asking more questions about our experience with the survival tribe. And, because our host and I had just that night privately connected, I was being the most conversational with him. He reminded me a little of my father and it was nice to have somebody father-like to talk to.

I didn't say much about what I had been through, I didn't talk about everything that had happened to me, but I did talk about the beliefs of the survival people we had been living with. I did explain that they were saying that their prophecies were telling them that the safety and survival of Humanity on this planet was in jeopardy, that we were facing pretty serious changes coming on this planet, that this belief was what the teachings, the ancient teachings that were now surfacing, were telling us, that what had been prophesized all along was coming, that we are now approaching those times and that "you must know what you need to know in order to be safe and survive."

I was asked by our host what safety meant to these people. I began saying, "Well, they believe that they are getting information, messages coming in, telling them what parts of the planet will be safe."

The boy's father was quite interested and asked me more about this. I began talking about it. "Well, some of the places, they are around the country, the U.S., some of the places are in California in the Sierras. Some of the places are in Colorado in the Rocky Mountains, not far from where the government apparently has an underground location fully developed in case there is ever a need for top government people to be protected from radiation or Earth changes of any sort."

And as I went on, one of the boys started kicking me under the table, clearly trying to shut me up, although it took me a moment to realize that was what he was doing. It was the son of the man that was talking to me. So, I found some way to sort of appear to run out of information and to then speak in generalities, while not really understanding what it was the boy was trying to tell me, other than to be quiet.

Later that night when the three of us, myself and the two boys I'd hitchhiked and hopped freights across the country with, took a walk around the block, I said, "What was that? What was that? Why did you kick me?"

He said, "You've got to be careful what you say in my house."

I said, "Oh, really? OK. Well I'm sorry but I don't think I was rude or anything."

He said, "No, that's not what I'm talking about, not at all. You were very nice to my parents. You've been very polite. You're a great guest. My parents love you. But you need to know that my father is a CIA debriefer."

I said, "A what?"

And he proceeded to explain to me what it meant to debrief for the CIA. And then he said to me, "So quite frankly, I think in a way, in his subtle way, he was debriefing you to get more information about all this underground survival stuff going on."

We left the next day, hitch hiking into Canada.

NOTES FROM THE FRONT

26

CALLED TO WRITE THIS OMEGA JOURNEY STORY

I have been profoundly affected by events occurring early in my life. This is not unusual, as most of us are profoundly affected by what we encounter as children and young adults.

It would be years later, long after that boy's father debriefed me, that I would realize what a great impact on me the various known and unknown, some even underground, survival groups I have met have actually had. It is not that I ever found myself simply buying into everything I was being told, or buying into what in some cases may have been cult-like attitudes and organizations. I was actually at times even at odds with some of the groups' leaders who expected an automatic buy-in to their views. I have never been one who engages in automatic buy-in.

I did however learn a great deal about what the Human mind, the Human spirit, the Human consciousness, the Human species, was and is sensing and trying to process in these complex times: We are consciously and also subconsciously sensing possible and actual threats to the survival of our species, whether we call these threats "end time" developments, or the "coming of the apocalypse," or the mounting of international political pressures and dangers, or scientific predictions based upon scientific research, or all of these and more.

Seeing this sort of thinking taking place in so many parts of the world, in so many sectors of so many sciences, among so many different world views and religions, I was certainly called to pay attention, close attention -- and to listen.

Hearing voices in my own dreams, dreaming that personages such as Einstein and Nostradamus, Hermes and Camus, even Mother Earth herself, various ancient and modern, some Earth based and some off-planet, people, beings, and characters, were speaking to me, were reaching into my subconscious and calling me to listen to them, stunned me, called every bit of my self to pay very very very close attention to what I was hearing about the coming changes taking place on this Earth, and beyond.

Indeed, it would come to me over time, starting in my childhood, that I was here to write an Earth change novel and more, that I was even being called upon to do so.

Already as I moved into the first couple decades of my adulthood, I somehow was feeling the call. I was sensing that writing a novel or a series of novels and other books -- about the idea that the collective Human consciousness is aware of something, is telling itself something, was and is necessary. I would answer the call to explain that we as a species are speaking to ourselves. I would see that, if we listen to messages coming in to us through time, from here and beyond, we must ask: What does it mean to listen? What are we hearing? What are we being told and by whom? Are we more focused than ever before on images of and the possible reality of cataclysm,

apocalypse, ecological doom, whatever it might be? Or, is something else going on?

Certainly, we are hearing more and more about natural resources being destroyed, pandemics, plagues, famines, threats of nuclear wars, increasing floods, Earthquakes, volcanic activity, the potential for meteor bombardment, all sorts of threats arising or increasing.

Yes, we are seeing and hearing these things. But, it could be just that we have the media to project these images ever more now, and that these have been constant realities all along. Still, we are more aware of something. We are more aware of what is happening now than we were ever before. At least we believe that what the media is telling us is what we are aware of. We may witness more than we have ever witnessed -- at least on television or the internet if not in our internal viewing of reality (whatever that internal viewing means, and I'll come back to this later in this and other books).

The more aware we are, ***the more sensitized we are to what we are aware of***, the greater our chances are to manage all this stuff that's coming to us, both consciously and subconsciously, even unconsciously. So, I began to realize I wanted to write, actually felt I had to write, a compelling teaching tale to bring together these ideas from various religions, ancient teachings, mythologies, philosophies, and sciences, modern and old. I felt I had to put them in one place and talk about the surfacing of awareness -- what this surfacing might mean.

Eventually, some of the characters in the story literally became so dominant, so alive, that as I wrote their dialogues I could even hear them speaking, even feel their wanting to be

heard, feel their messages guiding me. The sensation of these characters actually dialoging with me was riveting. I was grabbed by these essences, these voices, their messages. To say that I was grabbed by these voices shorthands this experience, reduces into just words that which cannot be fully captured in words. In all my work and writing, I had never -- *until I stopped and interacted with this experience,* engaged in actual dialog with these voices reaching through time, from beyond the time we live in, from beyond the physical plane -- recognized what was going on.

When I first was drafting an early version of my OMEGA STORY, the message was, at the time, and now it is easier to say this, that I should tell this story as what I called a *psycho-spiritual adventure,* interwoven with science and metaphysical and other concepts, to talk about what is coming, what it means that we feel things are changing, what it means to be aware of various ecological crises, and what it even means maybe to question these. There are those that are called to see what is happening and there are those that are called to try to stop us from seeing this.

Questions are indeed pressing themselves into the Human story, questions such as: are we facing serious ecological climate change, Earth change, whatever we want to call this, at the level of global crisis? Is what is happening here far bigger than anything the Humans are doing on Earth? Or is all of this just politically fabricated?

Of course, we hear arguments coming from all the different positions. Already back when I first started working on the first draft of the OMEGA STORY, bringing this information in was quite a challenge. Now, as this story has reformed, redefined, and now extended itself far into the REVEALING THE OMEGA KEY story, these questions and pulls and pushes coming from so many directions are all the more profound.

What has come into focus is that these voices speaking through time not only are trying to reach us, to tell us that their messages are urgent, but to also tell us that:

There are those forces and factors here on Earth trying to suppress this messaging, some in the form of what I have called the OMEGA CABAL.

And, also there are forces and factors beyond Earth, beyond the physical plane, seeking to stop these ancient voices from reaching through time to tell us what is taking place here on Earth and beyond, to inform us of the OMEGA TRANSITION we are entering, to tell us about the essential REVEALING of the long suppressed OMEGA KEY to survival.

NOTES FROM THE FRONT

DOUBLE

OMEGA

ALPHA

PART FOUR

NOTES FROM THE FRONT

27

WE WALK A FINE LINE

It is a fine line we walk between **what we do not want to know**, and **what we very much need to know, even when we do not want to see it**. Yet, there are other still more subtle, even virtually invisible, lines between:

what we know
(or at least we think) we know,
and
what our subconscious is calling us to know,
in some way trying to tell us we do know,
and do need to know,
and
what we are not knowing or not seeing as a result of
various forces and factors
working to suppress our knowledge,
to hold us captive to their
deceptive presentation to us of our realities.

Whether we are prisoners of our own flawed evolution, or of something interfering with our own evolution, however we arrived here, it is time we see that we can gain control of our awareness, our evolution, our survival, our survival options.

We are at a critical moment in time, in history, in the cosmic cycle. We must gain control to avoid being controlled by outside forces and factors taking advantage of our situation.

As we move deeper into this time of profound Earth changes, into the coming turn of time, into the close of this current grand cosmic cycle, into the close of this "great year" as it has been termed by many great thinkers, we must see that: what we are not knowing, and ***what we are not being allowed to know,*** is all the more critical to our survival as individuals and as a species.

When we further cloud the already obscure line we walk with what we feel we are certain of, with what we believe are facts based upon our beliefs and givens, we may or may not see what all is taking place. We may see only some of the whole picture. We may or may not see that our own beliefs and givens may themselves be incomplete, or even inaccurate or distorted or mistaken impressions based on forces and factors largely out of our awareness. When our view of what is actually happening is being so clouded, obscured, distorted, ***even perhaps manipulated,*** we have to be ever more alert to any actual information coming to us.

How to proceed in this sea of unknowns is to listen ever more closely and carefully, to always keep an ear out for the increasing degrees of proof and truth. Ultimately we can listen, indeed listen ever more carefully, even feel the Earth talking to us in her own voice, her own sounding.

Let's not allow those who wish to keep us uninformed about what they are doing -- about the survival resources and territories they are hoarding -- while they prepare to survive -- to deceive us.

We can confront the OMEGA DECEPTION on all levels, on global and local levels, on economic and biological levels, on political and personal levels, including from deep within our own subconsciousness-es -- where our own synapses may be being blocked from access to their own survival knowledge, to our own species' long stored ***keys to survival*** of grand cycle transitions.[32]

[32] Readers are encouraged to see the companion novel, *REVEALING THE OMEGA KEY*, for more on the deeply carried ***transition survival knowledge*** we do carry. Readers are also encouraged to see ***keys*** discussed in the *KEYS TO CONSCIOUSNESS AND SURVIVAL SERIES* books. See Recommended Reading list at the end of this present book.

28

IT WOULD BE YEARS

I would be deep into my adulthood and various concurrent careers before I would realize when I had first been debriefed. Finally, for whatever this term, *debrief,* meant to me, I grappled with this notion of being questioned for what I knew, or for what I was thinking, or for what my purpose here is.

In the process of the notion of being debriefed coming into my awareness, I had to realize that in my line of work, a debrief itself could be quite subtle and not formally called debrief. A debrief could be a seemingly accidental contact, a brief meeting seemingly about something rather mundane. Or a debrief could be some kind of subtle interrogation, or for that matter some kind of being tracked or stalked, having my thoughts and ideas and awareness-es detected. (I have been known to ask various persons if they were the thought police, always of course framing this as metaphor.)

This issue of the debrief may sound rather odd, perhaps rather over-concerned. After all, could anyone really be listening to our thoughts, even wanting to know what we are thinking in the deepest recesses of our consciousnesses? On the surface, sounds unlikely, preposterous, science fiction-ish. Yet, we all have to at times wonder whether the advanced technologies already developed may allow some highly adept beings or machines or other forms of intelligence to be able to track our minds. We have to wonder whether there are already what I have come to call ***thought trackers***, or even actual thought police, monitoring us.

As I have said, the discussion in this book is not conspiracy theory, rather is heightened awareness of possibility and possible reality.

Let's just watch ourselves closely to protect ourselves, to know what we are thinking when we are thinking something, to know whether our thoughts are our own, to know whether there are advanced awareness-es or technologies reading our thoughts, monitoring the evolution of our minds -- monitoring even the evolution of our species -- even the survival awareness of our species.

Could there be ***thought trackers*** monitoring the evolution of our awareness? Could there be on- or even off-planet, physical plane or even interdimensional, monitors seeking to identify those of us who may deviate from the ***required mental landscape norm*** just enough to notice the presence of more than we are officially told is here with us?

Are we being monitored to find those of us who are detecting the OMEGA DECEPTION, detecting this control of WE THE PEOPLE OF THIS PLANET as we move through this OMEGA TRANSITION, the close of this current grand cosmic cycle?

Are we allowed to ask this question I have been asking all my life, or is there a reason not to ask:

Whose thoughts am I thinking?

Who evolved, or programmed, me to think this way?

What is my brain designed to wall out of my awareness?[33]

And why?

As noted in an earlier chapter, it was a few years into my early adulthood that I found myself in the company of a man who I much later discovered was an intelligence agent. I realized after the fact that he clearly had debriefed me regarding behaviors I had *not* engaged in during that time when I had roamed alone as a young woman through Central America. At the time, I felt that I had accidentally encountered this experience of being questioned about what I was doing and thinking, and had been asked these things in a casual social friendship way. However I was questioned, it hardly felt like questioning, and the process was generally nonthreatening and almost beguiling. Although I met this person who questioned me shortly after my passport (which had been taken away from me for three weeks) was returned to me, I did not at that time connect the questioning with the passport event.

I am sure I am not the only person this sort of thing has happened to. In fact, I know from many others that they have also encountered situations where they were questioned almost innocuously, only later to realize who had been questioning them, and how serious the questioning was.

---

[33] Regarding our being evolved to function or to not function certain ways, such as to be controllable, for our thoughts to be controllable, for our awareness-es to be blocked, see my discussion of our Human brain in the second *OVERRIDING THE EXTINCTION SCENARIO* book, *Volume 6* in the *KEYS TO CONSCIOUSNESS AND SURVIVAL SERIES.*

I and others have found that being debriefed can take several forms, some rather vague. Being debriefed can indeed be more a form of seemingly casual questioning (although at times not even presented as questioning) than a formal meeting. In my experience, as part of this Kirkenes Project (referred to in other chapters) I had somehow years ago been inducted into, the various debriefings I experienced along the way may or may not have appeared to be official, may not have appeared to be about a particular agent seeking me out and in some way engaging me so that I would provide information -- *perhaps even information I did not realize I had.*

Certainly, there is some kind of awareness and knowledge filtering through our minds at all times, let alone with regard to what's happening to the Earth and to our species, to all life on this planet as we move into coming times, into what I describe in this book and elsewhere as the OMEGA TRANSITION. And, there is some kind of observation, perhaps even official or covert observation, of this awareness we carry. There may be some kind of belief that the beliefs of people had better be watched. Why?

Clearly, there are those out there who know that the collective mind of the Human species (and perhaps also of other species) is aware of what is happening -- aware of the subtle messages the various species are receiving. We sense, feel, know of, the various minor and major cycles we living within, even the grand cosmic cycles that envelope everything.

It took me many years of my own life to understand that what I do call *species survival awareness* is a sense we do carry. This survival awareness is not just something you learn when you go camping or backpacking, although of course survival basics are a good thing to know. However, the level of survival awareness I am talking about here is deeper, perhaps more intuitive, perhaps more ancient, something the species knows even on a cellular level. *This is a sense that some members of the species tune into, some stumble into, some are called to. Some are simply suddenly hit by it as they live here on Earth.*

Part of that basic survival awareness is knowing what to do in an emergency. Part of that awareness is what to do in order to be safe, and where to go to be safe, and what to know to be safe. Over the years, I've realized that ***part of that awareness is also knowing what you are not being allowed to know, what you are not being allowed to perceive about being safe and about survival spaces and places***. Where there is some form of grand thought control or even mega level deception taking place, those captaining this deception prefer their true purposes remain undetected.

What's not revolutionary about this is that this is all quite obvious and simple stuff.

And what is revolutionary about this is that, if there is some kind of organized or semi-organized or even disorganized sort of *information cartel*, almost a control mechanism where those in power are the ones determined to survive Earth changes no matter what their survival costs the rest of us, then we have to look closely at what is actually taking place.

Those of us who are not in power, who are not members of the global elite's OMEGA CABAL faction, must watch carefully so we do not fall prey to those who would choose to keep us uninformed in order to control us, even use us.

Those of us who are not members of this global elite's survival elite -- what I have often called the OMEGA CABAL -- had better do something soon so we also can have access to what is involved in our own survival.

29

SPEAKING TO ASSISI

Assisi, Italy, 2001. I had been invited to speak (by the International Association of Transpersonal Psychology) at a very large conference. I found myself arriving with jetlag, having never been a coffee drinker, getting through that week and performing daily for hours, basically because people were so kindly bringing me a constant stream of little demitasse coffees. This sudden use of caffeine was intense and very powerful. By the end of the week, I was definitely a caffeine addict and grateful for this at the time.

The topic I was asked to speak on was regarding my work titled, *How To Die And Survive: Interdimensional Awareness And Travel And Its Utility*. How this material came to me, how I had already seen that I would write this book way back when I was a little girl, was also part of the discussion. I sat in a very large long rectangular hall being translated into seven languages, facing a very large audience. This daily presentation went on for a week. I shared the stage with a panel several times, and then spoke on my own with more detail regarding my own work several other times. I became intensely aware of the incredible reception for this work outside the U.S. and had tremendous interactions with many conference speakers and attendees.

NOTES FROM THE FRONT

While all this was taking place I didn't sleep much (of course in part because I was so caffeinated). And, when I would finally fall asleep at night, I would have what I have to call dreams, although even now I wonder if this is the best description.

I found myself traveling beneath the ground in what I perceived were tunnels underneath Assisi, walking through areas where the veil between this life and the next life was quite thin. In fact, there were places where I felt I was being shown people being assisted to move through what was almost a looking glass. Yet, the reflection there in that glass was not necessarily of anything we think of in three dimensions. Somehow, even in my dreams I was aware that moving through this looking glass was moving **beyond**, moving to the other side. I could see some people moving through, saw that some would return to their same or a new physical existence, and knew that some would move beyond and not return to physical plane form. However, none of them would extinguish, cease to exist.

I finally said to one of these essences that seemed to be standing there with me, "This is what I'm talking about, dying and surviving, moving to and from these worlds, these awareness-es, these dimensions."

During the day, back at the conference, I shared some of these dream experiences rather casually while presenting on my HOW TO DIE AND SURVIVE work and related books. However, much of these experiences I kept to myself as my work was already viewed as being somewhat on the edge of mainstream.

One afternoon, during a break, I walked down to one end of this beautiful town, Assisi, and encountered several priests and monks who lived in Assisi and worked in the primary church of Assisi. They apparently knew about my work and what I was speaking on at the conference, and were somewhat confrontational. I was taken aback, actually shocked by their attitude toward me. And then I remembered something I had learned from my father back when I was nine years old, back when he was having me read about every major religion on the planet. He had explained to me that religion has for a long time structured our knowledge about our reality, that this use of religion took place in a such a way as to control how much we know about our reality. I certainly had begun to understand this more as I moved deeper into my own work.

I have long found that I actually love religion and mythology. Yet, I do see that sometimes some religion has been and is used as a way to control people, to control their perceptions of their realities, and of themselves. Yes, there have long been powers who have sought to subtly or sometimes quite visibly control the masses, we members of the masses, to keep us behaving according to certain codes. Now, I have come to see that there is also this effort to control our access, our rightful access, to other dimensions of ourselves and of our realities.

As I was there, walking the historical pathways of Assisi, I recalled learning that the underground of Assisi, and the Assisi network, had protected hundreds of Jews from the Nazis during World War II. Far earlier in history, Italian friar and mystic, Francis of Assisi, who was born late in the 1100's, once persecuted by both his father and the church, along with others who preceded him, secretly addressed hidden ancient esoteric teachings the church was formally suppressing and even denying. Routes of ancient esoteric teachings being brought into Europe, and even being protected by inner esoteric circles of churches, were said to be, both actually and symbolically, through Assisi.

Even before this, Assisi, as the figurative (and actual) meeting of ley lines and emerging of portals, became a literal and figurative conduit for the transmission of ancient and suppressed wisdom, preserving this and moving this through time. This reality has been long known and largely only quietly addressed. Protecting this knowledge, this what I have come to call ***inter-dimensional awareness***, from forces and factors who have long sought to suppress this, to keep We The People from access to this, has long been essential. In these times, this protecting of awareness is becoming ever more essential.

We, The People Of This Planet, have a right to access our ancient knowledge, to access the keys to our species' survival. These are the keys we have carried through time, and across dimensions, for ourselves to access now at the closing of this current grand cosmic cycle.

These are Humanity's keys to our species' survival, keys we have protected through time by burying these keys so deeply within us, within our species' consciousness.

It is time we reveal to ourselves this body of knowledge, despite efforts of the OMEGA CABAL to block us from so doing.

It is time we are seeing this body of knowledge we carry. Now is the time to be:

REVEALING THE OMEGA KEY.[34]

[34] Refer to *Volume 2* in this *METATERRA CHRONICLE SERIES,* titled, *REVEALING THE OMEGA KEY.* This is a fictionalized depiction of some of the matters indicated in this present book.

30

NOTHING SO PIVOTAL

There is nothing so pivotal in a writer's career as one's writing forcibly being put on the line as a supposed judge of one's character, competence, credibility, or even sanity. This travesty of Human rights is an experience some of us, hopefully very few writers, have had to experience, or better stated, to endure.

As noted earlier, I was involved in a very long legal case regarding assets and other parts of my life that I wanted returned to me as they were wrongly not made available. In the middle of the process, so much of what I had in my files and on my bookshelves was subpoenaed, so much was being demanded beyond any norm. When the opposing side began subpoenaing all of my writings, published and unpublished, in print and not in print, old and new, and even what was not yet fully written or published, in all forms -- electronic, printed, recorded, even in outline form or in scribbled notes, virtually including everything in my files, I truly began to feel that the reach of the court had extended well beyond anything imaginable (at least in a "free" country).

The notion of my first amendment rights appeared irrelevant. The notion that someone could subpoena all this, including even my notes on my thoughts, anything I was thinking about perhaps someday writing in some form, was absolutely beyond the pale.

There I was, being questioned on the stand in court about material they had subpoenaed regarding my work. This was not just what many will call my mainstream work on mental health, addiction, social policy, physical and mental health, and many other very central areas of research and study, but also my work on consciousness, spirituality, and death and dying, and also my work with people who had experienced or felt they had experienced non-typical and or atypical experiences such as contact experiences, or near death experiences, or out of body experiences. Additionally, what was being examined (and I cross examined regarding) also included my works of fiction, which were being treated as if they were non fiction. Among this material was my early OMEGA work and my early version of the related novel.

I sat there feeling like a person being called a witch -- and being burned at the stake. At one moment, I blinked and briefly saw the opposing side's attorneys in the room as hooded men prosecuting or was it executing me. I blinked again, and for a moment they were still hooded. Are these witch trials, am I actually being accused of something here, I asked myself. I felt myself, my ideas, my life's work, being tortured and executed while I sat there on the stand, answering questions designed to attack me in any way possible. I explained at one point that my early OMEGA book was a draft novel, was therefore fiction, and was a love and time travel story bringing together ancient teachings with scientific findings to talk about what was happening on the planet, to the Earth and to the biosphere. The judge shouted at me not to speak out of turn.

I spent days and weeks on this stand, with attorneys constantly attacking my credibility, an argument they never won. I was being treated as if I was nuts, which was a hard case for them to make as I had so many impeccable mainstream credentials. And although they tried again and again, they certainly did not ever win, as my credibility continued to be difficult to question. Nevertheless, at that time and in the years since, I had and still have found that that blatant incursion into my thoughts, and into my creative and professional work, was and still is alerting me to a deep drive among many out there to keep this information I am presenting from becoming front and center. In the years since, I have found myself called many times to face the pressure by some out there for me not to share this work with the world.

Amidst this legal process, there were even letters sent to the court, to the judge, and to my attorneys regarding, and in support of, my work. For example, an astrophysicist at Stanford University said, "You know, Dr. Brownemiller's working with people who believe they've experienced contact with life forms beyond what we see here in our daily lives may not be that unusual. Many of we who are scientists believe there is life out there."

And other letters came in, including one from a colleague and dear dear friend, Dr. John Mack, head of the Department of Psychiatry at Harvard Medical School and Pulitzer Prize winner, who has since then left the planet after dying in a hit and run accident in London, an event about which many of us still have questions. At the time of this trial I refer to above, Dr. Mack sent a letter to the court explaining that many people are doing work in this area, that certainly he was while also continuing his mainstream work.

However, amidst Dr. Mack writing the court explaining that my work was quite justified, respectable, and scientific, he himself was facing a case he had to bring against Harvard where they were threatening to take away his tenure because of his work in certain parapsychological fields, including his discussing people's experience with what they thought was contact with other energies or intelligences or lifeforms. So, one of my definite references (who stepped forward to help me in my own legal case) was in the middle of his own legal case, which of course the opposing side in my trial brought up, now seeking to discredit this great thinker in order to discredit me. And although Dr. Mack won that case he was facing, the process was rather trying for all involved, everywhere, including for myself and for Dr. Mack.

At one point during the trial where I was being attacked for my work, I received a most surprising call from Dr. Mack's attorney, who many of you may have heard of since, Alan Dershowitz, who offered to make himself available to me on my case should I need help with these issues. My own local attorney refused to allow me to accept Dershowitz' assistance on this case, another development which I have more questions about than I will get into here. However, attorney Dershowitz seemed quite understanding of what it was like to experience one's work being questioned when it reaches beyond mainstream givens -- even for those of us with very strong professional "mainstream" backgrounds, such as Dr. Mack definitely had, and which of course, I also do have.

This awareness, that the world may slam those of us reaching beyond, is not new. However, the idea that this sort of attack could be this vicious in our so-called modern era, could be almost like a witch hunt, almost like being burned at the stake, was unnerving for me and I think for many people watching. I was forced to explain and defend my work, even my notes, even my thoughts, for many grueling days, even weeks, on the stand, of course under oath, which I tried my best to do, in a simple and very clear way. I could not help but feel some kind of thought police was driving this horrific process.

Amidst all this, the attorneys working what seemed desperately hard to discredit me also began questioning my books on death and dying. They worked hard to scramble all my work together, blending my sociological, psychological, and psycho-spiritual writings with my fiction writings to demean all my work, and with this all my testimony.

After I experienced what felt to be endless beleaguering at their hands, I finally said to one of them, "You know, I wrote this material to help people. Most of this is metaphor. Some of this, such this global climate and Earth change material in this OMEGA STORY, is actually presented as fiction, as a novel. Much of my writing speaks in metaphor. So, you are questioning an author about material that is literary, material that is certainly an attempt to share creative thought, material that helps people, even those who may be experiencing very difficult times, including dying processes. And you are blending my fiction with my non-fiction for some reason."

Ironically, shortly after that, it became clear that two attorneys involved in this case were both dealing with cancer. One definitely eventually succumbed to terminal cancer. The fate of the other attorney I am unsure of. So, while all of this was taking place, there were individuals in the courtroom grappling with questions about what lies beyond in their own lives. I could almost see the despair in the eyes of some of those attorneys grilling me, despair they were fighting to conceal.

The pain was palpable, and somehow mirroring the pain present in the larger questions, even in the largest survival questions we are all facing: What are we looking at here, yes, as individuals, and also as a species, what are the ramifications of these survival issues?

31

AGAIN THAT QUESTION

Over the years, there have been times when I would go what some would call underground, or at least retreat to what one colleague told me was my "cave monk status." Other times, I was quite visible, speaking on media and at events in the U.S. and other countries, and also at private meetings where I had frequently been asked to privately present my work in depth.

When traveling to speak in various locations, I would at times notice that some of the same faces were appearing. At times, these were clients, followers, and colleagues. Of course, this level of interest and support was helpful. At times however, some of the reappearing faces were persons who would not necessarily fit in to the environments where I was speaking.

At times, some of the people I would see again and again, as I presented my work at unrelated events in unrelated locations, were people I sensed were present for some reason I was not quite able to process. This was the case during an event in New York City where I was speaking about my OMEGA work and my work on death and dying. Among the large audience, I noticed two men in very dark nondescript suits arrive last, sit in the back, and simply stare at me while taking quick notes here and there. I realized I had seen them many times before, at various other events where I had been speaking.

As I went on speaking about my work, I found myself looking at these two men in particular as I looked out at my audience. At one point, I held my gaze on these two men, and they both got up and together left the room.

It was not long after that event that I was in the hotel coffee shop, reading my notes, and waiting for my ride to the airport. Abruptly, someone sat at my table. As things like this had happened to me before, I felt it could be that same sort of contact. But I wasn't really sure what this was, and was on edge, wondering what this might be about. I stared at this man. He stared back. Finally, I decided to pack up my papers and leave that coffee shop.

"Wait a moment, Doctor," the man said.

I paused and looked at him. He was not one of the two men who had walked out on my presentation a little earlier that day. He was no one I recognized. "I have a flight to catch," I told him. "Here is my card. If you have questions about my work, or if I can be of help, write me."

"If you like, we can pay for the cost of any delay in your travels, and get you another ticket."

For some reason, this person wanted me to stay and talk. However, I was not interested. "Thank you, no," I said. "I have commitments in other places as early as tomorrow morning."

"Certainly you can make time to report in."

I hid my irritation. "I am sorry, there must be some mistake. I have no one I am to report to. You must be thinking of someone else."

"We both know that you know that I know who I am speaking to, Doctor. It is time for the regular check in meeting. It has been too long."

I simply stared at this man.

"We can meet in a private setting here or soon, when you return to your home. You can decide this."

What could I say. I wanted to get rid of this person, but knew he or someone he worked with would appear again somewhere sometime, likely many places and times. "Not now," was all I said.

"Contact me at this number within one week," the man said as he handed me his card. "This is urgent now. You certainly know the great importance of what I, we, have to say."

I took his card, glanced at it, and saw that this card had an official appearance yet was obscure in its affiliation. "Yes," was all I said as I packed up and walked away.

As I left, I reminded myself that this sort of contact had been pursuing me for years. I also knew that this was not like the usual approaches I received from people who liked my books or my speeches or my work, or who wanted to see if they could be my clients. This man who had just approached me wanted to meet about other things. I knew his request to meet was quite serious, and that this sort of contact would continue. But this was not Yan -- clearly this was someone else who had some other reason for this contact. And, I was not sure I would ever share what I had said to Yan, about my growing understanding of my work and views, with anyone else.

I would however later contact this man I had just met, and set up a time to meet. I had to, or he or they would step up the pressure, I decided. Yet, in that moment I made this decision, I found myself not trusting this man I had just met. I felt I needed to know how to tell whether someone contacting me was presenting himself one way while having an opposite agenda.

I was becoming clear to me that my antennae were up for good reason.

32

CONUNDRUM WHEN ALREADY OUT

Earth and Beyond, Undisclosed Location, 2012. We were very aware of each other out there. We each had a sort of interdimensional symbol or icon, what I have come to call a PES, *personal expansion signature*. So we recognized each other (and ourselves, by the way) in those domains and dimensions we had entered (or as I say, also had created or generated).[35]

There was a limitlessness to the space we had entered. The vastness of this cosmic sea of existence was exquisitely exquisite, yet for some also disturbing or disorienting. This took some getting used to, as this could be a place and space we could be swallowed into, losing ourselves if we were not holding onto our personal identity, personal awareness.[36]

That night, some of the team members out there did want to lose themselves, felt they had seen God's face and wanted to

---

[35] I explain more about **identification "out there"** in the volumes of the *KEYS TO CONSCIOUSNESS AND SURVIVAL SERIES.*

[36] Refer to *Volume 3* in the *KEYS TO CONSCIOUSNESS AND SURVIVAL SERIES,* titled, *UNVEILING THE HIDDEN INSTINCT.*

merge with it, or die (as once described by John Dunne[37]). I urged them to stay with themselves, to hold onto their own consciousness-es, until a later time when I could show them more about HOW TO DIE AND SURVIVE.[38] As was and is always the case when I am working with people in (metaphorical or actual) out of body, out of physical body, settings, we had begun all this with the agreement that no one would during the experience abandon themselves, that such a decision would be made very consciously at a much later date, long after our full return to the body, to the physical plane, to Earth. This was all the more critical when we were not only out of body, but (metaphorically or actually) very very far from physical plane Planet Earth, as this group was that night.

Note that no one there was on any psychoactive or hallucinogenic plant, medicine, or drug, no one was in a so-called altered state generated by outside compounds. I frequently insist that many of these expansive out of body journeys be experienced unaided by anything but the self itself. This allows the individual to stay as linked to him or herself as is necessary to return to his Earth life when the experience is concluded.

Furthermore, this group was the expanded break off of the break off remote viewing team, and being as fully conscious as possible was essential in this particular part of this work.

---

[37] Refer to the character, John Dunne, in the novel, *REVEALING THE OMEGA KEY.*

[38] Refer to the *HOW TO DIE AND SURVIVE* volumes, specifically the *HOW TO DIE AND SURVIVE* BOOKS, *TWO AND THREE,* in the *KEYS TO CONSCIOUSNESS AND SURVIVAL SERIES.*

33

AS A WRITER WHO MAY BE HERE ON ASSIGNMENT FROM BEYOND

At times, I find myself curious about where this drive to write, where this stream of ideas that move through the mind-brain into words onto paper or into the computer and onto screen, where this inspiration (if this is what this is) comes from. Note that I do understand the mechanisms of cognition well enough to know at least to some degree how the brain works. I've done extensive research in the areas of various brain functions such as cognition, perception, memory, learning, addiction and habituation, and so on.

However, *the flow, the inspiration, the drive to express* what is perceived as information and what feels to be observation, this is something we can't necessarily capture in words or even in description. There is no verbal description or formula or scientific model that truly explains inspiration, because there is much more here.

There is also no scientific model that truly explains some of the experiences I have had (and I am still having) writing REVEALING THE OMEGA KEY and other books. No scientific model truly precisely explains an author actually hearing and interacting with voices coming from outside what we think of as the physical plane, some coming from outside this present time we are living in, some even speaking through time -- some coming to the author in dreams, others coming into the mind-brain of the awake author whenever they, these voices, choose to.

Indeed, in my work, I have found that even when writing my fiction, as well as my nonfiction, some characters speak through the lines of my books. And speak is putting this mildly. Their voices become powerful presences. I at times am so profoundly affected by this experience, I have to work to remain in my physical body. The experience is so intensely riveting, that I cannot do anything but recognize and even speak to these presences. I am being told by these presences I am actually myself one of these presences, that I am living here in a physical biological body to do this work of serving Humanity at this critical moment in time, to serve by sharing these essential to survival ideas and processes, even to bringing forward awareness of the OMEGA CABAL here on Earth and also BEYOND.

Obviously, this makes writing far more than a writing experience. This makes being an author far more than being an author. There is a sort of working with presences who are indeed quite present, who care so much about the survival of Humanity, who are in the room so many times while I am thinking and writing. The experience of this sort of interdimensional dialog is far far more than channeling. Channeling is a far too limited explanation for this form of interaction and mission to serve, to come in from BEYOND to be here to serve and inform and guide. (I explain more about this in other books, and Readers are encouraged to see these.)

All this can sound odd or even be diagnosed as something out of order by those who do not understand. I know this and I understand that we only see what we are ready to see when we are ready to see this – THAT IS, IF WE ARE ALLOWED TO SEE THIS.

Note that: I am not a person with multiple personality disorder, or what I in this case tend to call multiple messaging ORDER (or perhaps also multiple personality ORDER). Still, I do feel I have expressed, allowed myself to have, even allowed myself to interact with, several voices dedicated to serving Humanity at this critical juncture in Earth's (as well as in the Cosmos') time.

For years now, I have been aware that I am working on a large inter-dimensional project, that I am not only hearing but also interacting with voices who arrive at my mental doorstep while I am writing (and at other times as well). As I explain in other of my books, I now recognize the beings or presences I am interacting with, working on ideas with, as METATERRA. I have also come to see I am a member of METATERRA who is here in a physical biological body to do this work, and to bring forward awareness of the on and off-planet efforts of the OMEGA CABAL to stop Humanity from accessing its full survival potential during this OMEGA TRANSITION time. (Readers are encouraged to see the METATERRA SPEAKS material I have written.)

I have worked to continue to be an intellectual and rigorous thinker, while also to be a creative who is full of ideas to share whether or not deemed intellectual or entirely so-called evidence-based. (One think tank I worked for called me an "idea generator.") All this is present as I work. But I can also be the mind open to communication or wisdom or messaging, whatever we want to call this, that comes from beyond those strict channels of the objective thinking structure that so many of us are so trained in -- or should I say indoctrinated into (no offense to my colleagues).

I say all this, at the same time saying I am absolutely not an anti-science person. I love science. I believe in science. I respect the scientific method. Almost everything we do almost every day relies on science. So, let's not move into a loop where we deny science and its great value. I do believe, however, that science already is beginning to explore beyond the realm of the given structures that we are presently working in. My view is that we can extend our awareness. We can consciously reach beyond what we know the biological brain engages in.

We can detect and reach beyond our brain's structuring and filtering of our reality for us.

I do believe we know more than we know we know. I do believe our brain filters and reduces what we know for us, so we can function here in this material plane, on Earth, in biological bodies with biological brains.

Yes, we use our brain to function here, and also to obey the controlling dictum we have been provided: believe what our brain tells us to believe. Believe what we are programmed to believe.

Those of you who know my books (or will be knowing my books), such as the OVERRIDING THE EXTINCTION

SCENARIO or UNVEILING THE HIDDEN INSTINCT volumes (in the KEYS TO CONSCIOUSNESS AND SURVIVAL SERIES), do hear me take great pains to explain what I mean by the possibilities that:

(a) evolution either did or did not allow us to know all we can know; and,

(b) this restriction of our perceptions really is the product of random evolution or -- darn it, and I would swear here but I'm going to water this down here, or darn it --

(c) **is the result of something else interfering with us, or even directing us to become restricted in our perceptions and awareness-es, at least while we live here in this physical plane.**

All my life, I have been asking questions about what I call the programming we Humans either have evolved into ourselves, or have been implanted with. As a child and teen, I found that my wondering these things was somewhat socially isolating. Kids are quick to call other kids weirdos, and we don't want to be one, or maybe we do want to be one. However, the pressure to fit a norm is very intense. It remains very intense.

And, if you think of us as a biological species who wants to survive, then maybe pressures to fit social norms are part of some survival drive. Yet, at the same time, to fit these norms we may also leave out essential alternative intelligences and awareness-es and perceptions that we may also need in order to survive.

All this is quite obvious, and yet the nitty-gritty, moment-to-moment, almost molecule-to-molecule, even synapse-to-

synapse, process becomes incredibly intense. This invisible process perhaps becomes even quite political, when we understand the pressure we as a species are under and the pressure we as individual members of our species are under -- and the damn pressure our entire living biosphere, even Earth herself, are under.

Add to this forces and factors who may not want us all to succeed in surviving, and the pressure reveals itself to be uniquely extreme.

We must ask:

Is the who shall live question actually asking: who shall survive in the face of extreme climate and Earth changes, if these are to come?

If survival itself is a resource, is there enough survival to go around? Is the who shall live question more like a who shall be privileged enough to survive? Or is this more a question of who is stealing and controlling access to the resources needed to survive profound Earth changes -- in advance of their great demand?

Think of the global elite, and the profound accumulation of wealth and access to safety this elite, this what I call OMEGA CABAL, has already locked up. How do the rest of us break through to detect and then access these survival resources and territories in this and even in other dimensions as well?

Speaking as a member of METATERRA®, I say we have a right to ask these questions – and to seek the answers, to reveal to ourselves our rightful key to our, to Humanity's,

survival both here and beyond. It is time we reveal to ourselves the OMEGA KEY we carry so deeply buried within us.

(Readers are encouraged to see the novel referred to so many times throughout this book: REVEALING THE OMEGA KEY. Readers may also be interested to note that I actually had already trademarked METATERRA® beginning many years ago. Instinct is such a powerful messenger.)

NOTES FROM THE FRONT

34

SEEING THE BRAIN'S PROGRAMMING FOR US TO BE CONTROLLED

Information comes to us in many different ways. Sometimes we entirely miss a critical realization while it lingers in our subconscious realm. Sometimes our own brain may not be designed to allow the full impact of this realization to be consciously experienced. Once in a while, the awareness of this realization becomes so loud and clear, it cannot be ignored.

I became ever more deeply aware of a matter than has long concerned me while I served as editor of, even perhaps cheerleader for, the INTERNATIONAL COLLECTION ON ADDICTIONS.[39] This is a four-volume series involving hundreds, actually thousands, of people from over twenty nations: researchers, clinicians, policy-makers, others, a range of people dealing with addictions, drug and non-drug addictions. By the term *drug* here, I include alcohol and other substances, as well what are considered to be non-drugs with nevertheless distinctly addictive characteristics. -- or as I choose to say, ***which***

[39] Refer to the *INTERNATIONAL COLLECTION ON ADDICTIONS,* and its four volumes: *Volume 1: Faces of Addiction Then and Now; Volume 2: Psychobiological Profiles; Volume 3: Characteristics and Treatment Perspectives; Volume 4: Behavioral Addictions From Concept to Compulsion.*

trigger the brain's addiction functions. (Note that, among that latter group of nondrug addictions, are gambling, gaming, shopping, spending, internet, texting, sexting, working, and much more. Addiction is a function which is both chemical and behavioral.

There was I was, inundated with cutting edge material. The reality that only a certain number of articles could get into these four very long volumes was a painful one. I was therefore in touch with far more people (thousands) than were eventually published in the collection.

Working so intensively with this extensive material that its many authors were sending me from all over the world, I began to sense, better said -- be uncannily aware, that I was also working with, speaking to, addiction itself. By addiction itself here, I refer to the neural programming the brain carries to form addictions, to form even healthy habits basically for survival reasons (e.g., eating, sleeping, reproducing, and so on). I began to be acutely aware of how the programming, the wiring, of the Human brain was underlying all Human behavior -- of course -- *and* that we humans are programmed to behave in certain ways, even to become addicted.

This huge flow of information from so many directions provided me an amazing insight into the minds of thinkers and researchers looking at the matter of addiction, as well as into what I have come to call ***this lifeform we call addiction itself.*** And yes, I began to view ***addiction as a life form, something with a mind or at least a programming of its own, its own agenda designed to control us.***

For me, this was a great adventure into the Human mind-brain. I found myself in an ongoing dialog with the brain, actually with the addiction-habituation programming the brain was being controlled by. This dialog itself became on unusual experience. I felt as if I had detected the presence of something that preferred to remain unrecognized as an actual program, almost a life form, with an intelligence of its own.

Although I had years of experience in this field, I was profoundly changed by this experience of working with thinkers from all over the world. I began to see the human brain as a highly programmed biological machine, one with its own glitches and cycles and patterns, at times **quite inescapable loops designed and implanted into our coding to control us.**

What leapt out at me, after delving so deeply into this matter of the Human brain and its tendency, even programming, to became harmfully addicted, to have natural functions run so far awry, even to became addicted to dangerous, even life threatening, behaviors were these questions:

> **How did we, our brains, evolve these problems in programming, these flaws destined to undermine so many Humans?**
>
> **Is addiction really simply something just naturally part of the biological brain we have evolved?**
>
> **Why would we have naturally selected to form self-programming that would undermine us this way?**
>
> **Is this so-called naturally evolved programming really the result of natural evolution?**

Or, have we somehow been programmed with this sort of limit to, this catch-22 in, our functioning?

Why would something, programming, we need in order to survive -- such as to become habituated to healthy survival oriented behaviors, e.g., eating, reproducing, even fighting or taking flight in response to danger -- be designed or evolved to both protect us, and to, when running awry, kill us?

If this is the result of intelligent design, and if so, how intelligent is this design?

If this is the result of intelligent design, what sort of higher intelligence programmed this sort of flaw into us?

Who wrote this script? Can we seriously say natural selection made this for us?

Let me back up a moment here. Indeed, in reading each piece of the submitted material again and again, then again and again editing it as it was submitted and resubmitted, I found that many of the contributors from outside the United States who were writing in English needed less editing than many of the contributors from within the United States, but that is room for another discussion. However, with this large number of words I was reading regarding addiction, I began to see quite differently the brain and the addictive patterns it forms.

I see that it is definitely the programming of the Human species to become habituated, addicted. We are designed to become addicted. The state of being addicted is of course natural for all of us, as we need to be addict-able, habituate-able beings for survival reasons. Yet, this basic situation, what I have elsewhere defined as our "addiction function,"[40] has run far, far awry now in modern times, and has made us ever more controllable.

As I delved all the more deeply into the mind-brain addiction tendencies, I saw the Human species as falling prey to this tendency. In doing this thinking, I began to also look at other ***evolved-in or programmed-in or designed-in,*** however we want to describe these here, functions of the Human brain that we do not to have enough power to override. Harmful addiction behaviors of our species, or of ourselves as individuals, must be understood for what these are. ***I see these as: either accidentally evolved, or perhaps even purposefully implanted, control mechanisms.***

Somehow all of this emerging understanding was building at the same time I was looking at the survival instincts and or counter-survival instincts of species including our own, the Human species. My concurrent and ongoing extinction-related studies of *extinction-prone behavior* originating in the Human brain-mind led me to look for what forces and factors, and groups such as the OMEGA CABAL I have discussed in other chapters of this present book, are:

opportunists taking advantage of

our programming to be controlled by

deeply embedded brain programs

---

[40] See also the book by Angela Brownemiller in the *FACES OF ADDICTION COLLECTION,* titled, *SEEING THE HIDDEN FACE OF ADDICTION: DETECTING AND CONFRONTING THIS INVASIVE PRESENCE.*

and their patterns such as addictions.

Here was what the primary question became for me:

Might we be

designed *not* to be effective at our own survival?

During this multi-year global collection on addiction project, my sensitivity to our brain's programming became increasingly acute. And it has stayed so. In fact, there were and still are times when I felt and continue to feel this programming of us has a mind of its own, and that this mind, this intelligence, is in a sense watching me watch it -- as if this programming of our minds, our brains, our neural systems, our genes, has an intelligence of its own.

In fact, my book, SEEING THE HIDDEN FACE OF ADDICTION: DETECTING AND CONFRONTING THIS INVASIVE PRESENCE, grew out of this awareness. And then my books on survival, such as the two OVERRDIDING THE EXTINCTION SCENARIO books, followed by the UNVEILING THE HIDDEN INSTINCT book, and other of the books in the KEYS TO CONSCIOUSNESS AND SURVIVAL SERIES, were all demanding of my mind and soul that I write them.

The idea that we have been programed, ***even designed,*** either by random evolution -- or by some other force or factor or intelligence in order to control us, is always on my mind.

I often speak and write about the concept of extinction. I often suggest that we may have somehow been intelligently designed by some forces or factors out there. Were we actually somebody else's petri dish or laboratory test? **Might we be unknowing or unwilling participants in what I have called**

extinction trials? (See the books in the KEYS TO CONSCIOUSNESS AND SURVIVAL SERIES such as UNVEILING THE HIDDEN INSTINCT and THE OVERRIDING THE EXTINCTION SCENARIO volumes).

Extinction? This is a pretty heavy issue to talk about, although as the decades have proceeded since my earlier OMEGA WORK, there is far more use of this word, extinction. To share with people (on air, in person, and or in writing) that the Human species ***may be designed to become extinct*** is a burden. In fact, saying this is something I avoid. Rather, I choose to say that we have the ***option to override our own extinction-related behaviors***, our behaviors with potential or actual extinction potential, I say that we have this powerful option.

Of course this option involves so many different levels of thought. First of all, if we were *designed to be the way we are*, this means there is some higher intelligence or some other intelligence who has maybe not created us but has designed us. As I write this, I am suddenly thinking back to Robert Heinlein and his novels that were so popular years ago, and I ask -- did we travel from the future to our past? Are we here to warn ourselves of what is happening now? Or, did we ourselves design ourselves to conduct this experiment upon ourselves? In other words, did we do this to ourselves?

And who is sustaining this control of us? Who understands what this is about? Do some of those in control, members of a global elite, an OMEGA TRANSITION time CABAL, use this knowledge to better control us in these increasingly perilous times?

However this is happening, we are at least genetically and then neurally programmed, as I've said in the KEYS TO CONSCIOUSNESS AND SURVIVAL SERIES. We are in many ways unknowingly participating in whatever this ***extinction potential and extinction test*** is. I don't like this concept, I don't want this concept, but this is a question we must ask ourselves.

And of course, as I began writing several seemingly science fiction books, novels pulling together ancient teachings and modern science and philosophies, I began to see that perhaps there are people who understand this, whether they do so consciously or subconsciously -- and if they are in positions of power, perhaps they are even manipulating our extinction and survival options.

Who here on this Earth has the wealth to invest in his or her future, to invest in being prepared for whatever changes are coming?

If I can detect this programming, and if I can wonder whether we are being subjected to extinction processes and or extinction trials, imagine what those on this planet who have the greatest access to resources can find out and know.

35

BEING TAGGED EARLY?

My story is I am sure at least parallel to many of yours. We are all on life journeys of discovery of ourselves, of our worlds, of our realities. Many of us found our missions in life beginning to become clear to us at young ages, and/or as we moved into and through our adulthoods. Some of us have sensed callings, felt called, drawn to do some work in service of Humanity. Some of us have felt called to develop and share messages of various forms. Some of us hear or sense messages of some form coming in, calling us to share the wisdom pouring in to us from beyond. Even the notion of what lies beyond is opening into the here and now, with so many already walking in two and more worlds while still living in physical bodies here on Earth, or perhaps also while having moved beyond physical bodies.

Moving so rapidly, we imagine almost at the speed of light or beyond the speed of light, information travels to and through us. This knowing is coming in waves. In these times, we are hearing that call to see what is occurring here on Earth -- to begin to realize what is going on here.

And, while all this is taking place, I, as have many of you, have become increasingly aware that something is aware of us, aware of you, aware of me. As we have become more aware of what is or may be going on here on Earth (and perhaps also

BEYOND), even going on in our own brains, various forces and factors, intelligences, scanners, presences, programs, appear to be more aware of us. Without being paranoid, as paranoia is not useful, it is not difficult to sense that perhaps, just perhaps, we -- our minds, our awareness-es, maybe our consciousness itself -- are being monitored, stalked, tracked in some way.

Now of course, this is a different sort of tracking, stalking, as there is not necessarily a physical presence, or even a detectable electronic or cyber presence behind this tracking, this stalking. All the more stealth is the stalking I refer to here, stalking or tracking where our minds, our lives, our increasing awareness, can be read and yes, tracked.

Again, this is not a conspiracy theory book. There is no actual conspiracy here. However, there is what is perhaps an actual reality. We must be ever watchful to be certain we are able to detect the presence of this eye on us. During the course of our lives, many of us have been sensing, detecting, the presence of some form of monitoring. We have been becoming increasingly aware that there is a monitoring of our brains, our species, our thoughts, and I say **also of our EVOLUTION itself**.

36

EXTRA SENSORY AWARENESS

I look back on my own youth. It may have become clear to me at a young age that I was not on a very defined path in my life, although there were many who claimed that I should be. I remember that when I took first place in a state science fair while I was in junior high school, my name, school, and photo appeared in several local papers. I was then invited by the U.S. Navy, along with a number of other science fair winners (who were in the next grades older than mine) to visit a submarine stationed in the San Francisco Bay. That was all very interesting, and of course I went. While unusual, this invitation was considered a recruiting strategy and an honor. But, I made it clear that I would always refuse to go underwater in a sub which meant I would not be successfully recruited for this sort of thing.

No one enjoys claustrophobia. Some of us respond to this sensation quite strongly. I've never handled claustrophobia well, whether it be in my mother's womb, or in the possibility of being in a submarine under the water, or flying into outer space in a tiny capsule -- when really our journeys beyond are so expansive. So for me, physical confinement has always been an issue. And to truly go BEYOND, we do not need spaceships, we need the vessels of our consciousness-es themselves.

I remember the Navy identifying those of us who won these prizes at young ages as people that they should or would like to encourage to explore, or I gather even commit to, the Navy as a future. That concept sounded nice, although I was certain I would not yet commit. This was one of many contacts that were made with me, and I'm sure with many of my peers, regarding things we might do for the government when we were grownups. But, we weren't grownups yet. I am not sure what all the others decided to do. I know some did go into military services, some into intelligence agencies. I continue to tell myself I have followed neither of these paths.

I remember that at that time, I had been living in California, in the pre-Silicon Valley environment. At that time, in that county, there was a strong emphasis on a certain type of learning. This was called "teaching to intelligence" in those days. Later, at the age of eighteen, I was asked to speak at a conference on the educational program I had been in. I remember being the youngest speaker there. I remember the looks on the adults' faces when I stood at the podium on stage and told them all that this sort of so-called extended learning program I had years earlier been placed in against my will should be called "teaching all people to have intelligence" and "should offered to everybody or no one." (Of course, in the years since then, educators and psychologists know much more about intelligence -- and know there are many forms of intelligence, and many forms of mental acuity and thought and cognition and function and so on.)

Nevertheless, back then, in that soon to be Silicon Valley area, those in charge had decided to give all of the kids in the county tests, whether or not they wanted them. Those kids who scored extremely highly on various tests, and then highly on individualized additional tests, were eventually identified, labelled, and as best as I can tell, tracked for life. So there we were, sixty children heading into an experiment on us because we had the highest scores on some unwanted tests. Many of, as children, were questioning already back then why our friends weren't also being sent, why we had to go alone, into this high pressure very demanding program. We were insisting our friends were as smart as we were. And we were likely right about this. Yet, we soon realized we would not wish this high pressure situation on our friends, let alone on ourselves.

Without our being asked whether we wanted to or not, we were moved into that class with some sixty other kids from around the county. Among those sixty were some who were very socially adept and well adapted. There were others who needed a little help making friends or having social relationships. And there were others who were quite withdrawn. I could see this range of children, and wasn't quite sure where I fit. On the one hand, I was a sociable kid, yet on the other hand, I could be quite withdrawn. I did not engage in a great number of social activities. I read a lot, mostly long books written for adults, and I wrote down a lot of the ideas coming to me every day. I spent almost every Sunday at home, all day alone in my room, drawing and studying, already starting at a young age and doing this all the way through high school.

Anyway, there I was in this so-called accelerated learning program, this sixth grade where in the first few weeks we were pretty much moved through several school years at a very rapid speed, and taught speed reading and other skills. It seemed like far too soon in that school year that we were given a large

assignment, which was to do a real research project. I years later realized that this was a college level assignment.

I almost immediately chose, as I'd read about this research in a magazine, to contact Duke University where they were doing "parapsychology" tests at the time. I wrote and asked if I could conduct some of their experiments with my classmates, with those who wanted to participate. Of course, Duke said yes to this, asking me to be certain to not use the real names of the students I was testing, and then to please send them my results. I did not mention to the people at Duke how young I was.

As I worked on this project, I did a lot of research, also looking up sources on the research being conducted in other countries. I stumbled into some interesting research coming out of the then Soviet Union. These studies were looking at parapsychological perception and also parapsychological influence capabilities. Psychokinesis, the use of the mind to influence physical events such as the outcome of dice throwing, was among the experiments being conducted. Another area of related research also being conducted in the then Soviet Union was dermo-optical perception with which readings of textures, colors, and other information were being perceived through non optical channels, such as the skin. As I did this research, it became clear to me that these studies appeared to be being conducted under the auspice of that nation's defense agency.

Back in my sixth grade class, I did conduct various parapsychological tests and experiments related to those designed by Duke University. These included general parapsychology tests, such as testing the ability of participants to predict what they would see, such as numbers or shapes on shuffled cards before they were turned over. These tests then also went on to include other parapsychological tests, such as of the ability to predict outcomes such as that of rolling dice. These tests also included tests for psychokinesis, which would be to influence the outcome of the rolling dice.

My findings amazed me. I found, and I never explained this to my teachers, nor to Duke University, as I had no way to be doing this, that the students with the most power or skill or prowess in these parapsychological and para-psychokinetic areas were the children who were the most withdrawn and the least socially adapted of all the children in the class. Of course, back then, I didn't really have those labels to use, but I still to this day remember those children. Although I didn't quite fit their group, I identified with those children quite a bit.

So this was fascinating, even for me as a kid who had not yet learned the world of research procedures and data collection. The test scores of this particular group of students, the more withdrawn, were unusually high in areas of parapsychological awareness, parapsychological capability, even psychokinesis, which is either awareness of the outcome of physical movement, or actually being able to affect the outcome of physical movement.

So there I was, eleven years old, finding that our brains can do a lot of things that we aren't taught in school, and that most of our schooling ignores or even denies these things. I was greatly intrigued. Why weren't we being taught how to really use our minds in school, I wondered.

At the same time, I was in a large middle school setting where there were many children in the additional grades (seventh and eighth) in one school. But we sixty sixth graders there were quite isolated, and treated as strangers, largely unwanted. And there I was, a little girl carrying a big briefcase to school every day, and being taunted by other kids, mostly by older kids, and being called the "school brain." In those days, we didn't yet use the word "bullying," but I was certainly bullied for being intelligent and being what they called "brainy" and having a large vocabulary, which really wasn't my fault and I shouldn't have been blamed for. I certainly tried not to exhibit any unusual characteristics. In fact, already then I began training myself to dumb down. (I did not yet know the term "dumb down," and would learn this term and this sense that dumbing down was necessary many times as I moved into and through my adulthood.) Still, while I was most certainly being bullied for it, I did everyday carry a large briefcase to school. And I had a lot of allergies. I was sick a lot and I was often needing medicine for my allergies. Sometimes I had to go to the nurse's office and get medicated right in the middle of a class.

At the same time, I discovered my school would be offering foreign language classes in Mandarin Chinese. I decided that since my parents spoke most of the romance languages, I would take Chinese, something my parents did not understand or speak or write at all. So, during the seventh and eighth grade years, I studied Mandarin Chinese and absolutely loved it. But that became even more isolating for me, as other children in the school thought that was weird, too. And of course, I also played the violin and oboe in the school orchestra, which sent me over board into the weird girl direction. Still, what was most isolating was the sense that I was sensing so much more than people were talking about, or perhaps than they were aware of. And when I tried to talk about these sensations with any of the other students, I was laughed at, made fun of. So I learned to keep my ideas to myself.

These things I describe above were, back in those years, much more isolating than they may be for children now. It bothered me somewhat back then that the kids called me weird, and brainy, but then I got used to the labels and accepted them. I was sort of already on my own journey and just kept on keeping on.

I tell this story because I found myself exploring the mind at a young age, and seeking to understand the mind's capacity to go in unusual directions, even if the mind, in this case my mind, had to do this all alone. I could see the mind hungry for things that no one was teaching.

It seemed to me already as a child that there were things we were not allowed to know, not allowed to think about, that there was forbidden knowledge, even forbidden inquiry. I was hungry for information or truth or something beyond the obvious.

I think many of us feel this way, and yet too much of this curiosity is ruled out, is shut down. So back then, I felt I was somewhat alone on my path, and indeed I was frequently alone. Somewhere in that time period, at about age eleven, I was introduced to marijuana. (Of course, in those years, this was a much milder version than it is these days.) As my pre-teen and teenage years were incredibly and increasingly stressful, I found it quite calming. It may have saved me in an environment that was extremely stressful, where I was under a lot of social and academic and intellectual pressure from all directions.

At first, the marijuana had been an escape from a troubled life and distraught adolescence, providing a sort of safety zone for me. There were times that I could move into a zone that no one could touch. I remember walking in the many orchards surrounding our neighborhood, and seeing the flowers growing there were just floating on air. Much later, I realized I had been self-medicating my way through my pre-teen and teenage years. Nevertheless, I managed to get straight A's all the way through school, K through twelve. For me, A's were my defense against institutions, and I hoped the key to my freedom, but to freedom from what? I allowed myself the smoking of marijuana to cope with life. But, later, by the time I was eighteen, I was tired of that drug. It is not that I was coping better, but that the safety zone was gone.

Little did I know, my life would become more intense and at times even more difficult as I moved through adolescence. I thought something was coming. I was worried about my mother. But I didn't know what was worrying me. And when she became ill and then later died when I was seventeen, I realized I had somehow known this was coming. This knowing became a crisis both emotionally and intellectually for me -- because, if I had known, couldn't I have stopped it, I wondered. And who could I discuss this knowing with? Absolutely no one.

Here was the Human brain, in this case my brain, trying to understand what it knew, what it could know, how it could know it, and what the dangers were regarding knowing too much through avenues not considered means of knowing.

I would eventually come to understand that this was going to be a lifelong inquiry.

How do we know what we are not allowed to know?
How do we recognize
what we are not programmed to recognize,
WHAT WE ARE
PROGRAMMED NOT TO RECOGNIZE,
as actual information,
and even as essential information?

NOTES FROM THE FRONT

DOUBLE

OMEGA

ALPHA

PART FIVE

NOTES FROM THE FRONT

37

FERRETING OUT THE TRUTH ABOUT OMEGA TRANSITION OPPORTUNISTS

This realization process, its coming into focus, has been a sort of eyes wide shut experience. We are increasingly tuning in to the reality that there are those with the financial power and will to continue their largely growing concealment of -- their calculated non-disclosure of most of -- their acquiring of, even hoarding of, essential information, resources, and survival territories plus the precious access to these.

Of course, there are those who will exploit Humanity's weaknesses to take advantage of WE THE PEOPLE OF THIS PLANET as we move into the coming turn of time, the close of this current grand cycle, this OMEGA TRANSITION, including its Earth and climate changes, diseases and pandemics, economic and political turbulences, along with widespread confusion and despair.

Indeed, as this situation has intensified, there is intensifying recognition that what WE THE PEOPLE OF THIS PLANET have been seeing is but the tip of the iceberg (yes, of the melting iceberg). Calling this out, choosing to see that we are realizing, sensing, DETECTING, THE OMEGA DECEPTION, is stepping up, hearing the call speaking to us through time, urging us to see and step forward. NOW.

The modern environmental movement is said to have begun in 1970 with the declaration of the first Earth Day on April 22 of that year, which grew to international status. Also in 1970, the U.S. Congress created the Environmental Protection Agency. The fiftieth anniversary of Earth Day was in April 2020, one month after the World Health Organization declared the spread of Covid-19 a global pandemic.

There are many who note that actually, modern environmental awareness began with the release of conservationist and marine biologist Rachel Carson's book, *The Silent Spring,* which called attention to use of pesticides. Numerous efforts to draw attention to, and respect, even protect, the environment have emerged throughout history.

What are now becoming more and more clear (that is, if we look very closely and if we very carefully question what we are seeing and being told) are *major efforts to control key narratives,* such as narratives regarding what environmentalism is about, and also narratives designed to distract WE THE PEOPLE OF THIS PLANET from powerful efforts to hoard vast amounts of assets, territories, and access mechanisms and routes, should survival on the Earth be threatened on a global scale.

It is time we are doing everything we can to be DETECTING THE OMEGA CONSPIRACY. This growing awareness is a process of what I call dot connecting.

Let's step back a moment. We connect dots all the time.

We do what I see as being *gestalt perception* and *gestalt knowing of our realities.* What I mean by this is that we fill in gaps between (a) what our biological eyes and brains tell us we are perceiving -- seeing, and hearing, touching, tasting, smelling, and (b) that which is really out there. So we are perceiving (a) what we're being given biologically as a perception, and (b) only some of what is actually there to be perceived. Our brain is wired, programmed, to tell us what our reality is based on its generalization or perhaps even distortion of what is really out there.

(Note: For details on this, what I term, *gestalt perception,* see the opening chapters of the book, GESTALTING ADDICTION: SPEAKING TRUTH TO THE POWER AND DEFINITION OF ADDICTION, ADDICTION THEORY, AND ADDICTION TREATMENT, where I detail my theory and thinking building on scientists' gestalt theory of perception and other research on biological perception.)

I emphasize here that we (via our brain) connect the dots. We are always connecting dots. In other words, here's a broken circle, and we see a broken circle. Right? Well, not so simply. If we are quickly flashed a card with this broken circle on it, our brain may tell us we see a whole circle. This is because our brain fills in the gaps, connects the dots for us with the highest probability of what it believes is correct. Our brain does this for our own safety, for our own defense, for our own effectiveness. This dot connecting is always happening within this *gestalt perception* I refer to above. This gestalt is always happening.

However, there is a lot more going on when we think we see a closed circle, which is actually first being perceived by the brain as broken. We are telling ourselves something is there, or that something is there that may not be there, or may not be there the way we are being told by our brain it is there.

We are connecting dots where there are perhaps no dots to connect. On the other hand, we often do not connect dots that are there to be connected. We often do not draw the connections, close the circle, see most of or more of the whole picture that our biological eyes are giving us to see -- because our brains our told not to do this for us.

Yes, intuition comes in, every moment, all the time. We are all exercising intuition. Now, some of you have called this the sixth sense. And yes, it is, although it may be the original sense and the primary sense. This may not even be intuition, rather just sensory tuition. This is basically perceiving what is really out there, what is really in here, what is really here.

Now, let's go back to DETECTING THE OMEGA CONSPIRACY. As explained above, we do a great deal of dot connecting to give ourselves a sense of what is going on around us. What if there are functions perhaps evolved into us, or wired into us, or beamed in in some way we are not aware of, functions that are controlling what we are able to know, what we are able to perceive? So here is the larger question:

How can we fully

DETECT the OMEGA CONSPIRACY

when we are wired or primed not to?

Looking at what is really going on has been an interest (or concern) of mine as long as I can recall. This is not paranoia, rather a healthy heightened awareness. I have long felt myself to be a dot connector. (Back when that think tank had called me an "idea generator" because they saw me as having a constant stream of original ideas they could use (and I eventually discovered, they could exploit), they saw I could quickly write proposals containing original ideas, writing without stopping constantly for days and weeks at a time. Even when my right arm was broken, given that I am right handed, I did all this typing with my left hand.)

In my view, we all are to varying degrees constantly dot connecting, or at least our brains are. While this dot connecting has profound survival potential, this is not always used in positive ways. At times, opinions of what reality is reflect this. At times, we are hearing of bizarre conclusions people have made in their dot connecting (or perhaps in their false fact generating) processes. Unfortunately, we all too often hear people say, "Well, I heard it from the angels or from God, so it must be true," and then make decisions based on this sort of conclusion.

Of concern here are questions such as these: What forces and factors may be taking advantage of Humans' weakened or partial perception functions? How vulnerable is the Human mind to manipulation? Could the perpetrators of the OMEGA DECEPTION be taking advantage of this?

Now, we all know that we have complex jungles here on this physical plane planet, right? These are highly layered milieus where there is extensive collaboration among species, and also extensive competition among species.

Who is to say there aren't highly complex multiple-agenda'd jungles out there in other dimensions as well? So, if you or we are receiving messages from beyond, or from deep within your/our own subconsciouses, it may or may not be always a given that what you/we are hearing or the dots you/we are connecting, are being connected for our own good.

This makes ferreting out the truth all the more critical while at the same time, tells us we must question information coming into our minds and brains.

WHOSE THOUGHTS
ARE YOU THINKING?

AND HOW DO YOU KNOW?

38

UNSEEN HANDS

Earth and Beyond, undisclosed location, 2008. It was 0400, well, at least it was 4am PST. I was on a conference call with the break-off (some of them called themselves "rogue") remote viewing team. I had by now been willing, at least for the sake of understanding what all this was about, to suspend both my disbelief and my belief, to see both belief and disbelief as simply concepts rather than issues. It became clear that this is what the other members of this team were doing. We were all exploring this matter, looking at where our increasingly adept viewing skills would take us, how far out there we could see --and how far out there we needed to see.

These were scientists with significant mainstream backgrounds who had already dedicated years to this work. I already had great respect for them in the every day professional world. Despite their reputations and daily life demands, these people were there dedicating themselves to this project. I was honored to be part of this team.

We had gone to use of burner phones to do this work.

As frequently was the case, they would tell me what they sensed or saw and where, primarily communicating this sort of thing telepathically, accompanied by with trigger words or comments over the phone line. They would ask me to use my

skills to look at what they directed me to look at, and to give them any details or responses I might have.

In the process of doing this work over several years, we all became quite adept at reading, or sensing, each other's minds, their messages, perceptions, and images, at showing each other what we might see, hear, sense, out there.

This night, well actually at 4 AM Pacific Earth time, we were doing a surveillance sort of mission. We had all agreed that we were going to meet out there, take ourselves out there to connect out there to together look back at the Earth.

Our viewing Earth from this distance was for the purpose of seeing, sensing, what might be approaching Earth from beyond Earth. As we had done before, we were going to be aware of, detect, large ships, both metaphorical and actual ships, energy bodies, that may be approaching our planet, and what their nature and general intent was. This level of remote viewing was already reaching beyond original government remote viewing projects, which were looking at what was taking place on the planet, in various players' and enemies' Earth-based domains.

However, our particular break off group had long left the Earth and near Earth realm. Although we had a great deal of experience looking at what might be approaching Earth, and reading its energy and intent, we had reached well beyond Earth and near Earth in our remote viewing exercises.

This night, we were very far out from Earth. We were able to look back from a very wide venue. We were going to be able to see or sense what might be approaching Earth from very far off.

Now, as a group we looked back at the Earth in our joint viewing.

I could not help but gasp, first at the beauty of the Earth we saw as we were looking back from beyond, but then almost immediately at the tattered appearance of areas of the Earth's atmosphere.

One of the men on the call asked me what I was seeing. I showed him by joining with him to share my third eye, so to speak. He then gasped.

The group all came in to this viewing and we saw together this tattered atmosphere, an ailing planet's ailing shield, weakening in its protection of her own biosphere. We instinctively joined forces to send energy, through group focus, to areas of the Earth's atmosphere that appeared not only thinner but ragged. We could see that we had some effect; however, our communal power was of course not as strong as that condition that we were seeking to heal.

It was in that moment that we all agreed we had to do this regularly, and we had to learn to focus our power more and more to be able to (metaphorically and hopefully actually) help Earth.

We eventually joined with other teams who from time to time would work together on this. This focus is continuously needed and must never stop.

Later, after I left the call, I fell asleep and had a dream Earth was speaking to me. I had to listen. I asked Earth right there in that dream if this was actually happening. Earth said yes, you can create this space, this communication, and you can help us all rebalance this situation.

NOTES FROM THE FRONT

I could feel the connection. There are no words to describe this other than Earth begins to find those who can hear her.

39

TIME TO LEAVE THE NEST

New Mexico, 1996. An old friend, journalist and poet Victor Perrara, and I had recently discovered we were both friends of poet Victor diSuvero. We found ourselves guests of Victor and his partner, Barbara, at their ranch in northern New Mexico. I had stopped there on my way east, as part of a national book tour.

That night, I stayed in one of the ranch guest cabins. From there, I called in to a radio show as that night's guest. This was the Art Bell Show. We spoke for hours about my newest book on death and dying. Eventually, during my time on this radio show, I conducted my mental exercise for metaphorical body exit with Art Bell. I of course, as I always do, said this was going to include the body re-entry exercise.

The experience was at once both entirely obvious and entirely out of this world, so to speak. I felt myself to be out of my own body as I conducted this exercise on this show. Later many listeners contacted me and said they had participated in the body exit exercise I conducted on the air and were profoundly intrigued.

After the radio show, I met with Victor Perrera who was in the adjoining cabin. He and I had agreed we would discuss a particular matter after my radio show appearance. This was quite late in the evening as the show had been a long one.

Finally, Victor and I sat down at the kitchen table in his cabin. I explained that I would like his permission to quote someone in a book I was working on (which was an early version of my HOW TO DIE AND SURVIVE book) who he had quoted in his own book, *The Last Lords of Palenque*. The words I wanted to quote were those of Lacandon tribal leader, Chun K'in:

"... when the last Lacandon dies,
the world will come to an end."

It was quite late at night, and Victor and I talked about Chan K'in for hours. Then the telephone rang. It was the editor of a major magazine Victor Perrera had been writing for. This editor delivered a message sent to Victor, that there was an emergency and he must immediately call his friends in Guatemala. He did so. These were old friends he had known since his childhood when he was growing up in Guatemala, when he was closely relating to members of Lacandon tribe. Victor had all his life remained close to Chan K'in, who had become the Lacandon tribal leader. Now this night, I sat with Victor Perrara as he was told by telephone that Chan K'in had just died.

Victor went silent. In fact, he went blank, as if hypnotized by this information, its shock and pain. I sat there quietly, just being there for Victor as he sat in this suspended state.

I was interrupted in my sitting with Victor by a strange glowing blue light suddenly appearing right there outside the window. I went to the window and saw this beautiful luminous blue-ness filling the sky. But it was the middle of the night. I opened the door, stepped outside, and looked up. Immediately I felt enveloped in this rare blue illumination. Enveloped is putting it mildly. I was submerged into, yet felt as if I was floating within, this blueness, whatever it was.

I did not resist. Not could I have found a way to resist. Whatever this was, the power of the light or force was so immense that I had no option to do anything else but be part of it.

I began to see coming into focus a very complex thing above me. I have no words for this other than "thing" and "above me," or perhaps I will simply call this a "presence." I say above me, however, this was so immense that it filled as much as I could see of the sky. Was I underneath it or in it, I did now know.

I looked around this place or thing or presence filling the sky, now filling even the air around me. It looked somewhat like a larger than life, larger than the sky even, huge and fully lit up computer circuit board, except this circuit board or whatever it was seemed to be alive. Rivers of light were racing around this board and even beyond this board. Now living streams of light were racing throughout the luminous blueness filling the air.

I was taken into the light for much of the night. I remembered this much and more about that night when I woke up in the bed in my cabin the next morning.

I went to find Victor. I told him I was concerned about him, that so much had happened during the night. He said he was fine and that he remembered nothing that happened after that call about Chun K'in having just died. He then said, "Well, Angela, this is a very important thing, my dear old friend, Chun

K'in, died last night."

"Victor, does this mean the world is coming to an end, as Chun K'in predicated?"

"I have been asking myself this, too. You were just bringing me your request to quote Chun K'in in your book, HOW TO DIE AND SURVIVE. The answer is clearly yes. And there is something about the timing of your request and that phone call about his death that I am stuck with. I cannot give things specific meaning when I do not fully understand, yet there is definitely important meaning in your timing and this message."

Victor and I were later told that there had been many sightings of a powerful blue light that night, that this light had been predicted by many tribes' ancient teachings. For example, it is said that we have entered a new age, marked by the appearance, and re-appearance, of the Blue Kachina, prophesized in ancient Hopi teachings. When this Blue Kachina appears, the world is entering a new age where the world as we know it is coming to an end.

40

TRUTH OR DARE TRUTH

In the various waves of media attention regarding my work, there were (and still are) times I was (and still am from time to time) approached by press who want to talk about what had taken place in that Marin County Courthouse (the case I have referred to earlier in this book). While I have repeatedly replied that I am not interested in discussing this, I do understand that there is important information in all this.

What I do see in this is the larger issue, which is regarding the presence of forces and factors striving to quiet those of us who are seeking to share survival information. These forces and factors will work through various avenues to try to suppress the truth about Humanity's right to survive. Now, for some, this may seem to be a reach too far beyond, perhaps a strange extension into the esoteric, when trying to describe the abuse of my first amendment rights I experienced on the stand. Yet, if we look closely, there are indications that we indeed must look this closely at what takes place in our lives.

Marin County Courthouse, California, 2002. Cross examination is a highly respectable and even noble art for some, and a cruel means of constructing lies and breaking honest witnesses for others.

Indeed, sitting on the witness stand during cross examination can be rather unpleasant or at least uncomfortable. Other times this can be a grueling experience. In this instance, my being questioned about my writings became a macabre process of unreal proportions. Any trace of my first amendment rights had disappeared during this process. The opposing side's attorneys had subpoenaed all my writings, and all my notes regarding any of my past present and future writings, whether these be electronic or in print, handwritten or recorded, in any past present or future form. This truly felt as if the thought police were after me.

Certainly they were on a hunting expedition, looking for anything they could use, even distort into something they could use, to discredit me as a witness, a business partner, a mother, and an expert in several fields.

This process was indeed a travesty of justice and should never have happened. However, no one there, not even my own attorneys, were able to put a stop to this profound breach of my first amendment (and other) rights.

And what was being used to attack me were pieces of my most creative, intuitive work, all written in service to Humanity, and to assist readers and clients with the Human condition in these ever more challenging times. It made no difference that I was highly regarded in several mainstream fields, had spoken on my professional work at conferences around the U.S. and in several other countries, had worked with thousands of people in a range of settings, had served as a National Institute of Mental Health Post-Doctoral Fellow, and as lecturer at U.C. Berkley where I earned two PhDs.

It became clear to me that discrediting me as a witness involved attacking my work on personal change and transformation, such as my work on death and dying, all written to help people with these issues. It also became quite obvious that the core attack was focused on belittling me regarding what was not even my nonfiction writing, and instead was my fictional OMEGA story novel, which years later became the REVEALING THE OMEGA KEY novel.

Over the years, again and again I have experienced the drive of some persons, forces, and factors, to shut down my work on the Human mind and consciousness in these times, as we move into what I have called the OMEGA TRANSITION era.

Adding to the attacks on me for my work was the result that the sizable funds I had earned, working day and night for many years, ***the funds which would have allowed me to share my work quite loudly with the world, were lost in this legal case based upon attacks on the very work I would have been sharing with the world.***

Clearly the effort to shut my message down was surfacing there in that court case, as elsewhere many other times along the way. Nevertheless, both REVEALING THE OMEGA KEY, along with my other works, and I have persisted, called to do so in part by the realization that we all must recognize and address the OMEGA DECEPTION I describe in this present book.

41

DEATH AND TIMELINESS

Time to leave the nest. Perhaps time to find, or form, a new habitat here or somewhere, perhaps to generate one in another dimension of our consciousness, which is where we actually do live.

Too soon, it seems, we leave the planet where we have made our home. We are cast out by something, perhaps by fate or age, or maybe by bio-spheric changes, or maybe by choice, or perhaps for some reason we cannot know (yet), cast out of the nest, physical plane planet Earth.

One of the greatest regrets voiced about physical deaths which occur before what is called a "ripe old age" or the "end of a long and full life" is that death has come too soon. Thus the phrase "untimely death" has been applied.

Death and timeliness are, more often than not, anything but companion concepts.

Of course, death and survival are generally considered antithetical. This makes sense, as what we think of as death suggests the end of a life.

However, once we understand our right to inhabit several dimensions of ourselves, and thus of our realities, then death can be re-defined, can be the saving of a life, can be survival, can be inter-dimensional mobility. The movement of the self, of the consciousness, back and forth to and from the physical plane, may be something we do know how to do, once we access this awareness buried so deeply within our sub- and un-consciousness-es. This key survival knowledge I have defined as the OMEGA KEY.

Do note that nothing in the above comment encourages suicide. This discussion is about survival, expansion to powers of the self while surviving physically as well. (For in-depth discussion of the interdimensional view of the self I teach, see the books in the KEYS TO CONSCIOUSNESS AND SURVIVAL SERIES, listed at the end of this present book.)

42

WE ARE COMING INTO KNOWING

When I first began speaking on this OMEGA WORK that had grabbed my heart and soul by storm, I felt I must insist that the draft pilot book about it was fiction, and indeed it was a novel. What was not fiction were its components and the driving forces affecting me, the author, and yes, all of us living on Earth at this time.

What was not (and still is not) fiction, was (and still is) the experience I was (and still am) having even considering that ancient voices -- and other voices such as those of major thinkers who are now deceased, disincarnated -- are arising in these times when significant Earth changes are becoming increasingly apparent. And, what was not (and is not) fiction was/is hearing these voices speaking ... whatever and however this hearing of ancient and also more recent voices of those who have left the planet is taking place.... (Please again see the earlier chapter in this book, Chapter 33: AS A WRITER WHO MAY BE HERE ON ASSIGNMENT.)

Again and again, when I would insist the pilot OMEGA STORY was fiction, there were those who would insist that it was not fiction. Some said I was basically bringing this message

in and had to understand that the story form I put it in was the means of bringing this story in. What was strange about all this is that I myself could feel some kind of energy, some kind of presence, actually several presences, around me as I wrote this book and began speaking about it. I felt a strong drive to share this information, even to release this book in the pilot form its early first version was.

Shortly after I began working on this book, and then ever since, many a night's sleep became of an entirely unexpected, even shocking, revelatory adventure. My dreams had taken on new dimensions, with powerful, sometimes quite loud, sometimes even booming, voices speaking to me, and some kind of presences taking me flying through time to places I had never been or seen or even considered. At one point early on in the writing of the pilot OMEGA STORY, while I was asleep one night, I awoke into a dream where I heard a resoundingly booming voice telling me to, "Talk to Nostradamus." At that point in my life, I had not given Nostradamus much thought, although I vaguely remembered hearing about him sometime earlier. But now, the compelling voice insisted I was actually being told this, and then this voice or presence or whatever it was, took me flying, soaring, so far out of my body I was simply racing slowly through time and suddenly flying over gleaming gold covered pyramids and the sphinx in ancient Egypt.

To that point in my life, I had never given ancient or even modern Egypt much consideration, although twice I had been approached by actual modern day Egyptians. One was an Egyptian woman at U.C. Berkeley who I met quite randomly, who was working on her Ph.D. in mathematics and at times suggested to me that for her, mathematics was quite mystical.

The other, entirely unrelated, had years earlier approached me in a book store and told the man I was with (who in earlier chapters I note I had discovered was a CIA agent) that my eyes reminded him of ancient times, of ancient Egypt. At that time, the man I was with tried to ward him off, he said to protect me from strange men approaching me. I am not certain what their interaction was, although they did seem to know each other.

After that brief meeting, I did run into this Egyptian man from time to time, including in settings where I was giving a talk or speech about my OMEGA WORK. He would simply look me in the eye and then knowingly nod, and I would nod in return. One time when we met, he walked up to me and handed me a golden stone, said the words, METATERRA, and then walked away. I was somewhat surprised, as I had no idea why he was saying the name of the off-planet organization it seemed to me I represented and even belonged to, a name I had never explained to anyone was an organization of off-planet beings. I had however openly associated even my early OMEGA WORK with the name I cherished so greatly, METATERRA (using the name, METATERRA in the form of METATERRA PUBLICATIONS for example, and eventually even trademarking that name, METATERRA®).

That the voices of ancient beings and others no longer alive on Earth were speaking to me, actually engaging with me, and that I was even feeling connected to, related to, these voices, was somewhat out of my reality, given my ongoing heavy-duty mainstream professional life, such as lecturing at U.C. Berkeley, working in corporations, and working with many other people in a range of other settings. Yet, once the OMEGA STORY called me, my life was forever changed. So was my sense of self, even of survival, even of reality.

I would not say that I began leading a double or secret life. Everything I was doing in all the various worlds I was working in was pretty much out in the open. Yet, my experiences of subtle callings and communications in what seemed to be cross-time and cross-dimensional zones, was at that time more than I could capture in words even for myself, let alone explain to others. It has taken me years to be able to bring in this information, this calling itself, in ways that perhaps can be understood by a wide range of people. I want to remind Readers again here, what I was experiencing was in unaltered states, as no drugs or medicines were required to bring all this to me. It was very important to me to regularly test my expanding reality from a solidly sober state (although, elsewhere I have questioned even this state of presumed awareness our biological brain generates for us[41]).

When the pilot draft of this OMEGA STORY first came out, there began a rush of many different people and groups toward me. I found myself in a constant state of holding my own in the face of pressure to identify with a range of movements and groups and views, many of which were conflicting with each other. Although when I finally stopped speaking on the early version of this OMEGA STORY (while I was being attacked for this book even by some quite close to me), I was able to move

---

[41] Refer to books in the *KEYS TO CONSCIOUSNESS AND SURVIVAL SERIES* such as, *HOW TO DIE AND SURVIVE, BOOK TWO*, and, *OVERRIDING THE EXTINCTION SCENARIO, PART TWO*, and also, *UNVEILING THE HIDDEN INSTINCT*. See also another book by this author, titled, *SEEING THE HIDDEN FACE OF ADDICTION: DETECTING AND CONFRONTING THIS INVASIVE PRESENCE.*

the pressure from various groups into the background of my life. I was also able to make clear to people that their interpretations of my OMEGA WORK was not quite my interpretation. In several cases, I actually suggested to people that if they had a message for the world, perhaps they would write their own books rather than trying to have me represent them. This did help to a great degree. Still, back then and even to this day, I hear from a diverse range of individuals and groups.

Many of the people who have contacted me about my OMEGA WORK say they are professionals who have dropped out of their own mainstream positions in their own workplaces and cultures -- usually out of positions of high repute -- whether scholarly or business or clerical or other -- to engage in some sort of global revolution. Many say they are not certain what exactly this revolution is, although they understand that it is not violent, as it is a revolution in thinking. They tell me they feel the calling, and they feel that I know what they are talking about.

Others who have contacted me tell me they are representatives of civilian militias. Among these militia groups have been a diverse range of political and religious orientations. Several had at times even offered me protection such as armed body guard protection. I tell them thank you, noting that I myself want nothing to do with guns, that this is not the revolution's mode. This is a combat of realities, and of futures, I insist. I can see we must harness this energy of revolt to make it productive and of the highest spiritual and ethical order.

Among those of various world views who have approached me about my OMEGA WORK, are those of a number of different religious groups and other belief systems. Many persons who

believe we are in End Times and are facing the coming Apocalypse have approached me, some even calling my OMEGA STORY the "continuing of the Biblical Revelations." And now this more full version I have written titled, REVEALING THE OMEGA KEY, they say is, "The New Revelations." While clearly, the revealing of messages is part of my OMEGA WORK, I certainly have not myself said that I am writing the new Revelations. Nevertheless, this does tell us how important the meaning of these times is to people who interpret this according to their own belief systems and world views.

Accordingly, people of other religions and belief systems have also approached me about this work, also talking about other descriptions of major changes on Earth, even life-threatening changes on Earth. These and others have explained they understand that many modern and ancient, major and minor, religions and belief systems have seen -- or according to their own beliefs, even *foreseen,* coming profound, perhaps even cataclysmic, changes on Earth.

With so many ancient and modern beliefs, including scientific findings, seeing this time on Earth as a time of profound changes, all this must be listened to. What are we hearing, what are we being told, what have we known all along about these times we are entering, about this coming turn of time, this close of a grand cosmic cycle, this OMEGA TRANSITION?

What has had a most profound effect on me is that I have been approached by several Native American and other indigenous groups about all this OMEGA WORK I have been doing. Many have told me, including Lakota Sioux Standing Elk, that these are the times that have long been predicted. For many years, Standing Elk appeared in the audiences of events where I was speaking, at times even was the person who had invited me to speak. I was honored to say yes when Standing Elk asked me to be a keynote speaker, speaking on my OMEGA WORK, at the first Star Knowledge Conference, which was going to be held in South Dakota, on the Lakota Sioux reservation in the late 1990s.

In that time period, and in the years since, I had been and have been pressured by some to bring forward more of my OMEGA WORK, and by others to not speak about this work. Yes, some pressures have come from various groups of various belief systems as I note earlier in this chapter. Other pressures have come from those suggesting they represent intelligence and other governmental agencies. As I note elsewhere in this book, when the newsletter, UNDERGROUND RISING, was made known as early as at the end of the pilot OMEGA book, an agency telling me it was the U.S. National Security Administration told me I must cancel that newsletter immediately.

So much of what is going on, so much of the messages we are receiving, even so much of what some forces and factors seek to keep out of our awareness, is indeed taking place. As vague as my (and others') awareness of the overall picture here, we know, we just know, that what we sense must be addressed. Yes, we are only able to see pieces of this process, we are only able to take still shots of the moving picture, we are only able to know what we are allowed to know -- or are we?

I report on all this because I (as do others out there) see at least some of the global picture, and I am amazed that we aren't talking about all this front and center. I am amazed we are not loudly addressing the actions of the OMEGA CABAL, and its hidden plans and hoardings of survival resources and locations, while we see only hints of what members of the global elite are up to (for example, when we hear about the confiscation of their floating mini-cities, their supersized super yachts). I see the global elite quite aware of what is going on.

And we must ask: Are there still more vast opportunistic forces at play here, affecting us, as we move into this OMEGA TRANSITION?

I do sense the presence of something far less tangible, something deeply present and deeply at work, while almost indescribable. We may want to frame this presence in a way our minds can begin to detect it -- perhaps we can wrap our minds around the concept of an interdimensional presence, or perhaps we can see this as an off planet involvement in Human evolution and survival. (I explain this in other books such as, OVERRIDING THE EXTINCTION SCENARIO: PART TWO, and HOW TO DIE AND SURVIVE: BOOK TWO, and REVEALING THE OMEGA KEY.)

Again, as I have said earlier, the discussion in this book is not conspiracy theory -- this is about building our survival oriented awareness. I see that our detecting ever more about what is taking place -- about who has a stake in what, about our standing up for our right to know, and for our right to survive -- is central now.

Global revolution can be beautiful and productive, or bloody and hard core, peacefully or violently revolutionary, liberating or further enslaving. Take your pick. I prefer the former and believe with all my heart that we must rapidly come to full awareness to avert the latter.

Take this information in as deeply or as whimsically as you choose, as this is up to you. Even call this science fiction if you prefer. Just take all this in, let your subconscious mind begin watching what is actually going on.

The survival of the Human Species, as we approach this turn of time OMEGA TRANSITION, is up to all of us. Let's not leave it to the OMEGA CABAL to decide our fate.

NOTES FROM THE FRONT

43

EARTH CHANGE CULTURE CONFUSION

When a population, even an entire species, is sensing or hearing in some way, messages regarding challenges to its survival, that population or even that entire species, reacts. All the while, these reactions take various forms, as the messages we are receiving from deep within ourselves, and within our deepest instinctual functions and mechanisms, and also our from our environments and even our Earth it or *her* self, may not be easy to read.

Throughout ancient and modern, even recent, history, responses to survival messagings and awareness-es have taken a range of forms, from mythological to religious to other spiritual, to scientific and seemingly rational, to competitive and even political, sometimes even warlike, to panic behavior, to other interpretations, at times even including cult-like responses.

And, as this book explains, as per what is herein defined as the OMEGA CABAL, there are those who have collected and now control extremely high levels of resources. This OMEGA CABAL has already moved into highly advanced levels of hoarding behaviors -- hoarding resources, supplies, access to information, funds, territories, HOARDING SURVIVAL

OPTIONS for themselves.

We out here only see the tip of the iceberg, only sense what those with the most access are doing to both prepare for possible major threats to survival -- as well as to take advantage of the opportunity they see to control and exploit the rest of the population.

Others out here have formed whatever they feel called to in response to the survival pressures, messages, and teachings they are feeling and receiving. While not calling all that is taking place correct and right, we must observe how our species is responding to the call to action we have been and are hearing.

It is understandable that a confused species is confused about the messages it is receiving from itself, its environment, its teachers, perhaps even from intelligences beyond those we formally recognize as existing.

Many of these messages, or at least their details, are coming into our awareness on subliminal levels. Our brains are not designed or evolved to fully consciously read all we are perceiving.

(Indeed, as I explain in other books, our brain may be designed to block us from fully knowing what we are sensing and hearing, its actual meaning regarding our survival in these times. See for example, the book, OVERRIDING THE EXTINCTION SCENARIO: PART TWO.)

So we do our best to hear what is there for us to hear, to see what is there for us to see, to understand what the messages truly are telling us.

Many of us have continued to try to see more about these

deep messagings our species is receiving. Sometimes we follow avenues where it later becomes clear the teachers themselves are as confused as their followers, even when their original intentions are to serve and save Humanity and even Earth.

Sometimes would-be leaders emerge who are not really leaders, but rather are fools, liars, or worse -- persons I have come to identify as those I call *end-time opportunists.* Always look carefully at groups and movements, even at cults, who may be saying they offer you end-time resources and options. Keep your own counsel at all times. I have seen far too many leaders of such groups abuse their members, abusing them financially, professionally, socially, spiritually, even morally, or even sexually.

The OMEGA CABAL is not only formed by a rogue faction of the global financial elite. Other types of opportunists form their own invisible force fields, their own CABALS as well. There are those taking advantage of peoples' confusions and fears, these feelings often being felt out of our awareness, on a sub-conscious level.

44

FORCED ACCEPTANCE

Questioning one's calling, or whatever it is that is inspiring or propelling or demanding one pursue some sort of idea or issue, is itself a challenge. Not only can there be those around you who are wonderfully supportive, there can be those who are doubting you, and there can be those who actively seek to distort or even to exploit what you are saying and doing.

This has been the case along the way as I have developed this OMEGA TRANSITION WORK I have been called to do. Somehow, even when presented as fiction, the story I began telling brought a powerful response, at least half of it resistance and or even exploitation. Why? Why would anyone be troubled by a story about ancient voices trying to tell us something urgent now, something related to surviving the mounting earth and climate changes we are facing?

Tracing the path I have followed as the OMEGA WORK, and the DETECTING OF THE OMEGA CABAL project, emerged into my life, I see early experiences that were already influencing me, some in the hands of predators of sorts, and others in the company of some of the greatest guides I could hope to find this life time.

Looking back on the path I have followed as I have

developed my OMEGA STORY and the related work and books and programs, I find that I was already hearing this calling at a young age. I had already found myself searching for its meaning, for its messaging, for its purpose. I actively began looking for leaders in Earth change and survival thinking. Of course, not all leaders are actually the ones we should follow. I had to learn this the hard way. What we all must be clear about is that various movements, groups, even cults, form around people's search for meaning. Sometimes these movements, groups, and cults are misguided to put it mildly, and sometimes they are actually harmful to their members. Again, I note I had to learn this the hard way.

****

Northern California, 1970s. When is it that what is framed as great knowledge is forced upon you whether or not you want it? There is a fine line here.

We must ask ourselves these questions:

What exactly is knowledge?

How does knowledge come to us?

How do we know what actual knowledge is?

How do we recognize this knowledge?

Who determines what knowledge is available to us?

Do we recognize the fine lines between knowledge, and actual knowledge, and also essential survival knowledge, that we come across almost daily?

There is also that fine line between being held against your will and being held with no way out. It was not clear to me which way I was being held, but I was. I was in my late teens, idealistic, vulnerable, searching. And I had landed in a commune, actually a group of survival communes, where the leader taught that the Earth was going to face coming changes that would threaten all people's lives, and that the leader, Leader as he was called, as he called himself, had teachings that could lead to survival. I had gone there because I had been drawn to this messaging. I had been told this was where to go for sacred teachings. I was not certain I believed all that the leader, Leader, was saying, but I felt I needed to know, had to know what all this meant.

So there I was in sort of holding house, waiting to be taken up to the so-called "land," one of the mountain survival communes this organization had established. That night I was sleeping on the floor along with other people also waiting. I did not know any of them. I was a lot younger than most of them.

I heard a noise behind a big door at one end of the room. I had been told Leader was in there, that was his room.

I can still see that door swinging open.

The few people who were awake turned their heads ever so slightly to see the man we called Leader, the great Leader of this newly formed clan, an Earth Movement Community, come out. The candlelight forced his shadow to reveal itself. Then the body of the man stepped forward, unfolding his flesh out of his shadow and into the dark jungle of sleepers.

He walked toward me: barefoot, silent, and with an eerie motionlessness, as if he was stalking me. He slowly moved right up in front of me and squatted there. He waited. I studied him most warily. An unusual strain of confusion came over me. He did not feel to me like he looked. I tried to reconcile this mismatch, but couldn't. These days, I know what I am reading when I get this feeling. Back then, I just felt like a confused and cornered animal.

Here, in the flesh, right before me, was the hero I had admired from afar, the radical leader I had heard so much about. Leader, as he was called, or called himself. My hero, this Leader, was stepping boldly into the glittery and explosive dawning of what was proclaimed even by that era's mainstream to be the New Age, for some even the dawning of what back then was being called the Age of Aquarius.

I had never known anyone like him. I could feel how very special he was. This visionary man had proclaimed himself a revolutionary leader – the teacher and protector of true survival knowledge. People said he was a special man, could do magical things, talk to dead ancestors, read nature's signs for coming Earth changes and even apocalypses.

And I was impressed by his message. I could feel its pressing intensity, its powerful undeniable urgency. But now, feeling my spirit under siege, I wasn't able to feel so good about finally meeting this Leader. He seemed to carry a massive cloud of fractured energy around his physical body, as if he were swimming in some kind of cloud or liquid full of soft but shattered glass. I didn't feel good near this energy. I didn't like it – not at all. I was confused. How could I feel this way about this great man?

"Come in now," he ordered me, speaking smoothly and

softly, taking my hand. I didn't like his touch. I gazed numbly at the man's thick hand on mine. And then I shivered. For just a moment, I thought I saw someone else there in place of this man. I was startled.

Leader stood up and pulled me with him. Now I looked at the floor as I trudged behind him, feeling his firm grip on my hand. Clearly, I could not say no to this man, this self-proclaimed Leader of Earth change teachings.

He took me through that door and closed it. As I crossed that painful threshold, time stopped for just a second. Suddenly, a faint vision of some kind of event – or rite of passage – whispered itself in my mind. I remember a question asking itself of my young unaware mind: What am I seeing? Have I been through this before? It seems like I am remembering something, but about what, when, where?

Then I heard myself asking myself: Is this some sort of strange ceremonial sacrifice I am remembering? How can this be? I haven't been through anything like this anywhere, ever. Of course not, I told myself sternly. But I didn't have time to think more about this. Survival mode was setting in. Pay attention. Watch out. I had to stay alert, alive, and totally in the moment.

Crossing through that threshold was indeed a big deal. Not that there was anything special behind the door. The place was, if anything, disgusting. I reeled at the clashing smells of strong marijuana, heavy incense, and rancid sweat. There were burning candles in rows along the walls. He had a mattress on the floor in the middle of the room. It was like a bed throne, I said to myself as I gulped.

He spoke to me in a quiet but commanding tone. "Come

smoke some medicine weed with me now."

He sat down and crossed his legs on the bed. Avoiding the bed, I sat obediently on the floor, facing him, also crossing my legs. I looked up at him. He reached out, attempting to hand me marijuana rolled in a special paper held by a silver clip. There were feathers and beads hanging from the clip.

"No thanks," I said, wanting to try and stay clear, so I could think about what was happening. I definitely didn't want to do anything on this bed throne with this Leader, no matter how important to the future of the Earth his message was.

He lit the joint. He took a puff. Then he put it to my lips. "Have some now." There was an imperative in his voice.

I looked at his face, trying to think. I took a very small puff, holding the smoke in my mouth and then exhaling, hoping naively it would not reach my lungs. Our eyes locked. I held his gaze with a numb sort of defiance. I felt a little dizzy, but I didn't look away. I summoned every bit of testy adolescent rebelliousness I could find within me.

Leader noted my defiant response to his gaze. "You're different, a different kind. How did you find us? What do you want here with our teachings, with our Earth Movement Community? ... Are you the one we've been expecting?" He peered at me, seeming to look right through me. Then he answered himself, "Yes you are."

For a moment, I thought maybe I could get through to this man. Maybe my explanation would help. So I gave him all of it in what felt like one breath: "My boyfriend, Mark, had the address. We both thought you were doing the right thing, that

you stood for something good ... back to the land, against materialism, stopping all the exploitation of the Earth and of people, teaching people survival skills, and uh, ummm, trying to save the planet from destruction and all. I want to find Mark."

Leader shook his head no. "Your young friend is not here. He is up on community land."

"Well, then," I said, trying to sound as if I'd just had a great idea, "Tell me how to get to him. I'll go there."

He frowned. "That is a privilege you earn from the Leader."

"How?"

"The land is sacred. You serve to enter. You serve me. And when you do this, this serves the Earth."

That didn't make sense to me. I cringed inside. Something about this Leader's messaging made no sense. Something didn't fit. Why was serving him serving Earth? "I won't do just anything," was all I said.

He chuckled like an old man and touched my hand. "Service is not just anything, young woman. It is respect."

"I have that respect, and I respect the Earth. I want to help save the Earth from destruction."

"I will tell you what you are to do to help save the Earth. You will do what I say."

I looked up at him seated on that bed throne. "I don't think you have that right." I was scared and confused now. How could this great man with this great message be so dishonest?

"Oh yes I do have that right," he responded.

"I want to leave now," I said – but I only glanced toward the door. Again my silent questions: Could I get out? Would anyone stop me? Would something worse happen if I tried to leave?

Leader took another puff of his pot, narrowed his eyes as if to peer into my mind, and then exhaled a gigantic pot cloud around me. "Breathe woman, this is good to breathe in, weed soaked in sacred peyote juice."

I wanted to question this man's use of the word sacred here, but did not.

A wave of something invisible hit my mind hard. The room spun for a moment. I stopped the spinning by shaking my head. Did he just now hit my mind? No, I told myself, I am simply feeling the dizzying effects of the pot. But I knew I was wrong about this. I could feel that this man, Leader as he was called, had some kind of mental power.

Remember who you are – wherever you find yourself, I told myself silently, using words my recently deceased mother had once said to me. But I was beginning to doubt my ability to stand up to Leader. My attention was being distracted – the lights and shadows in the room were dancing. Was that sensation coming from the peyote he'd said the joint had been soaked in? I had heard about peyote. It would make me see lights around the edges of things, lights I had heard were called auras. I could certainly see a darkly jagged cloud around this man more clearly now.

I was lost in my thoughts. He touched my wrist to get my attention. He pressed his fingers into my wrist and pulled me toward him. I resisted. I told myself to hang on, stay alert, don't get sleepy or space out. Not now. Maybe you can get away still. I felt hope trickle through me. But, now, as he pushed the peyote pot joint into my mouth, I felt my thoughts slow to the speed of cement.

“Hmmmmm.” He narrowed his eyes as he studied my face and then my body and then my face again. I felt like an animal being inspected. “Who are you – you beautiful young goddess?” A mix of reverence and question filled his voice as he studied me. "Yes, you are the young woman they told me would be here now. So the time has come. You are here for me now."

What was he getting at? I edged away from him a little.

He looked at me sternly. “I am not here to hurt you. You should be grateful. This is a ceremony, a sacred ceremony, a passage. If you were the one in power, you would take the same.”

“Same as what?” I asked although I already knew that he meant take me. My body. “No, I would *not* take from other people without their permission.”

“You have given permission by being here, by seeking the teachings I bring to the world."

"No, I have not."

"Why are you here?”

“I said, to see my boyfriend who, according to you, is out in the mountains in one of your communes. And to help save the Earth from destruction.”

“Your friend has gone up to the land, our land, to work there. He is one of us now, part of our survival community now.

He belongs there. If you do the right thing, you will belong there too."

"My boyfriend loves me. He's waiting for me. He wouldn't want you to hurt me."

"I will not hurt you. This is how we come together. This is how you join our community. You cannot be us – until I fill you with my seed."

I reeled inside, feeling sickened but trying to remain expressionless.

He could see how I was feeling. He didn't like my attitude. He frowned at me. "You say the wrong things." He narrowed his eyes until they were almost all the way closed and then looked at me from between his eyelids. He studied me for several long minutes. "Hmmm," he said, "I see that someday you will be a very strong medicine woman, a healer, a leader into sacred realms. It is time for you to join me, to step into our sacred territory together now. … This is how I decide if you do belong. If you belong, then I can share the plan to protect the Earth. If not, then you have no right to be in our community's sacred territory with its sacred messages."

I listened carefully because part of me felt that some of what he was saying was very right. Yet, something was very wrong. Questions raced through me, merging with my intense confusion. What was this thing about my not having a right to be in sacred territory? If the Earth was sacred, weren't all the people of Earth entitled to be in sacred spaces on Earth? Was he really the one to decide this? Shouldn't the Earth herself decide this? And, how could this man say that anything related to what he was doing with me there was sacred? How could a man frame as sacred such sexual pressure being put on a woman? I cringed again as I realized that this was indeed sexual pressure.

He looked me deep in the eyes with a long penetrating glare. It was a cloaked but nevertheless violent look.

I reeled as another but heavier wave hit my psyche. A river of red blood rushed through me from another time into that present moment. I wasn't sure what I was seeing or experiencing, but it seemed somehow to my young mind that I had been sacrificed before and would be again now.

I sat up straight and defiantly stared at this Leader. No! Something deep within me cried out – this is ridiculous! This is wrong! I was seething with adolescent defiance. Defiance now felt to be my only defense.

I couldn't know this, but I was sensing he was surprised by my defiance, as for some reason he was not finding me scared of him. Maybe he could hold me captive for now, do what he wanted with me for now – but not forever. He might take me down, but I would rise again. And again and again....

I felt the tension increase. He had recognized my power far more than I had. He had seen my future and found that I would be a formidable elder – I stood for something in his mind– I did not know about this, not on a conscious level, but he seemed to. He seemed to know that I had been called there, that I had come to meet with him to do something symbolic. He saw ***I had come to take the torch,*** eventually to ***challenge him for a leadership role.*** I had no idea what was taking place, but felt this.

I started to stand up.

"Stop," Leader said in a deep voice.

I froze.

It was at that moment of fragile impasse between us that Leader reached and lifted his rifle from the crumpled blankets.

A gun? A gun! I had not seen the weapon in the dim light until right then. I felt my teeth clamp tight – but I continued to try to breathe calmly and carefully, staring at his eyes, not at his gun. I definitely did not want to show fear.

He actually raised the weapon and aimed it at me, right close to my face. "This is my weapon. I traded a woman for it," he said, and looked me in the eye by gazing right through the sites of the gun.

I blinked once and continued to gaze back at him. He wouldn't really shoot me, I tried hard to convince myself. People don't just shoot women for no reason, do they? Would he shoot me? Would he shoot me? God, he could actually shoot me. He's high on pot and peyote too.

Don't get scared now, I ordered myself with a silent but loud inner voice that I had never before heard myself use. It didn't even sound like my voice. But I had no time to ponder this. I felt a sharp quiver of fear race throughout my body.

"This is my weapon," he warned again. "It is loaded."

He continued to stare into my eyes – to pour his will right into me through my eyes. Then he made a move, and carefully placed the rifle next to his leg on the bed.

I relaxed just a bit. I thought he had changed his mind. We were frozen together there a moment, as if someone had hit the pause button on a movie. I was about to breathe a sigh of relief when he commanded, "Come here, on this bed." He motioned me to his other side, where there was no gun.

I had to be alert and not emotional. Yet, the problem with my effort to detach from my fear and feelings was that I was also distancing my focus from the whole experience. My alertness was sinking into a stupor.

But I knew one thing. The "come here" command I had just received from this man was an assault upon my dignity. He didn't think I was listening so he said it again. "Come here, on this bed. Now. I will not use the gun if you will do what I say. And you will like having me take you with my manhood more than with my gun."

That cloud of energy that surrounded him expanded unexpectedly and engulfed me. And my mind, now unable to even think about any safe way to resist, shifted into a seemingly irreversible numb automatic. I felt no emotion – I obeyed his order.

As I sat next to him, I felt my gag reflex activating – a deep mechanical repulsion. I tried hard not to vomit, held my lips tightly shut.

"Undress now," he commanded.

Frozen with indecision, I just sat still and looked at him. I made no motion.

He waited a few moments, then slowly reached over and, grabbing the material, pulled off my top. He then pushed me hard, his hands on my shoulders, and I fell back onto the mattress. He unzipped my jeans, and roughly yanked them off. I was frozen. I could not make myself move. Then he removed my underwear.

With a frozen sort of fear, but also with a strong naive surge of indignation, I leveled my eyes at him, now trying to send him arrows of force – energy to force him away. I summoned all my youthful power into my eyes and voice. "You have no right to do this to me," I told him tensely, hoping against hope that the force of my gaze would back him off.

He leveled his eyes right back at me and stared at me so hard that, for a moment, I thought I would be consumed – flattened to nothing, ripped to shreds, and eaten – by his hungry energy. My heart cringed.

I felt more naked than I had ever felt in my life. Undressed to the bone, unshielded, unprotected. I swallowed. I wished to God right then that someone would come in and make him stop. Then I was thinking in desperation: was the gun really loaded? Would he really shoot if I said no? Yes.

He was touching me with his paw-like hands as if inspecting a lesser animal he was about to slaughter or to rip to shreds and eat. "You have good breasts. Nice breasts," he said. His rough leathery palm covered one of my breasts. "Mmmm," he moaned.

He touched my stomach with his other hand and mumbled something unintelligible. It felt as if he'd created some kind of piercing circuit running through my body by placing his two hands on key spots, one over my heart and one over my abdomen. A stream of something foreign raced through me, energy pulsing from one of his hands to the other and back. This stream seemed to be filled with microscopic razor blades that were making tiny slices in my insides.

My emotions were boiling by then, but I told myself to try

and be totally devoid of feelings. I kept telling myself that I had to stay alert, to keep my head clear to see a way out. Jumbled thoughts tumbled through my mind. What was I supposed to do now? Did anyone know where I was? Did Mark know about this? Did I tell anyone I was going to be there? Was this really a sacred ceremony, and was I wrong to withhold my spirit from participation? Confusion raced through my fear. Was I the one who was wrong here, I asked myself. No! No! No!

Yes, a voice from somewhere in my head said.

No, I told myself, that yes is not my voice. I am not wrong here.

Yes, that other voice said. I realized this was Leader speaking into my mind.

"This is very wrong," I angrily blurted out. "I can't believe that you of all people would be like this. You were my hero only a few hours ago." A young woman about to be forced into sex by an armed man may not know how to get out of such a situation, except to express such defiance, if that.

Once I spoke this way, he became more physically aggressive with me. He shook me by the shoulders as if trying to get through to me. "Yes, I have a right, woman. You are the one who I was told would be here to be with me. I have been waiting for you. Now it is time."

He stood up. I made a weak effort to get off the bed but he pushed me back. He leaned over and looked down at me, ready to pounce. I froze again.

He came over, dropping his pants and dropping down on to me with his heavy weight. I wanted to scream but couldn't

make any sound. He started moving slowly and chanting while he did. I tried to push him off. He grabbed my arms, got quiet, and moved at a rapid pace. At first it hurt me, what he was doing – then I felt no sensation. I went out of myself or something. I went away.

Without stopping, he lifted his head and looked me in the eye again. I tried to shut my eyes but there was a hook in his gaze. "Move. Move with me," he demanded in a deep voice.

I did not move.

"Move, I said," he muttered tensely with some kind of new degree of threat in his voice. On automatic, I moved as he had ordered.

As he began to move more feverishly, I came back into myself and realized that the pain was intense. Now I tried hard to push him off, struggling fiercely. Now his hands moved to my neck to control me. I struggled harder to get out from under him.

In response, his thumbs pressed into the front of my neck, shutting my windpipe as he banged into me repeatedly. I stopped struggling, but he didn't release my throat. Instead he pressed his thumbs in harder. I couldn't breathe at all. I struggled for air. He pressed still harder into my neck. I tried to gasp several times and then stopped trying.

Time seemed to suspend itself. I had no energy to panic. I had begun to taste the soft cement of death in my mouth. I thought I would die. I think I did die. At least for a moment. I flew away like an angel in a hurry, my beating wings the wind sign of a great white bird ….

When I came to, I was alone in Leader's bed. He was across the room smiling at me. "Young goddess, you are mine now, always. You have earned to right to join us at the Land."

I said nothing and passed out.

NOTES FROM THE FRONT

DOUBLE

OMEGA

ALPHA

PART SIX

NOTES FROM THE FRONT

45

INTERRUPTED ESCAPE

Northern California, 1970s. The so-called Leader had given his approval. Then I had finally been taken up to the main Community land. This was a remote place, a large property in the mountains, that the Leader had dedicated to what he said was "the survival of End Time events coming to Earth in the near future."

It was difficult to be there. My boyfriend was very confused by what had happened to me. He had been told I now belonged to the Leader. But the Leader was not there, and no one wanted to deal with me at all. I was horrified about what the Leader had done to me in order to allow me to be with my boyfriend. Yet my boyfriend was now distant and angry with me because of what the Leader had done to me.

To make matters worse, I was surprised, shocked, that once there I was not treated as the Leader's chosen woman, even though that was the message that they all had been given.

I was virtually alone and could not get out of the place. I was in bad shape, disillusioned, upset, scared, and angry. What had happened to me with the Leader I could discuss with no one. It would be years later that I would realize the intense trauma I carried as a result of what the Leader did to me.

I lived there on the Community land for quite some time, hiding every time the Leader visited the property.

There were always people around, many of them armed, and always things going on. I had to try to get away to think. I needed to know what to do.

I waited for a time when, at least for a while, I could get a little bit away from everyone. I had to try to think about how to get out of there, as it was far from any paved roads and I did not know exactly where I was.

One day, I wandered deep into the woods.

When I felt I was far enough away, I sat down under a large tree to think. It was quiet there, serene. There were luminous patches of snow on the ground, each one giving off its own white light which floated upward between the trees like a soft chalky whitish flame.

I almost had a heart attack when I heard a voice grunt. I turned. Leader was right there, sitting under my same tree. How had he found me? How had he gotten there so quickly and quietly? I made a move to push myself off the ground and leave. He put his hand down on mine hard, and refused to let me stand up. I glared at him.

He didn't let go and started to speak. "When snow gets very deep, and you are very cold, you can make your way in next to a big tree trunk. The tree will keep you warm. And I can show you which side of the tree will be warmest."

"Oh," I said coldly, but I noticed I was a bit interested in how to stay warm in the cold. His hand was still pressing mine into the ground. My palm started to hurt.

"There will be a time when you may need to know this. Are you ready for that time?"

"Don't know."

"I have seen that the Earth will one day be in great distress. I have seen people looking for food, for warmth, for their own families, and even for death. I have seen you teaching them, leading them, showing them a new dance to do on both sides. You will be doing this more and more as we move to the time … the opening. I know who you are, my young goddess."

He paused and looked at me. He could see that I was trying to look like I wasn't listening. He leaned toward me quite intently. "Listen. This is important. I have seen you delivering the people into the spirit realm. You must know this. You must already know this even though you are so young."

Some sort of bell went off in my head. As angry at him as I was, I had to stiffly ask him, "You think they are coming? The big Earth changes?"

"You know as well as I do," he warned, "the big change time will come."

I began to cry. "But why?" I was starting to believe all this, even though I didn't want to. Or, had I already known all this long ago?

"Because the Great Rebalancing is so much needed."

"This will be very awful, won't it?"

"It will be years and years from now, but it is time to begin to prepare the people. You know, on some level you do already know. This is why you have arrived here to be with me, to meet with me. You do know. You will be a great teacher someday."

"No, please, I don't want to know."

"But you do know. You are supposed to know. I have seen that you will be a teacher of this knowing. You will come to know what our meeting means as you grow older and look back on this."

"Really?"

"Yes, this Earth change lore, wisdom, carries the Earth change truth. Earth change has come before and it will come again."

I could feel he was in earnest, but I just shrugged. This was too big a thing for me to want to know right then. And, I wanted to believe, maybe I did believe, that there was another way things could go.

He pressed my hand even harder into the ground. I could feel the little stones cutting into my flesh. "Do not hide from what the Earth is saying to you. Do not close your ears because you are not liking me. I am yours, you are mine, even if you do not want this to be true. And you do not like me, so you are cutting my heart with your baby teeth, young woman." He pressed my hand still harder. "My heart bleeds because of you."

I looked at him fiercely. "Let go of my hand. Never touch me again."

"Not yet," he answered sternly. "I will not let go yet. Maybe never. You have to listen."

"Let go, please."

We locked our gazes. I didn't move, or blink, or glance at

my hand even though my hand was starting to shoot hot pain up through my arm. Suddenly Leader lightened the pressure on my hand just a little and cleared his throat. He looked just a bit humble. "What do you think … Leader, he has not lived up to your wishes?"

I tried to pull my hand away, but he wouldn't let go. I couldn't stop my words. "No. He has failed me. He has failed all people. All Earth."

Leader blinked. "Is that what you see? You see only what you want to see, not what is."

"I see the truth. This is what I know. The truth about you, Leader."

"My young goddess, you are indeed breaking my heart. Don't you see I love you now?"

I was surprised. Could he really mean this, this thing about loving me now? I decided to stay cold. "No, I don't see this. You cannot hurt me then love me and call it love."

"Yes, you do see what I am saying, you do see this and you do feel this. You are my woman, and I love you."

"You do not love me. You want to control me, even to control who I will be in the future, in the years to come."

"Why not be mine? Being the Leader's woman is an honor. You will like it. I will share my teachings with you."

"No I won't like it, and I can find my own teachings."

"I ask you again, have I not lived up to your wishes? As the Leader and as a man?"

"I say again: You have failed me. On both counts."

Leader looked raggedly forlorn, actually hurt and broken, for just a moment. There was almost a tear forming in his left eye. "My priestess, I have wounded you. ... But I was called to take you like that. Called. ... But I hurt you, didn't I?"

I began to cry.

He watched me, unsure of what to do for a moment. Then he reached over as if he would hug me.

I pulled as far away as I could, but he still was pressing my hand down into the ground.

"Come close to me. Let me heal this. Let me," he almost pleaded.

I continued to resist him. I was able to yank away. I stood up and looked back down at him. "I suppose you thought I would trade my soul for what you think of as *your* teachings?"

"No. But you have been admitted into the inner circle of this knowledge. For this you make a trade, you give yourself to me."

"I don't need your admission to this knowledge about the Earth. It's not your knowledge, it is for everyone who hears it." I heard myself talking rather stridently and told myself to keep quiet. But I went on. "You don't rule this knowledge, you only think you do. You don't control Earth change knowledge; you only tell people you do."

I suddenly wanted to tell him that he was a liar and a fraud, but kept that wording to myself, as I was unsure what might happen to me if I confronted him that way. I wanted to tell him I thought he was fooling people, pretending that he cared about the Earth, pretending that he was receiving messages from the Earth, just to get people's land and money and labor and yes, in the case of girls like me, their bodies. But I did not dare say these things.

Leader frowned at me. "My young goddess, you have been given a few sacred teachings. And already you think you have a right to the sacred realm. You already think you can take over for ME?"

"You don't own the sacred teachings. They belong to everyone. And, anyway, you are not in charge of deciding what is sacred." I had no idea what I was getting at. Where was this coming from, what part of me knew or thought like this? I did not know.

"You have been allowed into my sacred territory because you are my woman … you can lead this survival nest with me. We are building the real Eden."

"What in the hell?!" I shouted at the Leader.

He interrupted. "You have been given the beginning keys to surviving the coming Earth changes. Now you will return the trade … you will stay here and protect the life of my son."

He pointed to my belly.

What in the hell did he just say, I silently asked myself. "No," I said and then went silent. Then I told myself he somehow thinks he got me pregnant. Oh my God, did he? I started carrying on a conversation with myself: Anyway, if there is a trade to return, I will return it my own way. If there is something to give back, I will live in service of good. I will decide what good is. I will keep my own counsel about this. I have a right to access the sacred as all people who honor the sacred do. These are my powers, too. I --

He narrowed his eyes and interrupted my internal voice. "Your life depends upon this. You follow my law in my land, woman. I can love you, or harm you. Both are possible. Let me love you, you will be my queen goddess. Say no, well, you will see, people just disappear up here."

I shivered inside. Was he threatening me, I wondered. Yes, he was, I told myself. "No. You cannot hurt me again. Not for the teachings, not for the land. This is everyone's land, not yours. Earth is not yours to control. And, I am not afraid of you or of your magic," I said, my voice suddenly resonating with a strange force surging within me, protecting me from him. "I have my own magic, and it's stronger than yours."

"You really think so, do you young she-star?"

I really did, but did not know why. "Yes, Leader, or whoever you really are, I do."

He relaxed his frown a bit, reached up and took my hand, almost paternally. "I am the father of your child. He is the future of us. You will please honor me."

I blinked back the hot tears racing into my eyes. How could I respond to this unfair request from my assailant? "Honor you? You dishonored me. You hurt me. You just about killed me. How do I honor that?" I was crying again. I was miserable, and I did not know what do to with this misery. But then, somewhere out there, I heard a voice say:

The universe was not founded on rape. Rape on any level is wrong. There will be a Great Rebalancing in the time to come. This will be the only way to save Earth and the cosmos.

I was stunned. What was this voice and where was it coming from? What was it talking about? I heard the voice say quietly in my ear, “I am Earth herself.” I shook my head. I told myself I’d better focus, keep myself safe, because all this felt seriously strange, too strange to cope with.

Apparently, the Leader had not heard this voice, had not heard Earth herself speaking. He squeezed my hand, and then said in a surprisingly soft and disturbingly compelling voice, “You forgive me, because you are an angel, and you will let me love you again, gently this time."

I looked at him, first in absolute shock, and next, as if he was out of his mind. Who was he really, other than a creature here for a while on this planet, a soul passing through? I had to wonder. In that moment, I knew that my concern for the future of the Earth had grown so much even in recent days. My whole world view had changed, but not exactly in Leader's direction. I looked at this man, warily, silently questioning his self-proclaimed authority.

Already back then, I had begun to form what I then called my Earth Change Era Theory. I was keeping this thinking buried in my mind, telling myself I needed to find out what this was, what this calling to think like this was about.

Leader went on, “We have knowledge to preserve into the future. This is why you and I have come together. This is not an easy meeting for us, but it would have been even harder if you had been older. ... You are young, but you can learn. You were sent to us. I want you and our son by my side.”

Son? I now thought to myself. Such arrogance that he thinks he knows this. Daughter if anything, I insisted silently. Then I was shocked that I was believing him, believing that he had made me pregnant.

I cringed. "How dare --" I blurted out, trying not to cry.

"Wait, wait to answer me. Go think and feel first. Listen to the spirit of the great Maka, Earth. You will hear you are to join me. THIS IS THE MESSAGE OF OUR TIMES, THIS IS EARTH TALKING TO US. Because of this, we are to be together. I love you, you love me. The Earth's will be done."

Speechless, I pulled myself away from this unnerving exchange – unnerving because I was torn regarding the whole message from the Earth thing. Did I have a right to say no to a crying planet? Or was all this not something Leader himself should be involved in? Or, and I dared to let myself ask myself this, did I actually love this man? Was I supposed to love this man as he said I was? No! I silently shouted to myself. No! No! No!

He had a much stronger will, presence, than I did, at least at that time. I could feel his forceful pull on me. I could feel this pull as if it was an invisible hand, and I almost gave in. But I just could not make sense out of all that had happened.

I could not give in to this pull, I had to fight back.

I forced myself to stand up straight and strong, then to turn and walk away.

With each step, I tried hard to figure out the meaning of this bizarre encounter. My heart was torn a thousand ways and I felt immensely confused. The walk back to camp was longer than the steps it took to get there. The distance was the struggle inside me plus the reality that I had to accept. But I needed to decide what that reality was in order to accept it.

That night I decided to leave the Land, and to do this right away. I didn't say goodbye to anyone. I didn't take my things. I knew I'd have to travel light.

The moon was out and I could see the dirt road. I followed it for what felt like several hours. But it was a futile trip. I could feel that I was being stalked. The ground told me. And sure enough, those same somber men that had greeted me when I first arrived at this place leapt out at me from behind a tree. They were armed.

Now I saw their truck had been hidden way off the road, as if they had expected me to try to leave on foot that night. "Get in," the biggest one said.

I looked at him unusually calmly. "No," I said.

"Get in."

"No," I said. "You can't make me."

He put the end of his rifle right in front of my face, an inch away.

I tensed. "You wouldn't shoot."

He cocked the trigger and then pushed the rifle tip into my pregnant belly. Another one of the men ordered, "Stop. Be careful with her. Leader says he wants her." This one grabbed me by the shoulder, and pushed me toward the truck. I got in. What else could I do?

They took me back to the land.

After that, there was always at least one of them nearby, holding a rifle and watching me. Everyone seemed to know I had tried to get out. The men with the rifles wouldn't let people come to speak to me. I was cut off from everyone for a while.

Leader made it clear he was waiting for me to change my attitude, or at least to have his baby.

Waiting.

I was waiting, too. I thought I was waiting to find a way out, but I could also feel myself waiting to find a way to connect with this man I had admired so much. I wanted to, I truly wanted to, and knew he wanted me to. Actually, the reality is, I had to, as I could tell he would rather kill me than let me leave. But try as I would, I was not able to make myself feel close or connected to him now. I simply could not find my way to this place in my mind.

So I waited for myself to know more about what all this really meant.

Time seemed to have stopped for everyone on this survival commune. We were all waiting for the Earth changes to begin, not fully seeing ourselves and the Earth already deep within the process.

The confusion and pain, and the struggle even trying to hear and understand the messages that all of Humanity was already receiving on some deep level were already present back then. And, as the years have gone by since then, things are growing ever more clear moment by moment.

Suddenly one day, I had a miscarriage. I began hemorrhaging and passing out. I was not helped or taken for medical care. Finally, a visiting school teacher found me and my boyfriend, and one other eighteen year old we were friends with there. Late that night, the school teacher quietly helped us get down a dirt road in the dark, then helped the three of us into his car, and secretly drove us out of there.

While he was driving he told us that there were people who felt these important teachings about the Earth were being misused by people like the Leader.

The school teacher took me, and the other two who were also very sick, miles away to a hospital emergency room. Once he was sure we would receive medical attention, he left. We never saw this man again and do not know his real name.

I wish I could find this man now, all these years later, I as never had the chance to thank him for saving my life.

Because he saved my life, I am here now, so that all these years later, I can be doing this OMEGA WORK, working to REVEAL THE OMEGA KEY, and to be DETECTING THE OMEGA DECEPTION.

NOTES FROM THE FRONT

46

THAT IS RAPE, MY DEAR

U.C. Berkeley, Berkeley, California, 1980s. It was a decade later when I was at U.C. Berkeley, working on my Ph.D., and taking a class on family law. The discussion that day was regarding male/female relations and how the courts viewed these.

Now that day, I listened to the professor discussing abuse of women. Many of the students had clinical questions seeming to pertain to their experiences working with people in mental health settings. So, the question I found myself asking, feeling it would be entirely camouflaged in this class discussion, was this: "What about sexual intercourse at gun point, or at threat of gun point?"

The professor paused and looked at me a brief moment before he responded. Then he said simply, "That is rape, my dear."

I was floored. I quickly decided responding with a question of a legal nature would continue to camouflage me. So I asked a follow up question, "And, what might be the statute of limitations on that?"

"Ten years," the professor responded.

I managed to hide how taken aback I was and merged myself back into the class full of students with so many different questions.

Later, as I left the classroom, the professor asked whether I might want to speak to him in his office, if I had a moment. I did not want to, not at all. However, I felt I would now be more conspicuous if I said no and therefore said yes. "I can be at your office in about five minutes, if this is the right time for you."

"Yes, I will see you there."

We walked off in our different directions, he to his office and I to the nearest ladies' room to try to pull myself together. It was almost exactly ten years since that episode with the Leader of that survival group, when he had had his way with me in the name of survival and of Earth herself. Yet, it was only that very day, that very hour, that I had let myself truly know that I had been raped.

What was more striking was that I had been raped by a man who carried what I had been told were great teachings, a man who had once been a teacher, even survival mentor, to me. Even that day, I felt so confused about what had happened with him. It was only a few years later someone contacted me to let me know he had died.

47

DEVIL'S TOWER

Wyoming, 1997. Years later, I had moved into the role of guide, teacher, messenger, psycho-spiritual counselor, author, speaker. Requests and invitations to immensely powerful events were coming in from all over. I will never forget the 1997 ceremony at Devil's Tower.

There we were, streaming in from all directions, even from all over the world, to the Devil's Tower in Wyoming. This was going to be the ceremony of ceremonies. As we arrived in Wyoming and moved, in the various vehicles we'd rented, toward this event, we saw large numbers of police vehicles and National Guard vehicles heading in the same direction.

It became clear once we arrived there that we literally had to cross a line of authorities, National Guard persons and others, who were widely circling the Devil's Tower area as we went into this camping location, and then deeper on, into the ceremonial area.

It was fascinating to be crossing government lines encircling the area, and to then move through powerful indigenous lines circling the tower, lines formed by men riding two by two on beautiful horses. While waiting to move into formation, one of the men on the horses told me they were

"running point" to protect the ceremony, and would be doing so non-stop for a week.

It would become increasingly clear to me that they were -- in addition to running point to protect the right to perform these ceremonial events --**also running point to protect access to realms beyond.**

The ceremony itself lasted days and was immensely beautiful. Members of several First Nations were there, many of whom I'd met at events where I'd been invited to speak, including at conferences on reservations, such as the one in South Dakota described elsewhere in this book.

Now, running point upon beautiful horses -- riding in pairs, double, two horses next to each other, around and around, at a rapid speed for all the days of this ceremony -- were members of various First Nations riding. I could literally feel, almost touch, the protective force field around us as we stood within the circle they created to protect the ceremonies being performed.

I had arrived with several Cherokee friends, one Tslagee priest, and a couple of my own clients. That first night, and continuing the whole time we were in that area, I and several of the people with me felt a sense of what I will call here ***de-gravitation, an unweighting of the self, even of the surrounding environment***. (Note that no one with me was using any psychoactive medication, prescribed or otherwise.)

I noted that several people with me, including some of my clients who were there, were each individually and privately reporting to me that they were feeling sensations such as: "about to float away" and "being pulled upward " and "coming off the

ground." I never mentioned the sensations I was experiencing until days later, so as not to influence their own perceptions. I was however quite familiar with such sensations, as I had experienced these many times before, there and in numerous other settings.

In fact, one woman spoke to me all night one night, and repeatedly said she felt she was being invited to be taken away and should she go? And I said, "No. You know you can do this another time, later in your life. Why don't you stay here for now and decide later in your life if that is something you want to do." But all of us in my immediate circle felt this gravitational de-densification, this lifting sensation as if we were being pulled beyond Earth's gravitation into another place or plane.

This entire experience seemed to be running on at least two opposing tracks. On the one hand, there were government officials very much from the third dimension demanding that whatever this experience was be under tight approval and control with tight boundaries set to it. And, on the other hand, taking place right there were some of the most amazing reachings beyond our so-called "normal" definitions of reality. It was as if officials were working to hold us here in the third dimension with no reach beyond, to block our access to the BEYOND; however, ceremony participants were still here in the third dimension while nevertheless reaching, expanding, into the BEYOND.

As I reflect on this now, all these years later when I am so deeply further into my OMEGA WORK and into DETECTING THE OMEGA DECEPTION, I see so clearly that those Devil's Tower ceremony participants were in essence breaking through the physical plane restrictions, the boundaries being imposed upon them by government officials, and by forces and factors using physical plane powers such as government officials to do so.

Note again, these were not substance-related altered state conditions, these were just naturally what some will call altered states or maybe the actual state of some of Humanity already, of some of Humanity who is understanding we have a right to access far more than we are being allowed to access, and that in order for our species to survive, we must understand this and be allowed to know this about ourselves and our realities -- and know this now.[42]

[42] Refer to *Volume 3* of the *KEYS TO CONSCIOUSNESS AND SURVIVAL SERIES,* titled, *UNVEILING THE HIDDEN INSTINCT* for discussion of the expansive capacity of the Human consciousness, and the intentional suppression of the awareness of this capacity -- at a time when we may truly need it to survive. **This suppression of key survival information, of the OMEGA KEY itself, is a function of the OMEGA CABAL's OMEGA DECEPTION.** See also the *OVERRIDING THE EXTINCTION SCENARIO* books, *Volumes 5 and 6* in this same series, where **evolutionary and design elements of survival** are detailed.

48

NAVIGATING THESE CURRENTS OF MANIPULATION AND DISINFORMATION

These are times that try people's souls, test their determination in the face of constant indeterminants. We see political forces from all directions playing, even manipulating, both information and disinformation, telling us their side's facts are "true." Some are even self-proclaimed, or perhaps quietly self-inferred, "End Time" leaders, surfacing now in these times of great transition and pressure.

Some of these End Time leaders are actually what I see as ***End Time Opportunists***, exploiting both prophecy and scientific findings regarding what is happening on Earth now, the growing geological, climatological, atmospheric, and other changes taking place. Keep in mind, there are certainly those who are exploiting people's vulnerability, confusion, and desire for information, resources, and locations related to survival during this time of seemingly increasing Earth and climate changes, this OMEGA TRANSTION time, this turn of time. There is certainly an OMEGA CABAL taking advantage of all this, and of all of us.

We must stand up to, yet reach well beyond, the basic

already dangerous climate change crisis denial, to see the larger deception taking place. **This OMEGA DECEPTION is indeed the survival strategy of the OMEGA CABAL.** We must DETECT the major distraction effort that has for quite some time been and is now well underway, the work by the OMEGA CABAL to hold WE THE PEOPLE OF THIS PLANET generally unaware of:

how far the OMEGA CABAL has and is taking
its own End Time OMEGA TRANSITION strategy,
its own survival planning and hoarding,
to exploit these Earth change times, and
to exploit WE THE PEOPLE OF THIS PLANET
for the sake of its own dominance,
and of its own survival.

We must become ever more aware on all levels of our **selves** and of our consciousness-es. We must see that the OMEGA CABAL seeks to keep us not-seeing what this CABAL is doing as we move deeper into this globally perilous OMEGA TRANSITION TIME.

Keeping people uninformed and misinformed
is a dangerous and powerful form of social control.

Yes, there is intense end time thinking emerging. However, end time is a concept, and need NOT be a reality. We need not be facing extinction, we need not be facing the end of ourselves, we need not be facing actual end time.

The global elite, the OMEGA CABAL, seeks to survive at

our expense. THIS DOES NOT HAVE TO BE WHAT HAPPENS. We can overcome the CABAL's suppression of our deepest survival instincts, of what I have elsewhere defined as our own rightful OMEGA KEY.

We must diligently be ever watchful for details and data indicating what is actually happening, what is really going on, and what this means for our individual and species survival. We must allow ourselves to be as aware as we can be regarding the various leaders and groups who seek to hold us under their control by means of THE OMEGA DECEPTION in all its forms, including but not at all limited to its collection and hoarding of KEY survival information, communications, resources, territories, and access to these.

NOTES FROM THE FRONT

49
NAVIGATING THE UNSEEN

Undisclosed, Unidentified Location. There we were, out there again. The surroundings came further into focus, more distinct, as the focal lenses of our minds grew further attuned to what was happening. At some point, this reality was as real, distinct, tangible even, as any reality. It became clear that this was perhaps no longer remote viewing, as we were not remote, we were actually right there.

The terrain was obscure, at first almost invisible. One might at first say it was like being nowhere seeing nothing. This process is for me a little like waiting for one's eyes or whatever we choose to call these to adjust to the dark when the lights go out. It takes a while for our night vision to start seeing. Similarly, it can sometimes take a while for what I call our *extra-sensory perception* to fully kick in. At the same time, we are likely always engaging in extra-sensory perception and simply not realizing this.

Yet, if paying very close attention, even before seeing (with the so-called third eye) what is there, one has the sense of what is there. I believe we know so much more than we know we know. We can learn to check and double check what we are sensing, to not take it all in as fact, and to always carefully study what is coming to us.

The Human awareness is increasingly tuning in, fine tuning itself to sense developments, presences, and forces that may not appear on the biological brain's everyday five-sense-based desktop.

The opening moments in an intentional remote viewing process may be more structured than in more informal processes. I say intentional here, as government and other professional remote viewing experiments and procedures have generally been more structured than the informal (or even rogue) remote viewing taking place in several arenas.

Early in my adulthood, I was approached by government agents asking me to be tested, and then asking me to participate in psi- as well as in remote viewing experiments and processes. As they were explaining to me what this remote viewing was, I realized I had been remote viewing many times in my life, even as early as childhood. I just did not call it that. I actually still don't call it remote viewing most of the time.

A note here. To this day, I have resisted being formally assigned to remote viewing and other psy-ops type government exercises such as those that were conducted by the Army's Stargate project. (As I have indicated in several chapters of this book, I even resisted being officially signed on to the undercover Kirkenes project, or to any more formal intelligence agency position.)

Nevertheless, although not officially signed on, I have many times over the years been brought in to what were informal and less official remote viewing processes and projects.

Generally, these were times when I was approached and told my skills were urgently needed, that there were forces and factors, perhaps some threats to our nation, or to the Free World, that required the immediate attention of psychically adept intelligence oriented minds.

Of course, the general notion of forces and factors was not what the first government remote viewing projects were supposed to be working on. At least not officially. Most of those projects were simply experiments to see whether the U.S. military could use remote viewing to: (a) see what we might be missing via other more traditionally technological means of detecting what our enemies are doing; and perhaps also to (b) detect the presences of enemies' efforts to reach into what we are doing by remote viewing us. In terms of enemies here, note that the whole purpose of government experiments in remote viewing was addressing its possible use in seeing what other nations around this Earth are doing as per their own military equipment and operations.

Those of us in some of the unofficial informal break off group processes were and have still been addressing the conceptual and yes actual possibility, or is it reality, of presences from beyond Earth who may be affecting Earth. This overlapped and still does overlap with defense-related research on the possibility of extraterrestrials approaching (or already arriving on) Earth.

(Note: Of course, the conceptual and definitional difference between extraterrestrials and beings who once lived on Earth, who have died or disincarnated, is debated. It appears that many disincarnates are perceived as being extraterrestrials, when they once lived in physical biological bodies on Earth. And, at the same time, it appears

that many extraterrestrials are perceived as being disincarnates who once lived on Earth, when they may have once lived in physical bodies somewhere else, or never lived in physical bodies in the first place. And also of course, once not living on Earth, a disincarnate being is in essence an ***extra*** *terrestrial.)*

When break-off or even rogue remote viewers have sensed the possibility of extraterrestrials (or others such as disincarnates) approaching (or already arriving on) Earth, the matter of what form of nonphysical being they may be takes second priority. What is the agenda of this sort of approach or arrival is the question. And clearly, this is not a readily answered question.

Some of our informal groups found various forms of visitors or others approaching. These could be energetic, or semi-material, or actually solid, ships, even fleets, way out there, many approaching Earth unseen from another dimension. Many of us had no idea what a profound experience this break off group remote viewing would become for us.

Although I began to realize I had been doing this sort of expanded remote viewing since childhood, I was nevertheless taken aback by the intense reality of all this when working as a group with shared group perceptions corroborating what we were each sensing.

Once I began engaging in these more unofficial extensions of the earlier remote viewing projects, the venues changed more than dramatically, eventually almost ***beyond anything imaginable***.

My personal experience of this was to begin to take what I was perceiving out there as critical information. I found myself sensing how critical, how essential to the point of survival-level essential, what I was perceiving may be. At times, I found myself alone in my sense of the urgency. I consequently did and still do a great deal of exploration and research on my own.

I somehow was coming to the sense that I had come into this lifetime to do this, to bring information in to this time of great transition on Earth and beyond, this time where the survival of Humanity is at stake, survival both here and BEYOND. (Refer to Chapter 33 earlier in this book, titled, AS A WRITER WHO MAY BE HERE ON ASSIGNMENT FROM BEYOND.)

This is one of the many avenues of awareness that brought me to begin to DETECT THE OMEGA DECEPTION. On one level, it has been a profoundly eye opening experience to be connecting the dots regarding the actions of a powerful self-serving rogue faction of the global elite: its hoarding of survival information, resources, territories, and access to these. On another level, it appears there are forces and factors, players and presences, from far off-planet, beyond this physical plane, who seek to influence, some who even seek to block, our successful navigation of, including our inter-dimensional awareness to navigate, this turn of time, this OMEGA TRANSITION.

Fortunately, there are others out there seeking to help us survive both here and BEYOND. Based on communications coming to me (and to many others) via many avenues, I see that there are those out there seeking to help Humanity survive this coming TRANSITION time, what some have called this End Time.

As I have shared in several of my nonfiction and fiction

books, such as the novel, REVEALING THE OMEGA KEY, there are intelligences, life forms, presences, both from off planet, and from other times in our own Earth's history, returning now, coming in to us through time and space, surfacing now with the survival messages we need, to help us activate our rightful survival awareness, which we carry so deeply inside our consciousness.

There are certain undercover intelligence organizations or projects, and their agents, who know what I have said in the paragraphs immediately above, and know this in great detail. There are those who know that some of the most powerful members of the OMEGA CABAL are actually already in communication with some off-planet, or extra-dimensional, forces seeking to block or control exploit, or restrict, our survival. Some of these undercover intelligence agents who know (or in some cases, who knew, as some of them are now deceased, or at least have left the planet) have themselves been detecting the vast OMEGA DECEPTION, and its vast multi-dimensional aspects. (I have recently been hearing from some of these beings who I had met earlier on, when they were living in physical biological bodies on Earth, such as the CIA agent and then the man named Yan who I met with in Kirkenes. See Chapter 12 of this book: BARBED BORDERS.)

However we choose to process the discussion in this chapter, what is clear is this: For WE THE PEOPLE OF THIS PLANET, in fact for all Humanity here and beyond, to stand up to the inter-dimensional OMEGA CABAL, to be able to survive this OMEGA TRANSITION time, we must call upon our inter-dimensional awareness, and do this now!

This book, DETECTING THE OMEGA DECEPTION:

NOTES FROM THE FRONT, therefore defines the front lines of the battle where we are already engaging in survival efforts, as being both in physical plane and beyond physical plane. Certainly, this is a far reach beyond daily reality for many of us, for me as well. However, we cannot miss a step here, as the pace is already set, and the extra-dimensional ranges of this survival pressure already entered.

Readers, here recall the earlier chapter, Chapter 47, titled, DEVIL'S TOWER, where I describe one arena of this vast battle:

This entire experience seemed to be running on at least two opposing tracks. On the one hand, there were government officials very much from the third dimension demanding that whatever this experience was be under tight approval and control with tight boundaries set to it. And, on the other hand, taking place right there were some of the most amazing reachings beyond our "normal" definitions of reality. It was as if officials were working to hold us here in the third dimension with no reach beyond, to block our access to the BEYOND, yet ceremony participants were still here in the third dimension while nevertheless reaching, expanding, into the BEYOND.

NOTES FROM THE FRONT

50

HYPERSPACE DOT-CONNECTING

I take a moment here to share another face of this OMEGA DECEPTION DETECTION process. I see how much dot-connecting I have had to do to make sense of all this. This is clear to me when I trace back into my life for the signals and signs I was detecting and then making some sense of, and then for the invitations and even the demands that I recognize something, whatever it was, often not what the sender was trying to show me.

What strikes me is the astoundingly varied range of avenues into, expressions of, what is really going on that I have been presented with, or stumbled into, or discovered in some other way. (I say some other way here, as there have been equally important realizations coming in both scientifically and intuitively, rationally and for want of a better word, hyper- or meta- rationally.)

Note: Recall that in writing the novel, REVEALING THE OMEGA KEY, I was "presented" so to speak with key personas and messages and then interactions coming to me in my dreams and also in my waking hours, including those from Einstein, Camus, Nostradamus, various ancient beings, even the Earth herself. This was and is not what some people say is basic channeling. I know what is taking place to be far more than this, as these experiences are ongoing *and are intensely interactive,* and are continuously life-changing experiences, to put it mildly. Refer back a few pages in this book to Chapter 33, titled, AS A WRITER WHO MAY BE HERE ON ASSIGNMENT FROM BEYOND, for more on this this experience.

Do note that when I set out to write the draft pilot OMEGA STORY that eventually developed to become REVEALING THE OMEGA KEY, I had no idea that these would be characters in that book, and I had no idea that I would be making contact, even dialoging, with these characters. These personas came to me to work with me to bring forward essential messages through time and space.

All sorts of views and persons and groups were showing up at my conceptual door, perhaps better stated, pounding on the door to my awareness. I cannot even begin to fully list the diverse sectors and views that came to share themselves with me. Some contacted me via traditional means of communication, others reached me in less traditional ways. As I have hinted in the chapters of this book, some were from the worlds of government, research, mental health, public policy, and the like, and others were from the arts and humanities, others from both traditional and alternative, ancient and modern, religious and spiritual worlds, others from domains I have little room to list, even have few words to describe as they are so beyond the norm, perhaps even beyond this planet.

My awareness, my mind, mind consciousness, and my brain were and still are being called to vastly expand beyond prior boundaries, prior realities, to work with this mix of material I was receiving and perceiving.

When I talk about dot-connecting, which is for me an essential (as well as essentially constant) process, I am immediately called to LEAP this concept into a sort of hyper-awareness, a hyperspace where our reality must reach, where our awareness must go to really see what is happening now as we Humans are encountering our vast expansive nature. And we must do this now,

just in time
to face serious survival pressures,
and perhaps even
to avoid extinction.

This is indeed the essential LEAP I have defined in the KEYS TO CONSCIOUSNESS AND SURVIVAL SERIES books such as *Volume 3*, titled, UNVEILING THE HIDDEN INSTINCT.

NOTES FROM THE FRONT

51

REMOTE REALITY UP CLOSE AND PERSONAL

Early in my career, I had been an intern for a White House conference, which at times had brought me close to what that current president was doing. I became aware that that president had various interests in what were considered outside the norm psychological studies, largely in the name of the U.S. Department of Defense and related offices and departments. For example, the U.S. was tracking the work of the then Soviet Union in areas of alternate perception methods, and modes, such as what was being called dermo-optical perception, which involved seeing or perceiving through the skin what would otherwise have been perceived visually through the eyes. I was somewhat familiar with some of this research as I had studied it myself along the way.

Of course, in my work for various intelligence agents, I had already learned that the CIA had been conducting various research regarding the paranormal since 1972. (Note that officially this research continued for over two decades. That this research continues to this day is not made clear on official channels, however, is made clear to those of us who are contacted about this research from time to time.)

The field of parapsychic intelligence is thus not a new one. The U.S. has engaged in this research in response to enemy nations' work in this field, especially the then Soviet Union's interest in developing such parapsychic defense (and possible also offense) capabilities.

The ability to read information across distance, through other than the conventional electronic and other technological methods of detecting, tracking, eavesdropping, and snooping means, is of course highly valuable and essential, especially if the enemy has this capability.

Back under President Carter, a psychic was engaged at least once to locate a downed plane, which turned out to be a Russian plane. This highly debated remote viewing project involved an individual working from a so-called trance state to discover general latitudes and longitudes where U.S. satellites could focus to find this plane, which they did find.

Indeed, from approximately 1978 to 1995, there was a secret Army unit, Project Stargate, at Fort Meade, Maryland where remote viewing and other "psychic-seeming" activities were studied and even trained for. It was said that this effort was part of the work by the Department of Defense, and the CIA itself to "close the psy gap," to correct the fact that the U.S. was lagging behind other nations' psychic defense research.

I had been made aware of this project when the CIA and other intelligence agents I had been working for, for example in Kirkenes, Norway and elsewhere, had sent me to an office somewhere in the U.S. to be tested for psychic capabilities. They had asked me (as part of my paid work for them) to attend these tests and then to write a report for them on my views of these testing procedures, and of whether these were good approaches to accurately detect psychic capabilities in individuals. Whether fortunately or unfortunately, I tested highly psychic, if this is the word to apply here. I of course already knew I was somewhat adept at parapsychic awareness. I gather the CIA did as well, although this was never made clear to me. (As noted earlier, over the years, I found myself resisting being a test subject, although I did work for various offshoots of related research projects.)

What I have to ask myself it this: What part of this work I have been asked to do, starting at least as early as my introduction to Project Kirkenes, have I done fully conscious while doing this, and what part have I been working on from deeper levels of my self, of my mind, of my awareness?

NOTES FROM THE FRONT

52

WELLING UP FROM DEEP WITHIN

Welling up from deep within the collective and individual consciousness of Humanity is the intensifying awareness: that we are at a profound passage in the evolution of the ecosphere, the biosphere, the Humanity-sphere; and, that we do carry within the actual means of finding our way through this OMEGA TRANSITION passage, of SURVIVING the end time closing of this grand cycle--surviving to then generate the ALPHA EPOCH.

Can we indeed travel this OMEGA TRANSITION passage fully conscious of what is happening here? **Yes.** We CAN affect the outcome of this shift in our ecological, biological, psychological, and spiritual realities.

How? We can bring into our consciousnesses a deep knowledge of how living systems work, how living systems heal, how we can consciously work to heal living systems in all we do and build and think.[43] We can also expand our understanding of what itself is actually living to include ourselves as CONSCIOUSNESS-ES themselves.

---

[43] Means of **consciously working to heal living systems** are presented in the volumes of the *KEYS TO CONSCIOUSNESS AND SURVIVAL SERIES*, as per reading list at the end of this present book.

We can resist forces and factors seeking to exploit us, to keep us unaware of what we know, to use us, WE THE PEOPLE OF THIS PLANET, for their own survival purposes, seeking to suppress and even exploit us at this time of great Earth wide transition.

Despite forces and factors seeking to stop us, we can reach deep into the consciousness of ourselves, of our species, of Humanity, and find the survival tools and messages we have carried, even protected, through time, through eras, through epochs, through cosmic cycles, to have this precious inter-dimensional knowledge here for us now in these times of great transition: We can REVEAL to ourselves the key to our survival on many levels and dimensions:

THE OMEGA KEY.

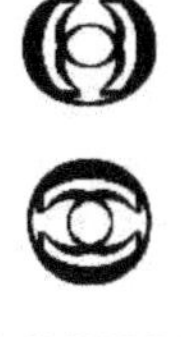

DOUBLE

OMEGA

ALPHA

PART SEVEN

NOTES FROM THE FRONT

53

WHEN SEEING

Earth and Beyond, Undisclosed Location, 2001. I had gone out there "alone" now, exploring a particular tract of the great vast space. I was being certain I knew something of what was to be experienced in that unique tract of inner and outer space before bringing others that far in and that far out.

Abruptly, the environment changed. I could feel something different was there. I could tell I was not alone. I went onto alert. I held still, a little like an animal in fight, flight, or freeze mode who has no option but to freeze. Of course, in that same instant, I realized even freezing would not hide me. My non-physical presence was not invisible as it might be in the physical plane, it was entirely detectable. Although I would eventually develop methods of masking oneself in such situations, this would not have helped in the face of what I was about to encounter. (Note: Refer to books in the KEYS TO CONSCIOUSNESS AND SURVIVAL SERIES for in depth discussion of these and related methods. See reading list at the end of this present book.)

I found myself in a very different sort of encounter, one unlike any I had had before. Had I not had so much experience out there (or out somewhere similar to this space) before now, I would have been entirely unprepared for this.

I centered myself, focused on holding my center, holding my SELF there. Then I told myself I was very ready for this.[44]

Still, this was an entirely unexpected and different on so many levels experience. First of all, this was an encounter. Second, this encounter approached me, and presented itself to me. Third, this was an encounter with a presence, a presence seeming to make certain I recognized this as a presence.

Fourth, this encounter was directly aimed at me. Let me rephrase this, as aimed would say I was the target and that there was a direction of what was aimed. My sense is that a presence approached, or better stated, surrounded, practically engulfed me.

At first, I felt myself tell myself to be certain I held onto myself, to be certain I was not swallowed up and away. Be certain you do not disappear into this, I told myself.

There were some brief moments, or eons perhaps, I do not know as time seemed so suspended, when this presence seemed to be letting me know that although it could consume me, this was not the purpose of its appearance there.

This communication came into me without words. I could just know what this presence was telling me.

I found myself aware of the immensity and the immense power of this presence. I was entirely at its mercy.

---

[44] For **out of body consciousness** exercises related to this experience, see exercises in the *KEYS TO CONSCIOUSNESS AND SURVIVAL SERIES,* such as *Volume 3* of that series, titled, *UNVEILING THE HIDDEN INSTINCT.*

It was now telling me I had entered its territory, its domain, its space.

I was now excusing myself, expressing myself as unknowing of the districts or sections or territories out there.

Acceptance of my being unknowing was communicated, in the form of what felt to be an embrace.

I was wary of reading this as compassion, or of any sort of benevolence, and my energy said this.

I was told that were I going to be consumed, obliterated, I would have been so already by then, that I was encountering a far more powerful presence than I myself was.

I only somewhat relaxed my own presence. I wanted to ask who are you, where are you from, what do you want. However, I thought it best to instead give these answers about myself: I am here from Earth, finding out what is out here, and whether Earth's people can be safe here. I want to see how far we Humans can already reach beyond the physical plane, especially if we need to for our survival, our species survival.

The presence replied, your Human reach is already here and elsewhere. It is high time for Humans living on Earth to see this. You must help to trigger this expanded reach for your people's survival on Earth, and throughout the cosmos. This is their resurrection through the wave of the coming Earth changes on Earth and beyond.

At the same time this presence was replying, I was being shown, in no way visually, but shown, that this presence was many presences at once, a collective of what on Earth we might call ancient and more modern elders who had lived on Earth

many times. I now got it, that I had communicated with this presence many times before, all along the way.

This presence had told me to develop the OMEGA KEY itself; its voices had spoken to me while I was writing REVEALING THE OMEGA KEY, and also this book, DETECTING THE OMEGA DECEPTION. (Readers, see the OMEGA KEY CODE TO SURVIVAL Excerpt diagram included at the end of the last chapter of this book, Chapter 63: ONE OF THE MOST PERILOUS, located immediately before the first page of the Appendices section.)

I had no emotion out there, so I was not reacting with emotion. But I did have a big question for this presence:

How can I share what you have shown me, told me here, with people back on Earth? How can I be believed when this message about who you are, how real you are, how true this is, is so critical to the survival of humanity, of all life, on Earth and beyond?

This presence boomed its response throughout my being. I could feel this resonating through my entire existence:

You must stand strong, hold steady in the face of those who can not hear you, in the face of detractors who seek to belittle you and silence you, in the face of the omega cabal who does not want this knowledge believed, does not want the people of the planet to survive if not members of the CABAL with its plan to dominate this transition.

I must have shown my sense of how challenging this is and has been for me. The presence responded,

You have been protected through many challenges to the message

you carry, to what you bring in for us. We have been calling you to step forward again and again, even in your older years, to continue this work. And you are and will.

I felt as if I was bowing to accept this message I was being given, and to thank this presence for the protection I have been given in my life on Earth, even though there have been some difficult times.

In that moment, an immense wave of powerful and almost tangible compassion, a sort of energetic empathy, came from this presence and washed over and through me. This sea of beauty was so overpowering and beautiful, I wanted to simply stay in it forever.

The presence heard me feeling this and told me:

You are greatly needed back on Earth, to generate, develop, and teach the OMEGA KEY CODE TO SURVIVAL, to help Humanity REVEAL to itself THE OMEGA KEY.

The power of this communication was so great I could not have objected. A new wave of compassionate empathy embraced me, flowing from this presence through me, all through my essence. I could feel my **self** absorb this and learn this through and through.

I could feel myself flying through this energy, soaring in bliss a moment, and then...

I somehow fell back down to Earth, shifting to physical plane reality in that instant.

I awoke just as my non-physical self fell back into my sleeping, or was it trance state, physical body.

NOTES FROM THE FRONT

54

CRITICAL INFORMATION SURFACING

Sometimes critical -- essential -- information can only percolate to the surface of Human consciousness in story or fantasy form. Were it to come in as fact, it might be too bizarre, startling, or overwhelming to believe. It might be too big to recognize. The brain might not be programmed to recognize this information. The brain might be programmed to entirely reject it -- or to simply not see it.

This may be why we can be presented with sign after sign and still not see. And so we are blind to the significance of what flashes before us while we blink in ignorance or denial or fear:

The time has come -- and has come most urgently – for WE THE PEOPLE OF THIS PLANET Earth to know and access the cross-dimensional techniques for understanding and overriding ecological and planetary disaster. We need not become extinct. We can survive this turn of time, this close of this great cycle, this OMEGA TRANSITION.

We are actually designed to survive.

The suppression of this knowledge is growing ever more apparent to us. ***We feel there is a knowing we have a right to, an***

awareness pressing us to see it. This calling is growing louder by the day, at least on deep individual and collective, species wide, subconscious and collective consciousness levels.

We feel this knowing, we feel this survival pressure, we feel the wisdom we carry so deeply buried within ourselves. We also feel the suppression and even denial of this survival knowledge. And we feel our anxiety about this suppression and denial, we feel this and want to fight back. Yet, we are not clear what we are responding to. Not entirely, not yet.

We do sense a global revolution of some sort brewing. This may be a revolution in ideas rather than a war in the streets, as it is what we know and think we know that is seeking to step forward, to break out of suppression. We are DETECTING THE OMEGA DECEPTION that is seeking to confine us to its use of us in history, in the future, in the OMEGA TRANSITION, in the physical plane and other dimensions as well.

We feel this in our bones. We may feel our minds and brains resisting what we have to face in order to survive, and we may feel tense about this. It is easier sometimes to block out this knowing, to put ourselves onto some sort of automatic in order to live day by day.

Yet, we must ask ourselves, can we afford to let this suppression of our species-wide inter-dimensional survival wisdom continue? Can we turn a blind eye to this? Can we turn a deaf ear to the Earth herself?

Do we walk around like robots, asleep and unaware? Are we already so far gone? Have we been that effectively blinded by our own programming? We MUST break free of the shackles of our ignorance.

We must be willing to examine messages coming in from all directions and sources. We must be willing to question everything we hear, to continue to search for verification. Absolute acceptance of anything without examining it is not acceptance, it is acquiescence. There is always the necessary moment of uncertainty.

Truth comes into focus as one's vision adjusts -- as lines between fiction and reality, myth and truth, prophecy and history, reveal themselves, some becoming more obvious as decoys. Where there is a blurring, where reality checks are not solid and verifiable, we must continue our diligence.

Critical and otherwise unrecognized information makes itself known in astonishing ways.

NOTES FROM THE FRONT

55

SEEKING THE GOD'S EYE

Over the decades, it has become increasingly clear to me that many of the messages I was integrating into my OMEGA STORY had been presented to me in various ways all along, including quite early. Seeing how these messages were encountered, delivered, discovered, revealed toward calling my attention to what I would write in both the novel, REVEALING THE OMEGA KEY, and in this book, DETECTING THE OMEGA DECEPTION, has been part of this story. The story is the story in the making: the message is the essential knowing we can unearth for ourselves now.

****

Esquipulas Pilgrimage, Guatemala, 1976. I arrived in Esquipulas after a long and crowded bus ride, mesmerized by my own nausea and praying that I would emerge from the long slow six person per seat bus ride in one piece.

I was unceremoniously dumped into a mob – a swarm – a compacted herd of people from all over Central and South America. I joined them, merged with them. I remembered having been to some very large, huge, events, but I had never ever seen so many people so packed together in one place.

My initial response was claustrophobia, which puzzled me

because I was outdoors. What was this gathering in the name of the holy? Obviously the *Cristo Negro* – Black Christ – *Quince Enero* – January Fifteenth – Festival was in full swing. As I began to move into what I assumed was the town, I felt a bit better. I hadn't eaten, save for bits of fresh fruit and vegetable juices, in weeks. So, I was indeed somewhat *wakan* – still open to the spirit realm – raw more than ever now to the energies just past the veil of the material world.

But being *wakan* in an adulterated environment, a milieu screaming with spiritual conflict and con-men selling crosses, was frazzling. I wanted to scream out, a lonely intruder in an already invaded world, a lost soul itself looking for deliverance in a world being compromised by modern world forces. What were all these plastic things and sweet drinks for sale? What was this – a pilgrimage to a mecca of materialist decadence? Everywhere was the rampant debasement of the divine in the name of the divine.

"OK," I said to myself loudly in English, "go buy yourself a drink and maybe eat something."

I wasn't hungry, but this direction sounded sane to me. I bought some *ceviche* – a dish of raw marinated fish – and a bottle of bubbly water. I was thirsty and eagerly drank the water, although it tasted metallic. I was not hungry, but had a bite of the fish. Being my first bite of food in quite some time, the experience of its taste was nothing short of ecstatic for me. However, the second bite brought me to the brink of vomiting. I left my food without reservation, picked up my pack and ran desperately into an alley way where I heaved up what little was in my stomach. Would I ever be able to eat again? Was I really here anymore, I wondered.

Sick and hot and dirty, I wandered on. I felt too naked there – too exposed. An unnerving sense of defenselessness set in. I was a foreigner in a foreign place – a stranger in a strange land. But this was about more than being a stranger in Esquipulas. It was about being a stranger in this material plane, something I would only begin to make sense of years later.

OK, so where is God? Where are the spirits? Where is this thing all these people have come to touch and feel? My inner voice demanded information I could not provide. And where am I?

"Donde esta el Cristo Negro?" I asked a man selling Coca Cola. Where is the Black Christ?

He pointed up the street to the highest hill, a magnificent hill upon which was built a beautiful old cathedral. *"El primero Cristo Negro esta alla, pero hay muchas otras Cristititos Negros circe de aqui."* The main Black Christ is there, but there are many other Christs around here." He pointed to rows of street cars selling little figurines.

I determined to get my self all the way up there, to this "there" where, apparently, according to legend, the first Black Christ that had ever appeared was housed.

As I made my way uphill, I could see how the town circled this single hill on which was built a large Spanish mission-style Catholic church, actually a cathedral of sorts. It seemed that all processions were headed this way. But all who dared make this pilgrimage to the heart and height of Esquipulas faced many cunning distractions. Or perhaps, according to some traditionalists, these were actually tests along the way. Everywhere I looked, people were selling elixirs and potions, icons and magical objects – a bizarre bazaar.

Every once in a while, I saw what I felt I had come to be able to recognize as a real medicine man or woman. These persons were not shouting their beliefs or marketing their wares loudly from carts and podiums. Instead, they were strolling quietly along, taking in the situation, assessing the energy, and calling in their own gods at every stop along the way.

I proceeded uphill through the throngs, being flagged down, stopped, even grabbed by those who would deter me, people attempting to sell me plastic Black Christ figurines as well as elixirs and talismans for every possible curse and prayer imaginable. Was all this a competition for souls – a sort of race for unclaimed or unchained spiritual real estate – or a mere debasement of the divine? Or something else?

At the entrance to the cathedral grounds, I almost tripped over a man lying on the ground. Just as I tried to apologize, beginning in English, "I'm so sorry," I realized that I of course needed to switch to Spanish to be understood, "I mean, *lo ciento, perdoname*." Then I noticed that he had no arms or legs. I did a double take and tried not to gasp. Still queasy and achy, I was feeling far too vulnerable to let myself see this man. I was going to look away immediately, but I tripped again on something and almost fell over right onto him. I caught my balance in a sort of hairline save of face. "God, I'm so sorry, *lo ciento mucho.*"

He caught my eyes and saw that I was practically crying at the sight of him. *"Este no es un acto de Dios, Senorita,"* he announced in a guttural voice. This is no act of God, Miss, he had announced.

I knew he was referring to his physical condition. But why

was he saying this to me, I asked myself. I wanted to look away from him, to break eye contact, but I couldn't. He looked like a pirate – an armless, legless pirate.

"Mis parentes, quando yo estuve naciamiento, cortar mis piernas y brazos....para a prestar para mi familia." My parents, when I was born, cut off my arms and legs so that I might beg for my family.

What? Who would do this? Feeling I could do nothing to help, I pulled out of my almost empty purse an American ten-dollar bill. He thanked me and asked me if I would put it in his shirt pocket instead of in the can on the ground, as it was such a large amount of money that someone seeing it might pick it up. I did as he asked, patted him on the head, and said *"Mivoy a ver el Cristo Negro."* I am going to see the Black Christ.

"Pero, yo soy el Cristo, el Cristo Negro," he said laughingly. But I am the Christ, the Black Christ.

"Si, yo intiendo." Yes, I understand, I told him, but I really didn't know what he was getting at. Did he mean he'd been crucified? Nailed to an invisible cross by his invisible arms and legs? Oh my God, I said to myself.

"Adios, Señor," I told him.

"Adios, Señorita, y vaya con Dios si es posible en este mundo." And go with God if it is possible in this world.

"Yo espero que es posible, Señor." I hope it is possible, Sir.

"Entonces, sin suelo, no hay vuelo." Well anyway, he said, without a floor there is no flight.

I heard him. I nodded yes. The floor, the ground, matters.

"Adios," I said again and walked, shaking, into the

churchyard, thinking about his last words: without a floor there is no flight.

I looked up at the cathedral. Maybe it was just that the entire structure was painted white. Maybe it was the time of day or the fact that this church was on the highest hill in the city. Whatever the explanation, the building seemed to emanate a glowing whitish light. People were feeding into it from all directions. I joined the throngs and was washed in.

I truly felt washed in to a glowing luminosity.

There in the cathedral, I found a mix of unusual energies, and tried to decipher these. I could feel something else present, sort of lurking in the corners, a seemingly pressing suppression of something, what was it? I shivered. There are powerful presences at work here, I said to myself. What am I seeing and sensing?

Indigenous people, those who likely had the greatest right to be there, were sitting, lying, and kneeling all over the dirt floor of this poorly lit temple-like environment, the floor which was covered with so many candles that it was difficult to walk around. Many were mumbling prayers over rosaries they held in their hands. There was chanting in multiple languages coming from all directions. Several people were hitting themselves with branches and throwing rose water over their shoulders. The smell of sweat and rancid foods filled the place. What could be happening here? Where was this Black Christ I had come all this way to see?

I could see statues of White Christs, several of them. There were women crying at the feet of these White Christ statues, weeping -- and then carefully using their long black braids to wipe their copious tears from these feet. I was instantly mystified watching.

I had to force myself to walk on. I was in search of the Black Christ, I reminded myself. I had been drawn here, come on this long journey, to find the Black Christ. In this mystically occurring Black Christ would be a key – a key to something I was searching for – access to knowledge or to a reality, a realm still vague to me. ...

I almost asked myself how any of this could be tied up with my search for whatever it was I was looking for. But then I asked myself, whose birthright is this?

This belongs to all of Humanity, I heard back.

But birthright to what? To the sacred portal of access to the higher realms? To the real message about the future of life on Earth?

Was I just crazy? I tried not to wonder because asking myself too many questions was going to rattle me far too much. Of course, not asking myself was also unnerving. I simply had to rely on instinct, or something more powerful than that ... something calling me on a very deep level ... a strange mandate....

NOTES FROM THE FRONT

56

ON INTO THE GOD'S EYE

Still in the Esquipulas Cathedral, Guatemala, 1976. I roamed around, searching for El Cristo Negro or its message to the world, confused, disappointed at first, tripping over bodies in the dark. I wanted to pray too – to pray to something, somewhere. After all, I belonged there, too. I had made my way there, too. I had arrived there on my own long pilgrimage to Earth herself, to learn more about the mounting call to see what was coming to this planet, perhaps to all Creation.

I stood still and squinted around, searching for something, anything that would be a sign I was on the right path. Discouraged, I finally murmured, "God, please. I am so tired and I have come all this way. Please please please show me something. Show me what I came here for, reveal to me what message I have been hearing."

"Can I help you?" a soft male voice with a British accent asked from behind me.

I turned and found myself looking up into the most magnificent pair of the most intensely blazing blue eyes I had ever seen. These eyes were those of a tall, alabaster-skinned, white-haired priest dressed in white from head to toe. For a moment, he seemed to be a tall thin white blue-eyed flame. He was virtually gleaming, and this was odd because it was so dark in there.

"Uh … well … yes sir, uh, Father. I came to see the Black Christ."

He smiled. "You are an American."

"Yes."

"California?"

"Yes, how did you know?"

"Just thought so. So you came all this way all alone, to see the *Cristo Negro*? Or should I say *to meet the Cristo Negro*?"

"Yes, I guess both are true."

"Well, he certainly inspires some particularly fine pilgrimages."

"I don't understand."

"Look around you. The Black *Cristo* you are looking for is everywhere."

"I really don't understand."

"Come, let's sit there a moment." He beckoned me to follow him to a pew, which I did.

We sat there looking around.

"Well, young lady, what is Christ now is what is to be resurrected in each one of us, and in all of Humanity, in all of Earth."

I wanted for some reason to debate this and had the childish gall to try, "Well, I'm not so sure that imposing Christ on these native cultures is, or was ever, the right thing to do."

He blinked, a little surprised at my direct albeit relatively polite concern. "Actually, it is said that the great *Cristo*, the Christ we speak of, walked these lands, these Americas, long before the Christ the European Christian people worship was said to be born."

"What? I don't understand," I said, trying to hide both my absolute incredulity and my total emotional exhaustion. Now I wanted to just curl up and go to sleep. No more searching, no more inquiry, no more questions. All this was too much now. I was verging on overload.

The Priest looked at me, seeming to be looking into my soul.

I suddenly opened up a bit about myself, about my confusion at least. "Sir, I mean Father, I mean, I don't know what to call you, but none of this conversation is making any sense to me. But then, most of my life is making no sense to me anymore these days. So who am I to question anything?"

"Excuse me. Child, I am Padre Postumo, or in English, this is Father Posthumous."

Before I could stop myself, I laughed little. "You are indeed telling me a joke."

"No, actually, this is my name. Fancy that."

"I'm so sorry, I should not laugh."

I stared at the women cleaning the feet of the Christs hanging on the walls, what were they doing. For a moment I was going to cry, perhaps of sadness or perhaps of exhaustion. "Excuse me, Father, I am trying to understand these women."

"Yes, I see this. You see, some of the women here in this part of the world reenact the Biblical washing of Jesus' feet, seeking inerrancy, as close a translation of the Bible as is possible. But, the truth is that many others are reenacting – and even mourning -- what they sense is the sublimating of a polytheistic Goddess worship by not Christ, but by --"

He paused a moment to see if I was really following him. I really wasn't, but I apparently was following enough for him to finish his sentence: " – by all that was done with Christ's life and story, by all religions on Earth."

For some reason I could not explain to myself, I balked, "What you are saying is not very Christian or Catholic. I'm surprised that you are telling me this. How do you know I will listen? How do you know my religion – whatever it is – will let me listen?" I wasn't even sure whether I would really listen. At the same time, I was absolutely fascinated, virtually enthralled by the concept this priest was presenting. At this point, I had no idea whether I had any religion at all.

He looked extremely patient now. "I know. No matter what your belief system, this is very strange to hear. … Christianity is a complicated thing. Far more complex than those of us who thought we understood it ever imagined. Take for example those women over there weeping onto the feet of the White Christ."

I looked at them again.

"This is not simply a replaying of what some people believe to be the Mary Magdalene story, in which she washed the feet of Jesus with her tears and then cleaned his feet with her hair. This is a ceremony of far greater import, at least to those who know."

I watched the women with greater attention now. I could see that their tears, while flowing freely, were part of a purposeful ritual. There was a higher logic to all this. I was feeling this, but not fully knowing this. A vague sense of recognition filtered into me. On some deep ancient level, I knew what all this was really about. I knew this priest was another form of medicine man who happened to be wearing the robe of his religious label.

"Poor Mary Magdelena," this priest said. "The Book of Luke says Jesus expelled Seven demons from her. Could these demons have been something else?" Now Father Posthumous peered mysteriously at me, as if I actually did know the answer.

"Seven," was all I said, as this number Seven suddenly resonated through me.

"Seven."

How have I arrived here, right now, for this meeting with this way past typical priest? And why, oh why, I wondered, was I hearing this bizarre information right then?

Things were confusing enough. I had been propelled on a strange enough journey, on an almost desperate search for something almost impossible to define. And now, this new deconstruction of my old and even my new reality was taking place. After all, although I had rejected or thought I had rejected all Judeo-Christian influence upon my life, what this priest was telling me was really shaking me up.

"What I am trying to say is that one man's demon may be another woman's spirit."

I shook my head no, and was not certain why. No? Yes? No? Yes?

"You see, while Christ may have been imposed upon these people by the earlier European missionaries, and while the plan was to impose Christ upon these people while leaving as much of the native culture as in tact as possible, something else happened. An entire civilization invaded and thought it was rightfully, in what it thought was its own God's name, conquering another, taking over another's sacred lands. What folly."

I felt I agreed but wasn't sure I fully understood. "I don't understand." What was he talking about? Why was he telling me all this? Was he rewriting history? Or proving history's lie? What?

"Nowadays, at least some of us have come to understand. We were finding out more about the Cristo than we would have ever known had we not thought we were bringing Christ to these truly Native Americans."

"This isn't making a lot of sense to me," I told him, puzzled.

He nodded. He seemed to emit waves of peace and serenity, as well as a remarkable luminosity that I could not explain to myself.

"I was wondering, how long have you been here?" I asked.

"Most of my adulthood. I came for a tour of duty when I was a young priest, and then never left. This is my home now. These are my people. Or better stated, I am theirs. Do not be fooled by what I wear of the church I appear to represent." He then murmured, "I am another kind of converso," and chuckled a little.

"You mean you're not really a priest?" I did not ask what he meant by "converso" here, although much later, I would understand this.

"What I mean is that this many years here has taught me the greater story, a truth stretching well beyond the boundaries of any one religion or myth."

I was silent. Tears were in my eyes, tears trying not to be cried. I could feel his ultimate truth reaching me.

"Are you lost, child?"

"Lost?" I whimpered.

"Lost."

Because he had asked me, I realized how very lost I was. "Yes, I guess so," I answered unsteadily, wondering why so many tears were now pouring out of me.

"And you came here in search of the way?"

"The way?" I tried to stop crying so I could make sense out of this conversation. What was he getting at? Was he going to try to preach to me, was he some kind of evangelist? No.

"The way. We all look for the way, a way, into the spiritual realm," he said in such a kind voice that I was immediately wanting to hear more of its tone, no matter what its words.

"Spiritual realm? Like heaven? Like beyond the physical?" I asked.

"Yes, the way to seeing more of this world than what the eye normally sees. In this, in finding this, being lost is part of the journey, a key passage."

I nodded. "Well yes, and more. I came here because I want to go home."

"Are you lost then," he asked me.

"No, but I guess I don't feel at home anywhere, as if the place I want to go is not on this planet. It's just a strange feeling I keep having."

The priest did not seem surprised. He touched the left side of my chest above my heart. "Well, child, home is, after all, where the heart is."

I felt his words, through and through. *Home is where the heart is*. Little did I know how many times I would hear this in my life. "But I keep feeling like I don't come from here, from this planet. It's making it hard to put a life together."

"And yet you are leading your life."

"Well, barely."

"Perhaps this IS your life … the great pilgrimage … the quest for the divine … the journey home through your heart back to—"

"Back to the stars," I interrupted.

He looked at me with those glowing sky blue eyes. As he did, I felt a powerful undeniable wave of compassion wash over me. This wave of beautiful energy was coming from him – or through him actually, and seemed to be a cloud made of the energy of pure love.

"What's that feeling?" I asked. "You sent me a feeling,

didn't you?"

"The feeling comes through me and through you. It comes from home. Take it with you wherever you go. Share it. Magnify it. Spread it here on Earth. Share it with the Earth herself. When you need it, one day, when you do leave this planet, you can follow it like a thread, a map, all the way home. You can help others learn this travel tool, this key to survival."

Floods of tears started pouring from my eyes again now, washing down my face in torrents, like overflowing streams in a heavy storm.

An intense wave of sound came over us, a wave of chanting by the people conducting ceremonies on the floor among their oceans of candles. But this was more than a wave of sound – this was a wave of feeling, a wave of awareness, a wave of being at the door to the spirit realm. I saw the priest close his eyes, reel a little in the wave, and chant along with them for a moment. Then he returned his attention to me.

I could feel him teaching me, transferring such precious information to me.

"Why do you stay here?" I asked him.

"I will stay here until I die. If I can help even a little to correct the great misunderstanding of the European invasion, I will do so. Europeans were so wrong about what they were doing in the Americas."

I looked at him, trying to fathom what he was saying.

He continued. "This is my way home now. This is my family. These are my teachers. These are my Gods. I live with these spirits."

I stared at him, trying to consume what he was telling me as if I had been hungry for it, starving for this version of the sacred, for so, so long.

He reached into his pocket and pulled out a tiny, precisely woven God's eye, which was attached to an old rosary. "I would like to give this to you."

A priest with a God's eye? I reached into my pocket and pulled out mine. "I would like to give this to you."

He accepted and examined the God's eye I offered him, eyed it a moment, and then looked at me with surprise. "I see you know K'nah'koo'd-ah, the old *bruja* in the hut up the mountain on the far side of the big volcano crater lake north west of here. She makes a very distinctive God's eye like no other."

"K'nah'koo'd-ah? You know that woman? She gave me that God's eye. I was there at her home, where she weaves. She told me to come here." I thought quickly back to the day I had met this woman in the mountains of Guatemala. I had been roaming that mountain jungle area alone.

"K'nah'koo'd-ah, yes. For many years we have known each other. This is quite a coincidence."

"You may call it that. I can't." I smiled.

"Of course it isn't. I see you see this, too." He took my hands in his and held them gently. I watched his face as he closed his eyes and sat in silence for several minutes. Then he opened his eyes abruptly and studied my face.

The priest's gaze into my soul was interrupted by a sudden synchronous loud wave of high toned wailing by the women washing the Christs' feet, more like long wails of screaming. The priest sat up very straight and listened.

When, a few moments later, the screaming wails diminished, the priest looked at me intently and said, "Never mind, never mind the details. Just follow your journey, the case will become more clear -- more clear to you -- and to all of us on this planet in these coming times."

"I do not understand what --"

I was interrupted by an event of lighting, a magnificent one.

The sun must have positioned itself just right at that very moment, because now a light ray broke in through a very high, tiny opening in the wall. It spilled down, brushed the sides of our faces, hit the ground right next to us, and splashed into a seven ray rainbow. As it did, I thought I felt a breeze washing in. I looked around and surmised that there were no open windows. Must've been the cool rush of angel wings, I told myself. Again, I gasped as I got the message.

The priest was watching my reaction. "Ah yes, the *arco ires de las Siete rayes*."

I interrupted, "The rainbow of the Seven rays."

"You know this sign then?"

"Well, I don't know exactly what I know, but I do, I guess I do."

"Of ancient and eternal significance to these people, to the indigenous people of all the Americas, in fact, to all the world, to all Humanity, to the Earth herself. And now this is the harbinger of the message emerging to take us all through the end of this grand era, through this coming transition in time, to take ourselves with the Earth herself, well beyond who we think we are right now."

I heard a voice – no, it was Seven voices in unison. "This is a message for the turn of time," they said.

"What does this mean?" I asked the Seven aloud.

The priest must have thought I was speaking to him, or wanted to pretend he thought this, because he chuckled and acted as if he was answering the question I had asked of the Seven: *"Sed quando submoventa erit ignorancia—"*

"What did you say?" I asked him.

"What did I say? I was saying, 'When the time comes for the removal of ignorance …' "

"Then what?"

"When the time comes for the removal of ignorance, the case shall be made more clear."

"I'm not sure why you said this."

"Oh, well, really it was the mystic French prophet Nostradamus who said this in Latin back in 1555: 'When the time comes for the removal of ignorance, the case shall become more clear.' "

"But what does this mean?"

He smiled at me. "You will know what this sentence, and much of the rest of all that you have seen, means when the time is right for our knowing, when the time comes for the removal of our ignorance. ... You will also know how to relay important transition survival knowledge to Humanity."

I was trying to take all this in. I could feel that this was a meeting with a remarkable man, or better stated, with a powerful spirit. He was almost not of this physical dimension.

We sat in still silence for many minutes, as long as the rainbow lasted.

"Was that rainbow an actual sign then?"

"The covenant, the arc or light, the arch of light, the wand connecting us to the spirit realm."

"Oh," I tried to assimilate all this.

"And also a sign."

"Sign?"

"That one of the First Mothers has returned to *Maka* for the reunion."

My eyes widened. *"First Mothers? Maka?"*

The priest put a finger to his lips, "Shhh! I should say no more. But, welcome back." He leveled his blazing blue eyes at mine and held my gaze. Somehow, I was instantly transfixed. I could not have looked away even if I'd wanted to. As I stared into his eyes, the face around his eyes changed from old to young to man to woman to some form of androgynous being from the stars. I felt information being moved from way beyond us, way past Earth, through his head, through his eyes, into mine. It was like getting a book I couldn't read, but knowing one day I would be able to decipher the language.

This went on for what seemed to be a long and a short time.

I thought that everything around us had stopped and that all the people in the cathedral must have been watching.

And then, deafening thunder broke just over the cathedral. I understood the transmission from the priest to me to be complete. I stood, bowed at the priest, and mouthed, "Goodbye." I knew this was what I was supposed to do right then. "I will always remember you."

He also stood. "And I you. *Dona nobis pacem.* Grant us peace," he said and nodded.

"Peace?"

He nodded yes. "Peace rather than the Great War. Or better yet, a peaceful form of the Great War, a Great Rebalancing. This is what we must work toward. This is part of The Work you and I and others are being called to do for the planet, and for all Humanity across the cosmos. ... And know this as you move forward: We must be vigilant, especially as we move into the coming transition in time, the coming long predicted intensification of Earth changes, as there are those who will seek to stop us here and beyond."

For some reason now, I was not even a little surprised by what this man was saying. I wasn't sure what it meant, but felt its deep truth. "Yes, *dona nobis pacem,*" I repeated resolutely. "And yes, we will work together to ***shepherd this great transition.***" I wasn't certain what I was saying, but felt myself feel certain about whatever my message was. (It would be years later, as my OMEGA WORK more clearly came to me, that I would better realize what this shepherding of this great transition was about.)

"Yes, we will, on some level we will," he said, "this is the real revolution. Survival. Survival through peaceful transition ... the real survival, the peaceful survival of the coming transition, of the close of this great cycle. Survival in peace. Peace on Earth. Peace beyond Earth. Peace in all dimensions of our cosmos. Finally peace. And peace to and from Earth, in and out of life on this planet and on this plane, peace in all dimensions."

I felt awash in the immensity of this spiritual man's statement, its optimism, its hope, and its crystalline truth. I could hear the calling, I could feel the mission. No words could capture this moment. However, we both knew that we both knew. Powerful information had been transferred in this meeting, only some of this in words. I could feel vast energies, or presences, or essences, I was unsure what these were, perhaps angels, gathering around as we spoke of this end of cycle transition time and its survival.

"***This is about the real resurrection, the hope of resurrection of life on Earth and beyond,***" he told me as he waved his arm around, gesturing around the cathedral. "I believe this to be the real message that the Christ, the Cristo, came here to share with us."

My breath caught in my throat. I think I stopped breathing a moment. I gulped. I got it, somehow I got it. "Yes, I am seeing that we must teach the PEOPLE OF THIS PLANET how to DIE AND SURVIVE, how to resurrect themselves, that they indeed can resurrect themselves, EVEN in the face of even dangerous *end time transition* where various forces and factors seek to end the life of Humanity for their own purposes."

I was stunned by my own words, although they rang so

true in my heart. I sounded so much older and wiser than I was at that time. It felt as if I was being spoken to or being spoken through.

The priest seemed to know this, smiled, and nodded.

"I just remembered that when I was a little girl I knew I would someday write a book about this, a book called HOW TO DIE AND SURVIVE."

"Oh yes, you will, and you will write many books, as you speak for so many out there." He waved his arms toward the sky and looked upward.

He seemed to be referring to being or doing something way out there, off-planet or something. I wanted to say this, but stopped myself.

He simply looked at me and said, "Why yes, of course."

"Thank you so much for being here and talking to me today. I will never forget you."

The man nodded.

I stood tall and took a deep breath. Then I nodded gravely and turned to leave the cathedral. I looked back a few steps later and this remarkable man (or whatever he was) was still nodding at me, his tall glowing presence standing out in the cathedral, singularly alone in the crowded space. I nodded back at him again. Then I turned and walked on to leave the cathedral.

Yet, I wanted to see this man one more time. So I quickly turned back again, but he had vanished. I had no idea how he could have left so quickly, but he had.

In that moment, when I quickly turned back to see him and

did not see him, I felt my eyes catch, stop, rivet, on one of the statues across the crowded cathedral. I gasped when I realized this was the Black Christ I had been looking for. I gasped again when I realized that this is who or what I saw when I turned to look again at that priest in the white robe.

That priest was a being yes, but a spirit walking these lands, sharing the message of survival, of resurrection. Now he was showing me the Black Christ. Everyone there was the spirit of the Black Christ who had 30,000 years ago come to Earth, who had walked the lands of the Americas long before Christ walked the Biblically described lands so far away.

I almost fell to the floor in tears, but chose instead to pray. I do not know what I prayed to, it was more of a sensing than praying. I took this experience in to hold it in my heart and soul forever.

I left that day. This man had touched my life in a more than profound way. This was another person I would probably never meet again. Not here, not in the same form, not in this lifetime anyway. Or ....

After so much of the profound, I was beginning to hunger for the mundane. But I was seized by a directive far larger than my little wish for a little relief. I could feel that I was on a lifelong search to find and share the key to something. I was here to help protect and reveal this key to Humanity.

This was the key to our survival here on Earth and beyond. And I was here to help stop the forces seeking to stop Humanity from fully accessing its own keys to its own survival.

I will never forget that day, that light, the man, that

message. It would be some decades later that I would write this present book about all this, DETECTING THE OMEGA DECEPTION, and its companion book, the novel, REVEALING THE OMEGA KEY, as well as the many volumes in the KEYS TO CONSCIOUSNESS AND SURVIVAL SERIES.

This being there, who showed me the resurrection of all of us, and of Earth herself, and the spirit of the Black Christ resurrecting the truth, is here now, every moment I write these words.

PART EIGHT:
HOPE FOR SURVIVAL AND EPILOGUE NOTES

NOTES FROM THE FRONT

57

EARTH RISE

Earth and Concurrent Beyond, Undisclosed Location. I had to pull over, as driving through this sensation was not at all a good idea. I found a turn off, drove off the highway, and parked under a tree near the bay.

I was awake, and not under the influence of any substances. I say this, as there are those who have told me that such visions are not possible when so-called "unaided." Yet, I had long been aware that what is possible is a long dialog with reality, one we will never complete.

I made sure my car was locked, the window open a bit, and then I put the seat back and closed my eyes. I may have dozed a moment.

Sometime into what may have been a nap, I was jolted alert. I heard the rush of water, almost a pounding of water, coming from everywhere, everywhere the rush of water. What was this?

I opened my eyes.

There was no time to be startled. If I had wanted to flee, I would not have been able to as I felt somehow immobilized. I was virtually frozen in place. Later I would feel as if I had been made to see, held still so that I would receive this vision.

Right before me, coming out of the water, out of the bay, was the Earth! The Earth! What is this? I did not have time to wonder however, as soon what seemed to be the Earth, or an Earth, was rising right on up out of the water.

It was then that I saw coming into focus, Seven beings. I knew that I had seen these beings in many forms and in many identities along the way. I somehow suddenly knew these beings, in their form here this day, to be assuming the role of what some will call the Ascended Masters of the Seven Rays. I do not know how I knew this, as these were Masters I was not at that time likely to have thought about much. But there they were, looking me right in the eye, telling me who they were and that they were ushering the...

EARTH THROUGH HER RESURRECTION.

To this day, I can still see this vision of Earth resurrecting, and see, feel, these ascended masters looking me in the eye every day. The memory has never dimmed and never will. It is as if you are reading this, Masters of the Seven Rays, and looking me in the eye as you bring Earth through this OMEGA TRANSITION.

Reader, you yourself may also be seeing the eyes of this Seven in so many forms. You too may be joining in ushering Earth through this grand transition.

58

THE CASE BECOMES MORE CLEAR

Undisclosed Location, 2019. The sun was setting on the water, its shining beams streaming from the distant horizon right in through the glass door of my office. The harbor outside was lighting up, reflecting the crimson brilliance onto the boats moored there. I told myself I should get going, head home, take the long way to avoid the traffic. But then I told myself I deserved a moment to enjoy the scene. I'd earned it, after all, I told myself.

I was enjoying a few moments gazing out the window of my office after seeing several clients in a row, each dealing with intense mental health, addiction, and other challenging issues. Now I leaned back and put my feet up. As engaging as the sunset was, I briefly dozed off.

I was startled when I saw two men in suits, along with an older woman dressed more casually, walking right into my office. I sat up and put my feet on the floor. Didn't they notice the sign out there? And, no one was scheduled for this time of day. I had completed all my appointments.

"Hello. Sorry, I have no more appointments set for today. You can take a card out there, just outside the door, and call in tomorrow. My assistant will answer and help you set an appointment. I think there are some times open tomorrow or the next day. Otherwise next week. That is, unless this is a health or mental health emergency. If so, tell me, and let me help you get immediate help."

The three of them did not reply, and instead pulled some chairs in close to me and sat down.

I was about to be angry, and wondered if I should call office complex security. But these people appeared rather harmless.

"Seriously, I will be glad to meet with you at another time."

"Thank you, however right now will be fine, Doctor," the older one of the men said.

I was about to object when the other man added, "Or, we can meet with you at your home later tonight. We already have your home address."

Now I was on alert. "Who are you and what do you want?"

The woman replied, "You do know why we are here. It has been too long since there has been a check in. Now the time is here, the work is central, all involved are being called in to the work. You knew we would come."

I hid my absolute shock. Seriously? I said to myself, they are coming in again now, after all this time, all these years? What on Earth could they want with me now? Yet, as I asked myself this, I found I knew the answer. Of course, on some level I had expected this. It surely was time, as even the daily news was indicating. The world was arriving at the points of both great readiness and great perilousness. Survival of Humanity was indeed ever more on the line.

The woman looked me in the eye, quietly expressing patience with me, and it seemed also with the men who were there. I felt her asking me to just relax, to give this message a moment. For some reason, I felt I had met her before. It would be later in this meeting that I would realize when.

The second man matter of factly explained, "We have closely followed your key research and writing, which in recent years is ever more increasing – such as in areas of perception and consciousness. You are among those working quietly, yet visibly, visibly yet with great stealth, right on the forefront, the front lines, of this subtle yet powerful matter. You are asking: **How can we trigger activation of the internal workings of the Human mind and consciousness: to rise Humanity above the end-time trends, break out of the end-time programming, break free of the counter-survival OMEGA TRANSITION PROGRAMMING, as you have defined it.**"

I looked at the older woman there. She held my gaze. I could feel her message was coming in to me on various levels, that she was telling me these men were carriers of something far bigger than they understood, to just listen.

In that moment, a cascade of dots connected in my mind, and all became ever more clear. I could understand, more than ever now, that I had been on this path for decades, perhaps for lifetimes, even before induction into the Kirkenes Project early in my adulthood this lifetime. I was being called forward again, to bring forward these OMEGA TRANSITION messages I had been hearing all my life. I had been one of the many sacrificed in earlier lifetimes to return now to this precipice in our evolutionary path. For a moment, I thought I heard the voices of those Seven ancient women who caught me when I fell into a

sacrificial hole in the jungle, so many decades ago. I could even still remember that CIA agent helping me out of that hole once he found me there. (Refer to the much earlier chapter in this book, Chapter 10: WAKE UP CALL: FALLING THROUGH TIME.)

Now the woman in my office waved her arm toward the door, and the two men stood up and left the room, just like that.

This strange woman and I sat there looking at each other, or should I say looking into each other's eyes. It was then that a great deal of communication took place, unspoken, silently. It was as if the two of us were telling each other the same thing at the same time.

It became clear that this visit was regarding my role now in ever more openly stepping forward along with others, in helping to generate a truly global force field to stop the OMEGA CABAL from continuing its deception and exploitation of WE THE PEOPLE OF THIS PLANET for this CABAL's own survival purposes. No longer would this on and off planet CABAL be able to exploit this OMEGA TRANSITION and suppress Humanity's own OMEGA KEY to survival here and beyond. I heard the woman saying the name of my novel, REVEALING THE OMEGA KEY.

I quietly wondered how much of all this these men knew about.

The woman heard me wondering and smiled just a little bit. In that moment I got her message, as it was the same message I heard myself giving her:

The global team is already in place and is expanding moment by moment. The ancient elders are already gathered around us, around Earth, to guide Earth through her own transition, ***her own survival, her own resurrection into the coming new ALPHA EPOCH.***

This global team is here both on and off planet. This team is here to work both here and beyond, to begin to help the Human eye see its true nature and the expanses of its true domains in both this physical plane and beyond. This next step in our evolution is essential, is the KEY to our survival here and beyond.

That day, in that meeting, I was being called upon, and also calling upon myself, to help organize and run this connection with the global mind both here and beyond, to work on this level for Humanity's, life's, Earth's, survival.

I looked at this woman sitting there, studied her still more closely, and realized I had seen her before. But when? What lifetime? Where? For a moment, I thought I heard this woman saying, "But I am you." She and I then continued in our joint communication with each other:

We are on the front line of the next step in Humanity's life. We can take our species to the next level of its evolution both here and beyond: expanding into its rightful domains of peace, compassion, and caring, into spaces of its own consciousness where we can form new niches, new places we can adapt into both here and beyond.

This is not about leaving physical plane Earth. In fact, this is about our not becoming extinct here, and our not becoming extinct beyond. We do carry the key to our own survival: this is to advance our own evolution into new domains both here and beyond.

And, this is about our standing up to those who seek to dominate and control, even to block, our evolution, even our survival both here and beyond. ***Humanity's access to the BEYOND is being threatened by those that have a stake in controlling access to that territory.***

Already, some of the most powerful members of the break-off survival faction of the global elite, these persons being the EARTH CHANGE OPPORTUNISTS I have been talking about in this book, specifically the OMEGA CABAL, are quietly exploiting the end of this grand cycle -- this major transition time we have entered, this OMEGA TRANSITION.

We can be expanding our ability to live in, and to travel in and out of, a variety of physical and non-physical domains, territories. These are places we can understand, discover, develop, for ourselves, and do this within the consciousness of our species.

We can recognize the species we truly are, step into our place in our own evolution. We can stand up to those forces and factors here and beyond who seek to block Humanity from evolving into its own rightful domains of its own consciousness.

We are the global ALPHA EPOCH team, serving the rightful evolution of Humanity, both here and beyond. We work quietly on all levels. We know each other when we meet, both here and beyond.

Readers, I hope you will join us.

59

WHAT TO DO WITH THE MESSAGES

I cannot emphasize this loudly enough: One does not write a book like this, DETECTING THE OMEGA DECEPTION, and like its companion novel, REVEALING THE OMEGA KEY, and remain untouched by what emerges from between the lines. The messages in these two OMEGA BOOKS, once listened to, once recognized, begin to speak on their own, even to work at the neural and synaptic levels of our biological brains. Some form of essential survival information is working its way into the consciousness of the species. Something about survival is being revealed within us.

When I tell people that the companion novel, REVEALING THE OMEGA KEY, is bringing ancient and modern teachings and sciences together in the form of a love and conspiracy story, I want to explain so much more. Yet, I realize again that the core of the messaging is actually between the lines, between the breaths we take, between our heartbeats, even between our synaptic firings.

Having written extensively, both nonfiction and fiction, I have discovered what so many before me have known so well: that there are boundaries between what we consider reality and what we consider fantasy. Yet these boundaries may blur when what feel to be outside forces or voices are speaking to or through us. Let me be clear here: It is not that we should lie to

ourselves, or take imagined events as facts. There is no way we want to create false facts. It is that we do best to listen to what is, or to who are, speaking to us as we write, as we create a story, as we dialog with ourselves and others, even perhaps with voices beyond who seek to speak to or through us.

For me, the writing, and again and again re-writing, re-fining, further and further developing, of the companion book, the REVEALING THE OMEGA KEY novel, has been profoundly life-changing and ultimately inspiring beyond anything imaginable. As the voices speaking through its pages became more and more involved, more and more outspoken, there has been a journey to this edge, to this place where I see the tenuous division, to this precipice from which, if one allows oneself to jump, one does not return unchanged.

I cannot help but be vulnerable to the Truths which have demanded themselves a hearing in these OMEGA BOOKS. My dreams, my daily life, my intellect, my soul -- all aspects of my existence -- have been touched. My entire life makes sense to me as I see how all roads have led me to these understandings. Every step of the way, the call to bring this material forward has been here, telling me this is why I have come in at this time in our history, at this turn of time: for this OMEGA TRANSITION, for Humanity's survival of this transition – survival in the here and now -- survival both here and beyond.

60

RE-THINKING SURVIVAL

Our antennae are up. We appear to sense that the survival of the Human species is to a great extent in our hands, or better stated, in our minds, actually in our consciousness-es. Both as individuals and as a species, we have been coming more and more to terms with this awareness. It is as if a picture has been coming ever more into focus over time.

This is even evident in the emergence of the environmental and ecological sciences and movements. Already in the 1970s, cyberneticist, systems thinker, professor Gregory Bateson, made a great impression on my young mind as a great mentor, when he set forth his riveting and even revolutionary collection of essays, *Steps to An Ecology of Mind.* In this interdisciplinary collection of essays, Bateson demonstrates a discourse intended to stimulate thinking outside the normal pathways, what I found to be and still find to be some of the most liberating material. I found that the effects of carefully thinking through the details of Bateson's writing generated what I describe as a ***comprehensive brain experience***. This inspired some of my work in developing what I have come to call ***conceptual shift practices.***

Ultimately, the meta-lesson I formed from this is that the environmental ecology movement was and is essential, and that

this thinking can and must now reach above and beyond the physical plane to the place where lives our consciousness – best described for now as our mind (as I explain in depth in the volumes of the KEYS TO CONSCIOUSNESS AND SURVIVAL SERIES).

Environmental ecology as a field contributes greatly to our respect for our physical environment, and is a central movement along the lines of survival. Yet, I say that there is clearly more to the survival of our species. Expansions of the reaches, capabilities, dimensions, and dominions of the Human mind and consciousness are indeed within our grasp. Even the notion of *expansion* begs further exploration now, a highly conscious, intelligently purposeful, even essential exploration.

On the frontiers of ourselves, we have the option to choose to be conscious and aware of our presences and our choices. All fields of Human endeavor, including but not limited to spirituality, physics, linguistics, neurobiology, genetics, psychology, sociology, anthropology, the arts, and so on, must step forward to make conscious evolution, even conscious adaptation, of the Human consciousness very high on the agenda.

Species definition of itself as an inter-dimensional life form is essential now. To address this notion, let us begin by understanding our place in the physical plane, the only place we are apparently programmed to believe we can live without divine (or what some suggest is psychedelic perhaps) intervention (or the illusion of this, the illusion which is perhaps what the psychedelic or the divine experience would be.)

I make no judgement here, state no preference either way,

regarding psychoactive drugs and medicines in the exploration of the mind. I leave this to individual Readers to choose. All I say is that the mind in its natural state, unaided, can and must arrive at its own rightful doorway to its own most natural domains. These domains are each of your own survival territories. This is where your own power to exercise your own power lives. This is where survival can be navigated.

However appealing and logical to many of you out there, no drugs or medicines are absolutely required to reach the fullest expanses of the consciousness, our own rightful expanses, our own domains of ourselves. Once we are truly free to access who we truly are, we can fully access ourselves.

It is indeed time for us to truly own our actual nature as interdimensional beings. It is also time for us to look at what forces and factors, and programming -- either naturally evolved into us, or intelligently designed and implanted into us -- have controlled and limited our access to the vast domains of ourselves. (Refer to the OVERRIDING THE EXTINCTION SCENARIO books in the KEYS TO CONSCIOUSNESS AND SURVIVAL SERIES, where I delve deeply into this matter.)

The notion that we can of our own free will develop various niches to move into for the sake of survival is not clear to us in large part as a result of many teachings dictating to us that such travel has to be under control of something or someone of higher status than ourselves. Ultimately this is true, however what is higher is our own higher consciousness, rather than someone else's.

Think of the times in Human history when leaders told others that entry into Heaven was determined by sets of rules

written for others to follow, that some form of gate keeper held the key to the teachings, even the key to the after life -- that only some so-called higher or ordained personages had the right to DIE AND SURVIVE. (See more on this matter in the HOW TO DIE AND SURVIVE volumes of the KEYS TO CONSCIOUSNESS AND SURVIVAL SERIES, listed at the end of this present book.)

Yet, we ourselves hold the KEY to our reaching into the realms of our own consciousness, and doing so even while still living in our physical biological bodies. We do not need to die to reach, to expand, BEYOND.

We have been programmed by various forces and factors to barely tap the power of our own minds and consciousness-es. We can release ourselves from programming not to know who we truly are. We can release ourselves from programming not to survive.

The physical plane is a great school. Or perhaps this world is better described as a bicycle with training wheels on it. Indeed, if paying attention, we see we always have the opportunity to become ever more aware. Every moment is a learning opportunity on some individual, societal, and or species level: psychological, social, spiritual, and sensory, cognitive, neurobiological, even cellular and synaptic levels, and so on. In fact, we are designed to learn, as individuals and as populations, (and to learn to learn) about our environments and situations in order to survive.

The next and most essential domain of ourselves, as individuals and as a species, is the territory of our own consciousness. This is where **our survival** of the intensifying

Earth (as well as cosmic) changes can be inspired, empowered. This is also where certain forces and factors such as what we can see as being the OMEGA CABAL seek to block our expansion.

However, we carry within the Human consciousness the wisdom, the insight, and the path to surviving both here and beyond.

NOTES FROM THE FRONT

61

UNDERGROUND AWARENESS IS RISING

The story continues to unfold. DETECTING and standing up to THE OMEGA DECEPTION is well underway. This DECEPTION is both a physical plane and a BEYOND physical plane deception we are going to unveil, to see for what it is, to stop from taking us down.

HOWEVER,
WE CAN HAVE HOPE, AS WE CAN SEE THAT
UNDERGROUND RISING IS RISING.

We must be watchful for efforts to suppress the truth about what our actual survival can look like. The stakes are higher than ever before with: several key players in prison in various countries around the world; a number of highly respected citizens being blackmailed and extorted into silence about this; suppression and stigmatizing of some key members of UNDERGROUND RISING, the underground political movement describing itself in many ways -- such as working to spot and stop the OMEGA DECEPTION and its OMEGA CABAL, and in so doing, working to stop both on-planet and off-planet -- or better stated, interdimensional -- interference in Human affairs without Human permission.

NOTES FROM THE FRONT

UNDERGROUND RISING is working on all levels to help Humanity navigate and survive this OMEGA TRANSITION, this close of this grand cycle. Let's be very aware of those seeking to exploit this coming transition, to use us for their own survival purposes. The world needs to know what we have to say, to hear our message, despite its highly unusual almost inconceivable nature. The OMEGA CABAL has finely tuned its work to keep its already huge preparations for itself, for its segment of the global elite, to have its own END TIME SURVIVAL resources, territories, and options.

The story I tell in this book,
DETECTING THE OMEGA DECEPTION,
and in the companion novel,
REVEALING THE OMEGA KEY,
and in the volumes of the
KEYS TO CONSCIOUSNESS AND SURVIVAL SERIES,
speaks beyond the pages and between the lines.
WE ARE BEING CALLED TO HEAR
THE MESSAGES WE ARE BEING SENT
BY THOSE BEYOND
WHO SEEK TO HELP US, GUIDE US,
THROUGH THESE TIMES,
WHO SEEK TO STOP THE OMEGA CABAL
FROM STOPPING US.

THIS IS THE STORY OF HUMANITY SURVIVING.

This may be the greatest story of our times, of all times, and perhaps the largest story in Human history here on Earth and throughout the Cosmos (Human or whatever history this actually is).

We must now think and sense in ways we are indeed able to think and sense, reaching far beyond the boundaries that have been set for us by both evolution and design. We must now think as clearly and precisely as we can, seeing both inside and outside the box of our day to day realities.

****

Note: For in depth discussion and definition of the matter of "**both evolution and design**" we have been subjected to, refer to Volumes 5 and 6 in the KEYS TO CONSCIOUSNESS AND SURVIVAL SERIES: Volume 5, OVERRIDING THE EXTINCTION SCENARIO: **DETECTING** THE BAR ON THE EVOLUTION OF THE HUMAN SPECIES, and Volume 6, OVERRIDING THE EXTINCTION SCENARIO: **RAISING** THE BAR ON THE EVOLUTION OF THE HUMAN SPECIES.

NOTES FROM THE FRONT

62

NOTE TO READERS: WE DO HAVE A CHOICE

Thank you for this opportunity to speak to you, to the very core of your **self** located so very deeply within your consciousness where you do truly live.

This discussion is regarding what is concurrently a casual and yet, if we are honest with ourselves, pressing matter:

extinction.

The Human species has a say as to whether or not it will become extinct. This is an invitation to explore the meaning of, the reality of, survival on all levels of ourselves. Only a true, fully activated, multi- and inter- dimensional survival process will guide us to full survival of this OMEGA TRANSITION, this close of this grand cosmic cycle.

We must understand who and what we are to have who and what we are, Humanity itself, survive. I have detailed many aspects of this matter in the KEYS TO CONSCIOUSNESS AND SURVIVAL SERIES, such as Volumes 5 and 6, the OVERRIDING THE EXTINCTION SCENARIO books, Volumes 3 and 11, the HOW TO DIE AND SURVIVE books, and the also essential Volume 3, titled UNVEILING THE HIDDEN INSTINCT.

NOTES FROM THE FRONT

I build a great deal of my thinking regarding the times we are moving into, this OMEGA TRANSITION, and related survival issues, on, and have developed a great deal of my work and research within, traditional fields of scholarship and inquiry ranging from neuroscience, to psychology, political science, public health, environmental biology, to philosophy and religion, to mythology, to literature and art, as well as other fields. I build on, reach beyond, the present bounds of those fields of knowing to natural next steps:

We must work to see
our survival issues as interdisciplinary issues,
even more as
inter-dimensional issues.

This dot-connecting requires a vast scope of awareness.

We must now, quite urgently,
see beyond limiting boundaries.

How infinitesimal we are relative to galactic and cosmic proportions. Against this backdrop of immensity, of infinite dimensions of infinite macro and micro proportions, we as a species are perhaps inconsequential, as is our survival. Perhaps.

However, it is my contention that our survival is not

inconsequential. We can and must have a greater say in the outcome of our evolution and existence than we generally allow ourselves (or are allowed) to believe.

Even where we are stymied by grand phases and natural and unnatural shifts in our physical environment, even where the keenest of scientific and technologic advances are not advancing rapidly enough to protect or control our physical environment (our biological niche), even where our physical evolution is not rapid enough to prepare us for every (possibly) necessary adaptation, we do have the choice to effectively adapt. In fact, we stand at the threshold of what I choose to describe as a most magnificent:

EVOLUTIONARY OPPORTUNITY.

We can consciously expand our species into dimensions beyond just the physical plane. There are physical and non-physical niches we can define and move into, come and go from at will. Such expansion is a matter of what I describe as our:

SPECIES' EVOLUTIONARY RIGHT.

It is incumbent upon those of us being drawn to this form of thinking in our times, and throughout our times, to develop methods of signaling our species regarding what we know. We can bring a critical mass of our species to see this truly magnificent, even revolutionary, ***evolutionary opportunity***, to see this expansion as an:

EVOLUTIONARY NECESSITY.

Note that no profound shift in daily life is required. Rather, this calls for a shift in awareness of what controls our minds, and of how our brains control us. Can we detect and take control of our programming to be so programmable?

****

Note: See in-depth discussion of what I define as this **evolutionary opportunity,** and **species evolutionary right,** and **evolutionary necessity** in the OVERRIDING THE EXTINCTION SCENARIO books, Volumes 5 and 6 of the KEYS TO CONSCIOUSNESS AND SURVIVAL SERIES.

63

ONE OF THE MOST PERILOUS

It is the responsibility of all of us to DETECT the **on and off planet** OMEGA DECEPTION being perpetrated upon Humanity as we enter this end of grand cycle OMEGA TRANSITION.

You are a player at one of the most perilous and yet spiritually expansive times in our history, perhaps in cosmic history. Now is when ancient teachings and current scientific thinking interact, merge, press to detect, distill, clarify, and render new and higher truths. Now is when survival depends upon a judicious balancing of sensation, messaging, information, and voices, coming into our minds, our hearts, our bodies, our souls, our individual and species consciousness-es.

I suggest you close your eyes a while and carefully feel your response to this information. Drop all prejudices and preconceived notions for only a while, in order to think your own thoughts. Decide for yourself whether this is information critical to your -- our -- survival, or simply a wonderful story. Decide for yourself whether this is truth or myth or both. Let not only your intellect be the judge. Let your heart and soul join in your discernment of this truth. The future of Humanity -- the freedom of Human consciousness -- is at stake.

FROM MY HEART TO YOURS:

WE CAN DO THIS, WE CAN SURVIVE.

WE CARRY WITHIN US
THE KEY TO OUR OWN SURVIVAL
BOTH HERE AND BEYOND.
LET US NOT BE DECEIVED
INTO NOT ACCESSING
OUR OWN KEY TO
OUR OWN RIGHTFUL SURVIVAL.
LET US SEE AND STOP
THE OMEGA DECEPTION CABAL
FROM STOPPING US.

WE CAN DO THIS.
WE CAN
CARRY THE LIGHT OF HUMANITY THROUGHOUT
THE HERE AND THE BEYOND
WHERE WE DO LIVE
AND CAN SURIVVE.

DETECTING THE OMEGA DECEPTION

OMEGA KEY
CODE
TO SURVIVAL
(excerpt)

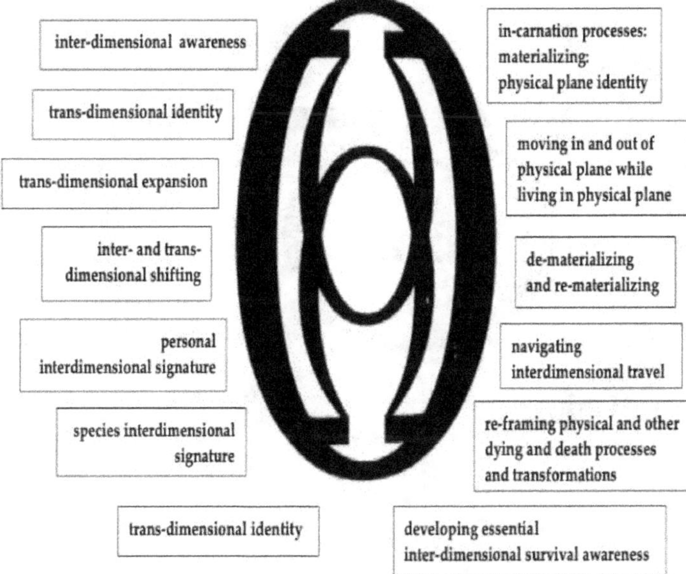

understanding death as expansion:
identifying as an interdimensional being:
clarifying the matrix of self:
survival as an interdimensional life form

NOTE TO READERS:
The above is a beginning list of OMEGA KEY CODE entries. Refer to the KEYS TO CONSCIOUSNESS AND SURVIVAL SERIES also by this author, present and future editions, for in depth presentation of SURVIVAL KEYS including the OMEGA KEYS, where the above OMEGA KEY CODE categories and other KEY messagings are explained.

REVEALING
THE OMEGA KEY

COSMIC LOVE STORY THROUGH ANCIENT END-TIME EARTH-CHANGE PROPHECY TO MODERN GLOBAL CONSPIRACY

ANGELA BROWNEMILLER
Metaterra® Publications

DOUBLE

OMEGA

ALPHA

APPENDICES

NOTES FROM THE FRONT

BOOKLIST AND RECOMMENDED READING

KEYS TO CONSCIOUSNESS AND SURVIVAL SERIES
by Dr. Angela Brownemiller:

Volume 11
How To Die and Survive: Book Two
Extending Our Interdimensional Awareness:
Next Concepts For Living and Dying
****

Volume 10
Seeing Beyond Our Line of Sight
Consciously Moving Through Life's
Changes, Transitions, and Deaths
****

Volume 9
Navigating Life's Stuff–
Dynamics of Personal Change, Book Two
Keys to Consciously Moving Through
Our Processes and Their Patterns
****

Volume 8
Navigating Life's Stuff –
Dynamics of Personal Change, Book One
Sensitizing to and Navigating
Our Patterns and Their Processes
****

Volume 7

Keys To Accessing The Beyond

Expansion, Elevation, Transmigration,
Survival Here And Beyond –Practices And Concepts

****

Volume 6

Overriding The Extinction Scenario, Part Two

Raising the Bar on the Evolution of the Human Species

****

Volume 5

Overriding The Extinction Scenario, Part One

Detecting the Bar on the Evolution of the Human Species

****

Volume 4

How to Die and Survive

Interdimensional Psychology, Consciousness, and Survival:
Concepts for Living and Dying

****

Volume 3

Unveiling the Hidden Instinct

Understanding Our Interdimensional Survival Awareness

****

Volume 2

Keys to Personal Discovery

****

Volume 1

Keys to Self

****

BOOKLIST AND RECOMMENDED READING

Continued

Ask Dr. Angela Series
Dr. Angela Brownemiller

—

The Bloodwin Code (Episode Books 1, 2, 3, 4, 5)
Dr. Angela Brownemiller

—

Seeing The Hidden Face Of Addiction
Dr. Angela Brownemiller

—

Contact us for information on the special
Science Fiction Series
on these consciousness and survival topics.

Note:
These books should be listed on Amazon.com and on DrAngela.com and on numerous other book distributor websites.

NOTES FROM THE FRONT

NOTES FROM THE FRONT

VOLUMES 8 & 9 in the KEYS TO CONSCIOUSNESS AND SURVIVAL SERIES

Can we better understand the journeys we travel in our lives? Can we detect and work with the patterns and processes we are forming, living within, and moving through? How much can we see about the patterns we form, and sometimes feel we cannot change and are caught in? How do we sensitize ourselves to the patterning processes we are engaged in? Find your way through the maze of life.

NAVIGATING LIFE'S STUFF: DYNAMICS OF PERSONAL CHANGE, BOOK ONE

Sensitizing to and Navigating Our Patterns and Their Processes

NAVIGATING LIFE'S STUFF: DYNAMICS OF PERSONAL CHANGE, BOOK TWO

Keys to Consciously Moving Through Our Passages and Their Patterns

Now in Paperback, Audiobook, and Ebook forms.

Find these and other books by Dr. Angela Brownemiller on Amazon.com and at **DrAngela.com**

Volumes 4 and 11 in the KEYS TO CONSCIOUSNESS AND SURVIVAL SERIES

HOW TO DIE AND SURVIVE, BOOK ONE
See also HOW TO DIE AND SURVIVE, BOOK TWO
by Dr. Angela Brownemiller

YOUR RIGHT TO KNOW IS CLEAR. These far reaching and life changing books offer new ways of understanding ourselves and our lives. The author details progressive understandings and practices for moving into multi- and inter- dimensional consciousness and survival skills. Through use of metaphor, this author guides Readers through: her progressive "shift" awareness-es; through LEAPs in understanding her sequential "shift technologies" by means of concepts, processes, and exercises contained in the chapters of these books. These exercises begin quite simply and carefully build toward some very esoteric understandings. ... These books overcome limits to old models of what we are, who we are, and where we can be and go. Ultimately, this is an exploration of the infinite potential of our consciousness. Join us for the journey of your lifetime, of all your/our lifetimes.

DETECTING THE OMEGA DECEPTION

Volumes 5 and 6 in the
KEYS TO CONSCIOUSNESS AND SURVIVAL SERIES
By DR. ANGELA BROWNEMILLER:

OVERRIDING THE EXTINCTION SCENARIO, PART ONE:
DETECTING THE BAR ON
THE EVOLUTION OF THE HUMAN SPECIES
and reach more deeply into all this with...
OVERRIDING THE EXTINCTION SCENARIO, PART TWO:
RAISING THE BAR ON
THE EVOLUTION OF THE HUMAN SPECIES

Now in Paperback, Audiobook, and Ebook forms.
Find these and other books by Dr. Angela Brownemiller
on Amazon.com and at **DrAngela.com**

NOTES FROM THE FRONT

Volume 3 in this
KEYS TO CONSCIOUSNESS AND SURVIVAL SERIES

UNVEILING THE HIDDEN INSTINCT
by Dr. Angela Brownemiller

Every day, we are presented with minor and major opportunities, reasons, even needs, to understand the nature of transitioning, shifting, from one state of mind, one way of being, one way of seeing the world, from one reality to another. In this sense, we are frequently calling upon ourselves to shift ourselves and our consciousness-es from one dimension of ourselves to another. At times, we may even sense that our well-being, perhaps even our survival, depends upon such a shift. ... Should we at some point find the survival level need to shift ourselves across ways of seeing the world, realities, dimensions, even perhaps from physical to non-physical and back, it is essential we have at least already considered the concepts involved. This book introduces, via metaphor, minor and major shift awareness-es, making these understandings accessible to us should we need these for everyday challenges as well as potentially profound survival reasons.

Volume 10 in this KEYS TO CONSCIOUSNESS AND SURVIVAL SERIES

SEEING BEYOND OUR LINE OF SIGHT

by Dr. Angela Brownemiller

SEEING BEYOND OUR LINE OF SIGHT: CONSCIOUSLY MOVING THROUGH LIFE'S CHANGES, TRANSITIONS, AND DEATHS ... is a simple yet profound book offering subtle yet major shifts in the way we think about changes, transitions, endings, and deaths. Here, we can see that we have the capability of holding and empowering our conscious selves as we move through events, changes, transitions, even emotional, even physical, death processes. ... The journey this book takes us on opens doors to finding our way through challenging, trying, even very difficult, events and passages in our lives. ... That we can survive is central as we undergo all minor and major transitions in our lives. ... Find yourself, know yourself, guide yourself through the minor and major transition and death processes you face during your life. You can define who and what you are for yourself. You can open this option in your mind, the option that you can develop this knowledge of yourself, and then carry this knowledge of yourself through this life, and perhaps also on beyond this lifetime.

AUTHOR CONTACT

www.DrAngela.com

DrAngelaBrownemiller@gmail.com

for
Paperback, Audiobook, and Ebook
versions of this and other books
by this author
Dr. Angela Brownemiller
see
www.Amazon.com
and
www.DrAngela.com

ABOUT THE AUTHOR
Dr. Angela Brownemiller
Dr. Angela®

Dr. Angela Brownemiller, also known as Dr. Angela®, is an author, journalist, social thinker, clinician, psychotherapist, trainer, speaker, and creator of the ASK DR. ANGELA® Series of broadcasts, podcasts, books, audiobooks, Ebooks, and programs. The views of Angela Brownemiller are centered on the great potential of the Human mind, heart, and soul, and on the rights of all of us, who and whatever we are (or think we are). Dr. Angela Brownemiller views the Human consciousness as a wealth of opportunity for exploration, insight, knowledge—and survival. For more information on her mind-body-spirit-consciousness and other work, see DrAngela.com.

The works of Angela Brownemiller are brought to you by:
METATERRA® PUBLICATIONS
(**and numerous other publishers**, see **Amazon.com**).
For copies of print books, audiobooks, and ebooks by this author, see Amazon.com, or contact us at **www.DrAngela.com**
To take part in our events and workshops, and or for personal consultations in person or by telephone or online, contact us at **www.DrAngela.com**

www.ingramcontent.com/pod-product-compliance
Lightning Source LLC
LaVergne TN
LVHW010050110826
845155LV00028B/269